Items should be returned on or before the last date shown below. Items not already requested by other borrowers may be renewed in person, in writing or by telephone. To renew, please quote the number on the barcode label. To renew online a PIN is required. This can be requested at your local library.
Renew online @ **www.dublincitypubliclibraries.ie**
Fines charged for overdue items will include postage incurred in recovery. Damage to or loss of items will be charged to the borrower.

Leabharlanna Poiblí Chathair Bhaile Átha Cliath
Dublin City Public Libraries

Baile Átha Cliath
Dublin City

Leabharlann Shráid Chaoimhín
Kevin Street Library
Tel: 01 222 8488

Date Due	Date Due	Date Due

D1380377

Rebel

R J ANDERSON

ORCHARD BOOKS

ORCHARD BOOKS
338 Euston Road, London NW1 3BH
Orchard Books Australia
Level 17/207 Kent Street, Sydney, NSW 2000

First published in the UK in 2010 by Orchard Books

ISBN 978 1 40830 737 3

Text © R J Anderson 2010

A CIP catalogue record for this book is available from the British Library.

10

Printed in Great Britain

Orchard Books is a division of Hachette Children's Books,
an Hachette UK company.

www.hachette.co.uk

To Steve,
who refused to settle for easy answers,
and Mark, who showed me it's never
too late to come home.

prologue

The Queen is dying.

The knowledge sat in Linden's belly like a cold stone as she hunched over the tub of greasy water, scrubbing her thirty-ninth plate. She'd promised Mallow, the Chief Cook, that she'd wash all the Oakenfolk's dishes in exchange for a second piece of honey cake at dinner, and at the time it had seemed a reasonable bargain. But now that she knew what was happening at the top of the Spiral Stair – that the faery Queen was lying pale and weak upon her bed and might never rise from it again – she wanted to heave up all the cake she'd eaten and throw the last few dishes straight back in the Chief Cook's face.

How could Mallow look smug, after bringing them such terrible news? The moment she'd spoken those words the whole kitchen had gone silent, Gatherers and cooks and scullions all staring in horrified disbelief. Yet the corners of Mallow's fat mouth were curled up in obvious self-satisfaction, as though the important thing wasn't Queen Amaryllis's fate, only that *she'd* been the first of them to find out about it.

Still, Linden didn't dare to question Mallow, or beg her for more details – unless, of course, she was prepared to bargain for the information. The other faeries in the kitchen must have thought the same, for they'd already gone back to work, downcast faces and trembling hands their only signs of emotion. But Linden could imagine the anxious thoughts running through their minds, because the same fears chilled her own:

How much longer can the Queen live?

Who will rule the Oak now?

And most of all: *Oh, Great Gardener, what will become of us when she's gone?*

Linden bowed her head over the tub until her long brown curls almost brushed the water. She squeezed her eyes shut and her lips together, trying not to weep. To be brave, like her foster mother Knife had taught her – but oh, she wished that Knife could be with her now!

'Don't forget these,' said Mallow's voice from behind her, and a silver tray clattered onto the counter by Linden's side. 'Not that *she's* eaten much, so be sure to scrape them first.'

In Mallow's language *scrape them* really meant *save all the good bits for me.* Linden looked at the almost untouched food – a plate of delicately carved roast finch with mashed roots and chestnut dressing – and felt sick all over again. If the Queen couldn't even muster the will to eat, how would she find the strength to do magic? If the spells that protected the Oak weren't renewed on a daily basis they would start to weaken, and then it wouldn't take long for disease, insects and a host of hungry predators to start gnawing their way inside…

'Someone else can wash the Queen's dishes, Mallow,' said a calm voice from the doorway. 'Her Majesty wishes me to bring Linden to her at once.'

Linden looked up, her tears draining into the backs of her eyes as she recognised the tall, grave-looking faery who had spoken. 'Me, Valerian? Why?'

But Mallow spoke up before Valerian could answer. 'Linden made me a bargain, Healer. *You* can wait.'

Someone gasped, but quickly turned it into a cough as Mallow swung round. 'Stop gawping and get back to work!' she barked, then returned her glare to Linden. 'Well?'

Anger surged through Linden, and she clenched her soap-slick hands. It was one thing for Mallow to bully her own kitchen workers, or a temporary servant like Linden herself. But to be rude to Valerian – worse, to deny a request from their own dying Queen – it was intolerable.

Yet what could she do about it? At fifteen Linden was by far the youngest faery in the Oak, and one of the smallest besides. She had no magic, no influence, not even a proper occupation yet: it was ridiculous to think she could stand up to someone like Mallow. Linden swallowed, nodded, and began removing the uneaten food from the Queen's plate.

'No,' said Valerian, walking over. She took the plate from Linden, gently but firmly, and set it aside. 'Her Majesty is not dead yet, Mallow. And even among faeries, there are duties more sacred than a bargain.' She bent and looked into Linden's face with her searching grey eyes. 'The Queen has need of you. Will you come with me?'

Not commanding, but asking: that was Valerian's way. And yet that simple courtesy was enough to straighten Linden's spine, making her ashamed that she had bowed to Mallow for even a moment.

'Yes, of course,' she said. 'I'll come at once.'

The Queen's apartments were nine floors up, at the top of the Spiral Stair. Through the window-slit on the landing Linden could see a rare view of the whole Oakenwyld: on the east side a matted brown carpet of meadow fringed with leafless trees, and to the north and west the withered hedges and empty flowerbeds that separated the Oak from the nearby human House. Drab though it looked now, in just a few weeks the garden would be glorious – but what did that matter, when the Queen would likely not live long enough to see it? With a heavy heart Linden closed the shutter and turned away.

'There is one thing I must tell you,' said Valerian quietly as she climbed up onto the landing beside Linden. 'If we should meet Bluebell on our way, let me be the one to speak.

And however she may press you afterwards, tell her nothing about your meeting with the Queen.'

Bluebell was Queen Amaryllis's personal attendant, a haughty but loyal faery who had served her for more than seventy years. 'Why?' Linden asked.

'Think, child. How do you think the news came out that Her Majesty is dying? If Bluebell would gossip about such a serious matter – and to Mallow, no less – then I fear she cannot be trusted with even the least of Queen Amaryllis's secrets any more.'

Sobered, Linden nodded her agreement, and the Healer parted the curtains and led the way inside. A distant bell jangled, and Linden braced herself for a confrontation – but mercifully Bluebell seemed to be elsewhere for the moment, and they walked down the corridor unchallenged.

The Queen's bedchamber was the most elegant room Linden had ever seen. Carvings of vines and berries surrounded every door and window frame, all the furnishings were antique, and the floor was carpeted in ermine, a white pelt thick and soft enough to bury Linden's bare feet to the ankles. But the moment Linden saw Queen Amaryllis, she forgot everything else.

She had the face of a goddess, untouched by age, and yet her half-lidded eyes held the burden of centuries. No faery could expect to live much beyond three hundred and fifty, and Amaryllis had passed that age seven years ago. Now all the warmth had drained from her skin, leaving it white as apple flesh, and she lay in the four-poster bed with her wings flattened beneath her, as though she already knew that she would never use them again.

'Your Majesty,' said Valerian, dipping a curtsy. 'I have brought Linden, as you asked.'

The faery in the bed stirred, and her faded blue eyes focused on Linden. 'Good,' she breathed. 'Come close to me, both of you.'

Valerian walked around one side of the bed, while Linden moved woodenly to the other. She couldn't speak, even if she had known what to say: she could only look down at the Queen's honey-gold hair lying tangled on the pillow, and gulp back the grief that threatened to choke her.

'I had hoped you would be older when this day came,' the Queen murmured. 'But I cannot delay it any longer, even for your sake.' She extended one soft, fragile hand, her fingers curling around Linden's. 'It is time you learned what your task must be, and how carefully we have prepared you for just such a time as this. For you are our people's greatest hope – perhaps our only hope.'

A tremor ran through Linden as she realised that she was about to receive her life's occupation at last. But the Oakenfolk's *greatest hope*…What could Her Majesty possibly mean?

'Do not fear,' said the Queen, but her voice thinned to huskiness on the final word, and though she cleared her throat she could not speak again. There was a painful pause, until Valerian spoke instead:

'Let me try to explain. By now, Linden, you must know about the Sundering, the reason we Oakenfolk can no longer work magic. Wink has told you the story, I am sure?'

Wink was the other of Linden's two foster mothers, a little redheaded faery full of affection and good intentions, but unfortunately bad at getting to the point. 'Some of it,' said Linden cautiously. 'I know it happened a long time ago, and that it was the fault of a faery named Jasmine.' She'd seen a portrait of Jasmine once, painted by the human artist who had once been Jasmine's lover: a strong-featured beauty with black hair and a mocking smile curving her lips. She'd looked proud and very determined – the sort of woman who might do anything. 'And I know she was trying to keep our people away from humans.'

'Yes,' said Valerian. 'Jasmine's experience of humans had been bitter, and she came to believe that faeries were better off without them. She thought that our reliance on human contact to give us new ideas and creative skills was mere laziness and habit, and if she could give us a way to maintain our population we would soon learn to thrive independently. So she cast a spell that would enable us to replace ourselves with eggs when we died, instead of having to take human mates or adopt unwanted human children as our own – but she used up nearly all our magic in order to do it. And though Jasmine believed the ultimate benefit to our people would be far greater than the cost, she was wrong.'

Wrong was an understatement, Linden knew. In Jasmine's day there had been more than two hundred faeries living in the Oak, but after the Sundering so many had been killed by predators and other misfortunes, and so few of their precious eggs had survived long enough to hatch, that only forty-five Oakenfolk now remained.

'I understand,' she said. 'But what does this have to do with me?'

'We need our magic back,' Valerian said simply. 'Queen Amaryllis cannot endure much longer, and once she is gone the rest of us will soon perish, unless we find a way to undo Jasmine's spell. Our only hope is to seek out other faeries who still have all their magic, and beg them to lend us some of their power. But how could any of us undertake such a long and dangerous journey, when we have so little idea of where to go, and still less chance of getting there?'

It was a good question: at their small size and with no magic to protect them, none of their people could possibly survive long outside the Oak. Linden frowned – then her face cleared as she realised what the Healer must have in mind. 'You want me to talk to Knife for you?' she said. 'Of course I will – but surely there's no need. She'd do it if you asked her, I know she would.'

But the Queen looked pained, and Valerian shook her head. 'We have no doubt of your foster mother's loyalty, or her courage. But she is human now, no longer one of us, and it is unlikely that any faeries outside our own Wyld would speak to her. Besides, it is Knife's duty to guard the Oakenwyld against crows and foxes, and provide food for our people. She cannot go.'

No, of course not, thought Linden regretfully. Especially not with Queen Amaryllis so close to dying, and the Oak more vulnerable than ever.

'But Knife has already done much to help,' Valerian continued. 'The time you have spent with her in the House, learning of humans and their ways, has given you a unique understanding of the world beyond the Oak. If the opportunity arises for one of our people to venture out in search of other faeries, no one is better equipped for the task than you.'

Shock froze Linden's blood in her veins, then set her whole body afire. 'Me? But I'm so...'

So small. So weak. So frightened. She wasn't like Knife, who even as a faery had been tough enough to take down a crow with a single arrow and fight off rats bare-handed. Linden had no fighting skills, and no magic either: how could she possibly do what they were asking of her?

The Healer's face softened. 'This is difficult for you, I know. But rest assured, we have not made this decision lightly. Nor does Her Majesty intend to send you out into the world without first giving you all the help she can.' She bent towards the Queen and said in a low voice, 'Do you wish to do it now? Are you sure you will not rest a little first, and gather your strength?'

Amaryllis's reply was barely audible, exhaled on a ragged

breath. 'Yes…it must be now.'

Valerian bowed her head. 'Then I will not oppose you. I only pray that Linden and I will prove worthy of such a sacrifice.'

Sacrifice? What in the Great Gardener's name was Queen Amaryllis planning to do? Linden's anxiety must have shown on her face, because the Queen's fingers tightened around her own, reassuring. Then she whispered: 'Do you give me your service?'

Linden's eyes welled up, but she bit her lip and nodded. Fearful or not, she still trusted the Queen, believed in her – even though what she was asking seemed impossible.

'Dear child,' Amaryllis murmured. 'You have been the joy of my old age. I wish I could go with you, when the time comes. But since I cannot…' and with those words a silvery glow kindled above her heart, and began to radiate outwards. Dim at first, but growing brighter as it spread, it rippled down the Queen's outstretched arms to her fingertips – and before Linden could so much as gasp, the light enveloped her as well.

She could feel the magic all around her, dancing sparks against her skin: she looked wide-eyed at Valerian, and saw the Healer surrounded by the same eerie glow. Linden started, but Amaryllis held her fast, and the light expanded until the three of them were contained in a swirling, incandescent bubble.

'*Half my magic I give to you, my ambassador,*' the Queen's

voice echoed in Linden's mind, clear as only thoughts could be. *'Yours are the glamours, the spells of illusion and temporary change. At need, they will conceal you from your enemies and confound those who would do you harm. But use them wisely and in good conscience, not for selfish gain.'*

'Your Majesty—' protested Linden, but the Queen had already turned to Valerian.

'And you, my chosen successor... you have always had the heart of a Healer; soon you must bear the burdens of a Queen as well. To you I give the Sight, to counsel you when your own wisdom is not enough, and I give you also the deep magics of protection and preservation, that the Oak might not wither before help is found. I only regret that I cannot give you more...'
And with that the light around her died away, and her arms fell limp to the mattress.

'Your Majesty!' cried Linden in distress, but Valerian held a finger to her lips.

'She is not dead, only exhausted. But she has given us all the magic she had – look.'

She lifted the coverlet, and grief stabbed Linden as she saw that the Queen's wings, once the most bright and beautiful of all the faeries, had completely disappeared.

'How long will she...' Linden could not bring herself to finish the sentence.

'It will not be long now,' replied Valerian, drawing the blankets back up around the Queen's shoulders.

Linden rubbed her arms, which still tingled from the

Queen's magic – no, it was *her* magic now; she could feel it glowing deep inside her, like a banked fire. But how to use it? She knew so little about spell-craft, she was afraid to even try.

'What are we going to do?' she asked.

'I do not know,' Valerian admitted. 'You are still too young to undertake your quest, and even if you were not, you will need human help to travel any great distance.'

'You think they're far away, then? The other faeries?'

'I believe so,' said Valerian. 'If they were nearby, we would surely have found them by now. Queen Amaryllis thinks that some may live among the humans, even passing for human themselves, as we Oakenfolk used to do before the Sundering. Perhaps in the great city they call London...'

London. It sounded almost like her name. A sign, perhaps? Could this be the Great Gardener's way of showing her where to go?

'But as I said,' Valerian added with more firmness, 'you are young. The Queen's gift of magic has bought us time, and there is no need to send you away, not yet.'

Linden looked down at her bare feet, brown against the white fur of the carpet. Valerian might think they could afford to wait, but she had no such confidence. Already the glamours that wrapped the Oak were weakening, exposing its doors and windows to human sight, and the wards that kept the tree safe from predators would soon fail as well.

By working together she and Valerian could perhaps

renew the faltering spells, and Knife would surely do her best to keep the Oakenfolk safe and fed. But those were only temporary solutions. There would be no security and no future for any of them until they had their magic back.

Linden knew she was young. But the Queen had given her an occupation – *my ambassador* – which meant she was no longer a child. And though the idea of going out into the world alone made cold worms crawl beneath her skin, neither could she bear to think of sitting idle while her people were in danger.

There was no telling when the opportunity for her to leave the Oak would arise. But in the silence of her heart, Linden vowed that when it came, she would be ready.

ONE

'I expected more of a missionary's son.'

The Dean's parting words still nagged at Timothy as he stepped off the train. He crossed the platform, pushed his way into the little station, and looked around the waiting room for a familiar face. But all he saw were strangers, so he dropped his bags on the floor and slumped onto one of the benches.

Suspended from school for two weeks – that much he'd expected, even counted on. And of course he'd known the Dean would give him a lecture beforehand, full of mournful reproaches like *You were such a fine student* and *Why did you do it, Sinclair?*

But bringing his parents into it…that was low. Timothy swiped the dark wing of hair away from his eyes and sank down in his seat, scowling.

A woman in a long winter coat swished past, and the guitar case he'd propped against the wall began to topple.

Hastily he grabbed the instrument and steadied it. Then his eyes fell to the sticker pasted on the lid: GREENHILL CHRISTIAN BOYS' SCHOOL, EST. 1956. LET YOUR LIGHT SO SHINE BEFORE MEN.

With sudden savagery Timothy dug a thumbnail under the sticker and began ripping it off piece by piece, until nothing remained but a gummy wad of paper in his hand. He shook it off into the nearby bin and slouched down again.

Minutes ticked by as he sat: five, ten, twenty. All the while people marched in and out of the station, most of them white-skinned and thin-lipped and walking as though they were in a hurry. Timothy studied their faces as they passed, but none looked familiar. Had his cousin forgotten him?

An icy gust swirled through the open door, and Timothy pulled his jacket closer. Six months in this country, and he hadn't got used to the cold: he might look like an English boy, but he still felt Ugandan inside…

'There you are!'

He started and looked around to see Peri, his cousin's wife, striding towards him.

'You've grown,' she remarked, scooping his rucksack from the floor and slinging it over her shoulder before bending to pick up Timothy's suitcase as well. 'I almost didn't recognise you. Nice lip, by the way,' and with that she headed for the door, her long legs carrying her down the steps with ease.

Was it that obvious? Timothy touched his swollen mouth

and winced. He grabbed his guitar and hurried out after Peri, arriving at the car park to see her fling open the back door of a small red car and toss the suitcase inside as though it weighed nothing whatsoever.

'Get in,' she said.

Was she angry with him, or just being her usual no-nonsense self? It was probably better not to ask. Timothy slid his guitar onto the back seat and climbed in.

As they drove away from the station, Timothy watched Peri closely. On the surface she looked just the same as she had on his last visit three years ago: still lean as a cheetah, with hair as pale as her eyes were dark and an unconventional, almost feral beauty. But there was no expression in her features, and she kept her gaze fixed on the road, not even glancing at him.

'So tell me,' she said as she steered the car round a roundabout. 'What brings you here? I thought Paul's parents were supposed to look after you if anything happened.'

'They are,' said Timothy, 'but they've gone to Majorca. They won't be back until the end of the month.'

'I see. So Paul's agreed to take you for – what? Two weeks?'

'Three, actually,' said Timothy. 'I've got half-term right after the suspension.'

'What's that?'

'There's a week of holidays after——' he began in a louder voice, but she cut him off.

'I'm not deaf. I'm asking, what's a *suspension*?'

For an intelligent woman, Peri had some surprising gaps in her knowledge. 'I got sent away from school,' he said. 'For hitting another boy.'

Her brows flicked upwards. 'That's an odd sort of punishment.'

'Not really,' said Timothy, thinking of the schoolbooks stuffed into his rucksack. Not to mention the thousand-word essay on the Beatitudes the Dean had assigned him as penance. *Blessed are the peacemakers...*

'Did he deserve it? The boy you hit?'

Timothy shifted in his seat. 'Sort of. But not really. I just——' He hesitated, wondering whether to tell her the truth, then suppressed the impulse and went on, 'I guess I just lost my temper.'

Peri looked sceptical, but made no further comment. Timothy glanced out the side window. They'd driven out of Aynsbridge now, and were speeding along a narrow road lined with hedgerows. At first the route seemed unfamiliar, but then he started to see landmarks he recognised: there on the left was the wood where he'd happily lost himself on his first visit, and further down lay the pond he'd fallen into the last time, trying to catch the biggest frog he'd ever seen.

'I suppose you've been wondering why we haven't had you come and stay with us before,' said Peri suddenly. 'You probably thought we were ignoring you, but…' Her hands lifted briefly from the wheel, shaping an apologetic gesture. 'We've had a lot to deal with these past few months. It's nothing to do with you. I'm sorry we haven't been able to make you more welcome.'

Timothy watched his own reflection in the window. He wished she hadn't brought that up: it just fired his resentment all over again. He'd expected to see a lot of Paul and Peri once he came to school in England, and visit them often at their big house in the countryside. But instead he'd spent all his holidays at his aunt and uncle's cottage in Tunbridge Wells, with neither cousin nor friend in sight. How long would it have taken Paul and Peri to acknowledge his existence, if he hadn't practically forced them to take him in?

'It's OK,' he said, trying to sound like he meant it. 'I'm here now.'

'Yes,' said Peri with an odd note in her voice, 'you certainly are.' She slowed the car as they reached the bridge, driving carefully over the ancient stones. The wood dropped behind them, bare trees yielding to a swath of brown meadow, and now Timothy could see Paul and Peri's house at last.

Oakhaven was nothing like the snug, whitewashed bungalow he'd left behind with his parents and sister in Kampala, and yet the sight of the old house gave him a sense of belonging he hadn't felt in months. He knew this place, from its foundations of warm grey stone to its ornamented gables, and everything about it said *home* to him in a way that no other place in England could.

Peri pulled the car into the drive and jumped out almost before it had stopped; by the time Timothy climbed out of the passenger seat, she was already hauling his luggage out of the back. 'I can take that,' he protested, but she strode past him, leaping up the ramp to the front door with his guitar in one hand and his suitcase in the other.

'Of course you can,' her voice floated back, 'but why should you? I'll just see if Paul's got dinner ready...' and with that she disappeared inside.

Timothy shut the car door and slung his rucksack over his shoulder, looking up at the house. From the outside it hadn't changed at all: a tall Victorian design with arched windows and a neat box of front garden. Nothing special, in itself. But over its peaked roof he could see the topmost branches of the oak that had given the house its name, and his swollen mouth tugged into an involuntary smile. He tossed his pack onto the front step and headed for the garden gate.

The first time he'd seen the old oak, Timothy had been seven years old. His parents had brought him with them to England on furlough – not a holiday, but a busy, exhausting time as they drove all over the country, visiting churches to report on their missionary work. And since his mother thought it wasn't fair to expect a child to do so much travelling, she'd brought Timothy to stay with her relatives at Oakhaven.

Timothy had been glad of the reprieve, but he was also disappointed. England was so different from Uganda, and though his aunt and uncle seemed kind, they were also very grown-up. Even his cousin, Paul, was too old for him to play with – and besides, he used a wheelchair, which in any case would have made it difficult for them to go swimming or explore the woods together. What was there, in this strange place, for a boy like Timothy to do?

But then his aunt had called him into the back garden, and he saw the tree.

It wasn't just huge, it was monumental. Its trunk could have held twenty boys his size, and its leafy arms stretched almost as wide as the house. Eagerly Timothy sized up the distance to the lowest branch, fingers clenched and toes curled with anticipation. He scrambled across the lawn and was just about to leap onto it when Paul's fiancée, Peri, grabbed him and hauled him back.

He'd cringed, expecting a tongue-lashing and a humiliating march back to the house. But Peri didn't seem angry; she'd only told him the old oak wasn't safe. Then she'd led him to the nearby wood, and shown him some trees he could climb there instead.

That was the beginning of a wonderful friendship, and for the next few weeks Timothy followed Peri everywhere. She knew all the local plants by name, and could tell him which berries and mushrooms were safe to eat and which were poisonous. She'd even taught Timothy how to snare a rabbit, skin it and tan its soft hide. Thanks to Peri there were plenty of exciting things to do at Oakhaven – but she still wouldn't let him near the great tree, and he went back to Uganda with his urge to climb it unsatisfied.

But five years later came another furlough to England – and another chance. This time Timothy had known better than to let Peri guess that he was still interested in the tree. One night he'd waited until everyone in the house was asleep, then sneaked out and climbed the oak as high as its branches would take him. It hadn't been unsafe at all, and he'd come back down with a deep and private satisfaction glowing in his heart...

The touch of cold iron against his palm brought Timothy back to the present. He worked the gate open and slipped through into the garden.

Until now he'd been picturing the oak as he'd last seen it, in its full summer glory. But it was too early in the year for that. The ground beneath his feet was black, wormed with roots and littered with the skeletons of dead leaves. Buds were forming on the tree's lower branches, but it would be weeks before they opened, and in the dim afternoon light the oak looked naked, a lonely titan shivering in the cold.

Timothy squelched across the lawn, skirting the empty flowerbeds, and stopped at the foot of the tree. How many times had he lain daydreaming under those branches?

27

Sometimes it had even seemed natural to talk to the old oak, when no one else was around. It wasn't like any other tree he'd ever seen: it didn't just have size, it had *personality*.

Of course, he was fifteen now and too old to be hugging trees, even this one. But it still seemed to deserve some kind of greeting. Timothy reached out and laid his hand against the oak's gnarled trunk, patting it gently. At first the bark felt rough and unyielding, the wood beneath it solid as ever. But then something shifted beneath his fingers, and he snatched his hand back in alarm.

A crack had appeared in the surface of the tree.

Timothy's heart gave a queer, uncertain beat. As a boy he'd liked to imagine that the oak tree held a secret door, and that it would open to him if only he pressed the right spot. But he was too old for such childish ideas now. If the black hole in front of him looked oddly neat and symmetrical, it could only be by accident.

But for the trunk to just *give* like that...it had to be rotting, dying from the inside out. And he'd just made matters worse by touching it. Shaken, Timothy stepped back, wiping his bark-crumbed fingers on his jeans.

'Timothy!' called Peri from the house. 'What are you doing?'

Her voice sounded sharp, even angry. Timothy was just about to answer when all at once his eyes stung and watered, as though someone had blown smoke in them. When his vision cleared, the crack in the oak's surface had vanished.

Disbelieving, he reached out to touch the place where the hole had been...

Don't be stupid. It's just an old tree. And why are you hanging about outside, when you should be in there saying hello to your cousin?

A prickling discomfort came over him, and suddenly Timothy didn't *want* to be near the oak any more. He pulled his hand away and was turning to leave when he heard a rasping croak from above. Two crows flapped out of the oak's branches, their silhouettes stark against the ashen sky.

Timothy shivered, stuffing his cold hands into his pockets, and began picking his way back through the garden towards the house. Yet even as he walked he felt his spine tingle, as though something – or someone – was watching him.

TWO

The watchful feeling followed Timothy all the way to the house, but once he'd made his way inside and shut the door, it soon faded. Inside Oakhaven was all light and warmth, wooden floors glossy with age and walls painted rich, spicy hues; modern design shook hands with classic architecture, and the furniture looked comfortable enough to sleep on. The place had definitely changed since his aunt and uncle moved out, but to Timothy's mind it was all for the better. He dropped his rucksack by the staircase and headed down the corridor.

He found Paul sitting at the kitchen table, chopping onions. 'There you are!' he said as Timothy entered, putting down the knife and pivoting his wheelchair to greet him. 'Good to see you, though I suppose we could wish for better circumstances. Have a seat.' He plucked a chair from beside him and sent it skidding across the tiles towards Timothy. 'Now what's this about getting suspended?'

'It was nothing,' said Timothy, squirming a little under his cousin's level gaze. 'I was just being stupid.'

'He says,' came Peri's voice from the open refrigerator, 'that he lost his temper.' She sounded perfectly calm now, as though she'd forgotten she'd ever snapped at him. 'Paul, have we used up all the mayonnaise again?'

'Look in the door,' said Paul, then returned his attention to Timothy. 'So was the other boy hurt? Worse than you, I mean.'

Timothy ran his tongue across his split lip. 'Not really. I just knocked the wind out of him. But fighting's against school rules no matter what, so…I guess I got what I deserved.'

'Hm,' said Paul. 'Do your parents know?'

'Not yet. I was supposed to call them when I got here. Only they'll be in bed now, so I thought…maybe I could send them an email.' Or pretend to, anyway. It wouldn't take long to fake an apologetic message and send a copy to the Dean, but what he really needed to say to his parents would take more time to figure out. A *lot* more time.

Paul looked sceptical, and Timothy held his breath. But in the end his cousin only said, 'All right,' then picked up the knife and began chopping again.

That had been far too easy. It wasn't like Paul – or Peri either; they'd always been patient with Timothy's mistakes, but when he broke the rules they'd given him no quarter until he put things right. Maybe they'd decided he was old enough to take responsibility for his own actions, but he couldn't shake the feeling that something was wrong here...

The telephone warbled.

'Excuse me,' said Paul, wheeling to answer. 'Hello, Paul McCormick speaking.' He glanced at Timothy. 'Yes, he's here. Did you want to speak to him?'

Timothy's stomach did a swan dive. It had to be his parents. The Dean had called them and told them what he'd done, and he wasn't ready. What was he going to say?

'I see,' Paul said. 'All right then. Goodbye.' He put the phone back down. 'Just the secretary at your school, making sure you'd arrived.'

'Oh, right,' said Timothy, his voice cracking with relief. 'They said they'd do that. So...what's for supper?'

They ate right there in the kitchen, which made Timothy feel a little more at ease: it meant Paul and Peri were treating him as family, instead of making an awkward fuss on his account. But even so, he couldn't shake the feeling that they were putting an effort into appearing relaxed and friendly with him, instead of just *being* that way.

'So,' said Paul as he passed Timothy the salad, 'how's your family?'

'Fine, I guess,' said Timothy.

'Uncle Neil still running that clinic for the poor, or whatever?'

'Yeah.' Kampala itself had good medical facilities, but his

father often travelled to the nearby village of Luweero to offer his services. He also preached at the chapel and led Bible studies in their home, but Paul probably wasn't interested in that. 'He keeps pretty busy.'

'And your mum? What's she up to these days?'

This was torture. Paul and Peri had never tried to make small talk with him before: they'd always talked about interesting things, like nature and art and music. He forced himself to answer politely, and was dreading the next question when Peri broke in:

'Tell me about Uganda. What's it like?'

Timothy was surprised: she'd never asked him about his home country before, and he'd assumed she wasn't interested. 'It's…different,' he said. 'Warmer mostly, and there's more sunshine and not nearly as much rain. But it's not all dried up or anything,' he added quickly. 'It's got plenty of green plants and trees and flowers. Kampala's the capital, so there are lots of big banks and hotels and lots of traffic…'

His memory conjured up the image of Entebbe Road at rush hour, crammed end-to-end with the blue-striped white vans that served as regular taxis while the motorcycle *boda-bodas* darted in and out of the chaos. His mother had begged Timothy not to ride the *bodas* when he went into the city with his friends, as they were so dangerous, but they were so much cheaper and faster than a taxi that he'd usually done it anyway.

'The buildings are mostly light-coloured plaster,' he went

on slowly, trying to put the images into words, 'and the roofs are red. Instead of crows and pigeons, we have these big ugly storks. And the streets are full of people, but it's not like here where everyone rushes around with their heads down and won't even look at each other. Ugandans are friendly, they like to talk and laugh, and when you meet someone they ask how you're doing and if your family is well and if you have any news...'

Paul nodded politely, but Timothy could tell he wasn't that interested. Peri, on the other hand, had a faraway look on her face, as though she were imagining herself in Uganda at that very moment. 'It sounds fascinating,' she said. 'Like nothing I've ever seen. I wish...'

Her words trailed off as Paul reached over and gently put his hand on hers. She looked down at their overlapping fingers, and her face closed up again. 'Yes. Well, never mind that. Have you had enough to eat?'

'The computer's in my studio,' said Paul, leading Timothy down the corridor to a pair of French doors. 'The connection's slow, though, and sometimes it doesn't work at all. I can't make any promises.'

Though the curtains were drawn and the room dimly lit, it only took Timothy an instant to recognise his aunt's old parlour. But now the built-in shelves that had once held porcelain figurines were littered with paintbrushes and tubes of oils, while an easel stood where the piano used to be.

And instead of family photographs the walls were hung with canvases, all rendered in the bold strokes and vibrant hues that were Paul McCormick's trademark.

'Here you go,' said Paul. He flicked a switch and the track lighting at the back of the room came on, revealing a computer desk in the corner. 'Help yourself. Any problems, give a shout,' and with that he wheeled back out into the hallway.

Timothy dragged over a chair and sat down in front of the computer. Despite Paul's warning the internet connection seemed to be working fine, and within a few minutes he had logged in to his school account.

You have one new message, his mailbox informed him.

Timothy's heart plummeted as he saw the return address. It was from his mother. Swallowing against the sudden dryness in his throat, he forced himself to click the email open.

Hello, dear one! Hope this finds you well and happy, as we all are here...

He relaxed. Just her usual weekly letter. She hadn't found out about his suspension after all: wouldn't, either, until Timothy was ready to tell her. Though when he explained the reason for what he'd done, the news that he'd picked a fight with the biggest boy in the school would be the least of his mother's worries, probably.

He skimmed the first few paragraphs of her note – which

included a report of how his little sister, Lydia, was doing at school, as well as a funny story involving one of the neighbourhood children and a list of requests for prayer – then slowed abruptly at the sight of a familiar name:

Miriam has been helping me with the children's club, and a wonderful help she is too! So good to have her lovely voice to lead the singing, instead of my feeble croak. She asks to be remembered to you, and says she will write soon. In the meantime I am sending you a picture I took of her and Lydia last Sunday...

Quickly Timothy scrolled down to the photograph. There she stood in front of the familiar whitewashed bungalow on Luthuli Avenue, one long arm draped about his sister's shoulders. Her hair was a mass of tight braids, with a colourful scarf tied around it, and her smile seemed to blaze out of the screen. Miriam Sewanaku, his neighbour and best friend.

He missed her, now more than ever. She'd introduced him to the music of Bernard Kabanda, who'd become one of his musical heroes; and when he bought his first guitar she hadn't laughed at the *muzungu* boy wanting to play Ugandan music, the way Timothy's schoolmates did. Instead she'd gone to a family friend, one of the finest guitarists in Kampala, and persuaded him to teach Timothy how to play.

Without Miriam's encouragement, he might have given

up. But now the guitar had become his passion, and he couldn't imagine a life without it. He would always be grateful to her for that – and lately, he'd come to realise that he might be a little more than just grateful. But she was a year older than he was, and he was a *muzungu*, and besides they were both too young to do anything about it. So he hadn't worked up the courage to say anything…at least, not yet.

Reluctantly Timothy closed his mother's letter and started a new message of his own. A few lines to his old email account in Uganda (which his parents never checked), a copy to Greenhill to make sure the Dean was satisfied…done. He shut down the computer and…

There it was again, that feeling of being watched. As though there were some *presence* in the room with him, invisible but uncomfortably real. Timothy sat very still a moment, then abruptly spun around—

No one was there. But on the opposite wall hung a painting he'd never seen before. It was a portrait of Peri, her narrowed eyes staring directly out of the canvas. Her feet were bare, and she gripped a long knife in her hand.

Timothy got up from his chair and went to examine the picture more closely. It was beautifully done, but something about it bothered him. It wasn't that Peri looked murderous, not exactly: if her expression was fierce it was only in a protective way, like the face of a guardian angel. In fact, the way the light filtered through the leaves behind her looked almost like a pair of translucent wings…

No, that was stupid, he was reading too much into it. But something about the portrait still made him feel uneasy, like it was sending him a message – or a warning – he didn't understand.

Timothy glanced around at the rest of the art displayed – mostly Paul's, interspersed with a few pen-and-ink sketches in a different style that had to be Peri's – then turned off the lights and left. But as he climbed the stairs, the image of that strange portrait still haunted him, like a voice whispering at the back of his mind:

Beware.

The guest bedroom had a four-poster and a window overlooking the front garden, and it was as big as the room he'd shared with three other boys at Greenhill. Timothy kicked off his trainers and jeans, flopped back onto the mattress and put his hands behind his head, thinking.

Maybe there wasn't anything wrong at Oakhaven. Maybe it was just him. He'd been confused and unhappy for so long, he just needed time to relax and get his head clear – that was why he'd come here in the first place, wasn't it? Maybe all he needed was a good night's sleep, and this feeling of constant tension, of being spied on wherever he went, would go away.

And yet out there in the garden, beneath the oak tree...he knew what he'd seen, what his hands had touched. That hole in the trunk had been real. So how could it just have disappeared like that?

Part of him wanted to go back outside at once, and investigate. But the sky was dark now, and there'd be plenty of time for that tomorrow. Timothy got up, picked a novel off the shelf at random and read until his eyes felt heavy. At last he turned out the light and settled down to sleep.

He was just drifting off when he heard a voice floating up through the grate beside his bed, muffled and tinny-sounding but still distinct:

'...*difficult with him here, but we'll have to manage somehow.*'

It was Peri, talking about him. And now that Timothy knew it, there was no way he could close his eyes and pretend he hadn't heard. He squirmed closer and dangled over the edge of the mattress, straining to hear Paul's deeper voice reply:

'*Of course. But we'll still need to warn the others. Make sure they know it's not safe to visit until we give the word.*'

Not safe? Timothy frowned. All right, so he'd hit somebody and got himself suspended, but Paul was making him sound like some kind of dangerous criminal. Or the mad cousin shut up in the attic.

'*I don't think they'd try it in any case,*' said Peri. '*Not with so many crows about.*'

Had she really said *crows*?

'*You're forgetting Linden,*' Paul remarked. '*Or was that wishful thinking?*'

Peri must have made a face instead of answering, because

Paul went on in an amused tone: '*Not my fault, love. She's her mother's daughter. Or –*' his voice sobered – '*as near to it as we're ever going to see.*'

'*Don't say that! I'm not ready to give up yet. And don't tell me you are, either.*'

'*What else can we do? We're only human. No offence.*'

Peri was silent.

'*And as for the rest,*' Paul continued more gently, '*remember what Amaryllis said. They've got to find their own solution. It's not your battle any more.*'

'*Whose is it, then? Hers?*' She was bitter now. '*If it is, it won't be for much longer. And how long will the oak survive once she's gone?*'

Timothy had done a lot of eavesdropping in his time, but this had to be one of the oddest conversations he'd ever overheard. He was still wondering who Linden and Amaryllis might be and what the oak tree had to do with anything when he heard Paul say in a husky voice, '*Love. Don't look like that. Come here.*'

There was a long silence, and then Peri said, '*I just want this to be over. I want to be able to leave the house without worrying that something's going to happen while I'm away. I want—*'

'*I know. If anyone was meant to see the world, it was you.*' Now it was Paul's turn to sound bitter. '*And I can't give you that. Especially not right now.*'

'*It's not your fault.*'

'*Isn't it?*'

'*Paul Graydon McCormick.*' Her voice was stern, but there was a shake in it that might have been laughter, or tears. '*You start wallowing in self-pity and I'll wheel you down the road and dump you in the pond myself.*'

'*I'd like to see you try,*' said Paul in a tone that was half-growl, and for a moment Timothy thought he was angry. But then their words slurred to murmurs, broken by pauses that were not entirely silent, and Timothy decided it was time to stop listening. He dropped a pillow onto the grate and wormed back into the middle of the bed, resolutely shutting his eyes.

But his dreams were full of dark wings and great trees falling, and he did not sleep well.

THREE

When Timothy woke, it took him a minute of staring stupidly at the ceiling to remember where he was. Pale light fingered the edges of the curtains, and the silence seemed expectant somehow, as though the house were waiting for its inhabitants to hatch.

The bedside clock glowed 7.05 – too early for Timothy's liking, but it was pointless trying to sleep longer. He stumbled out of bed, scrounged some clean clothes from the tangled mess inside his suitcase, and headed off to the bathroom.

He had just turned on the shower when he noticed something outside the window. Brushing aside the gauzy curtain, he peered out to see Peri striding across the back garden towards the house. She carried a vicious-looking knife in one hand, and the limp body of a dead rabbit in the other.

Timothy let the curtain fall and stepped into the shower, but even the hot water couldn't wash away the crawling feeling that had come over him. As a child he'd thought everything Peri did was wonderful, but seeing her now reminded him just how unnatural her love of hunting really was. As far as he knew, she didn't eat anything she caught, or sell the pelts either. Yet as long as he'd known her, she'd been killing wild rabbits and other small creatures on a regular basis...

'You're up early,' Peri remarked when he came down to the kitchen a few minutes later, still damp-haired from his wash. 'Did you sleep all right?'

'Not bad,' said Timothy, watching her sidelong while she wiped her hands on a tea towel. They looked clean, but as she turned them over he could see a dark line of blood beneath one nail.

'Well, I've already eaten and Paul won't be up for an hour at least,' said Peri, 'so you may as well go ahead and have your breakfast. There's fruit and cold cereal, or you can make toast if you'd like – here.' She pulled the toaster from a shelf and set it on the counter, hesitating fractionally before plugging it in with a quick, almost savage thrust. 'I'll be in the studio if you need me.'

One apple and two bowls of cornflakes later, Timothy piled his dishes by the sink and looked out the kitchen window. The sky was the colour of dirty wool, the garden dismal with rain. He still wanted to have another look at the old oak tree, but there was no reason it couldn't wait until the weather cleared.

All at once he heard a high-pitched cry, and a small brown shape flashed by the window, with a crow in close pursuit. Timothy knew more about marabou storks than he did most British birds, but he was pretty sure crows didn't usually hunt on the wing like that. Didn't they eat things that were already dead?

From the other end of the house came a muffled oath, and the sound of feet pounding up and down the stairs. Timothy stuck his head out into the corridor to see Peri wrench the front door open and leap outside—

Had she been carrying a *gun*?

Timothy raced down the hallway and skidded to a halt on the step. Peri stood barefoot on the muddy lawn, an air rifle raised against her shoulder. She squeezed the trigger, and the crow plummeted from the sky.

Shocked, Timothy was about to protest, but then Peri turned and the fire in her dark eyes silenced him.

'Go back inside, Timothy,' she said.

'What happened?' said Paul sharply from behind them. 'I thought I heard—'

'You heard me,' said Peri. She strode back into the house, propped the gun against the wall, and began wiping the dirt off her feet with a rag. 'But it's all right now.'

'Is it?' asked Paul.

Peri straightened up. 'I did what I had to do,' she said. 'And if those crows don't keep their distance, I'll keep shooting until they get the message.' Her fist clenched around the rag, crumpling it. 'How *dare* they!'

Paul opened his mouth, glanced at Timothy and shut it again. At last he said with deliberate calm, 'Quite. But I expect people might begin to wonder, if you make a habit of it.'

People meaning him, Timothy supposed. But it was a bit too late to stop him wondering now. 'I don't get it,' he said. 'It was only a crow.'

'You don't understand,' said Peri, and turned an appealing look to her husband. 'It was chasing one of ours, Paul. What else could I have done?'

'Ours?' Paul looked startled, as though this put a whole new complexion on the matter. 'Did it get away all right?'

'I don't know,' Peri said, pushing her feet into her shoes. 'I couldn't see her anywhere.'

'I didn't know you kept birds,' said Timothy.

'We don't,' said Paul. 'They're wild. It's just that we've been looking after them for a few years now, and we've become…quite fond of them.' He glanced at his wife, who had turned her face away, then continued in a crisper tone, 'The crows here are overpopulated, and they're becoming more aggressive all the time. If something isn't done to protect the other wildlife, we'll soon have nothing *but* crows.'

'I'm going to look outside,' said Peri. 'In case she's just hiding.' She snatched up the rifle again and disappeared.

'Well,' said Paul to Timothy, 'we may not get out much, but never let it be said we aren't interesting.'

He smiled wryly as he spoke, but there was no humour in his eyes, and Timothy's answering smile was equally thin.

Peri spent much of that morning in the garden and the neighbouring fields, searching for her lost bird. When she returned to the house her expression was strained, and Paul began to look anxious as well: they kept leaving Timothy alone and going off to consult with each other in whispers, until Timothy couldn't stand it any longer and went upstairs to play his guitar.

After five years of practising an hour or more every day, he knew the strings so well he could have played blind. He'd even started picking out some tunes of his own lately, though songwriting proved to be more of a challenge than he'd expected. The tune he'd been working on had an amazing chord progression; just playing those three arpeggios made his bones vibrate. But he hadn't been able to figure out what to play next, no matter what he tried.

Once again he felt eyes upon him, though he knew no one was there. Timothy steeled himself to ignore it, and kept playing. Arpeggio, arpeggio, arpeggio…

Then his fingers seemed to move of their own accord, leaping up the neck of the guitar to a position he'd never even thought of before. He'd found it! Timothy slapped the guitar in triumph – and amazingly, that was right, too. Arpeggios, strum, slap, repeat. Perfect!

He was playing the line over and over, cementing it in his

memory, when something small and brown flickered at the edge of his vision.

Peri's missing bird?

Timothy thrust the guitar aside and jumped up just in time to see the thing zoom out into the corridor. Beyond the doorway, a blur of distant movement caught his eye. *Aha!* He pelted down the hallway to the bathroom – to find nothing but his own reflection in the toothpaste-speckled mirror. He'd been chasing himself.

Maybe the bird had flown out the window? He'd only raised it a couple of centimetres after his shower, but now it gaped wide. Timothy was reaching out to close it when he saw Peri walking out across the lawn.

He was about to call down to her, but then she stopped and glanced back over her shoulder, as though anxious not to be seen. Instinctively Timothy ducked out of sight, and when he dared to look again Peri was standing at the foot of the oak tree, one hand raised to its massive trunk. She knocked once – and then, to Timothy's surprise, she kneeled down on the muddy ground and bowed her head.

It couldn't be what it looked like. She must be pulling a weed, or picking up a bit of rubbish, or setting another rabbit snare. But as he watched, she took something out of her pocket and tucked it between the roots of the tree. Then she folded her hands in her lap and her lips began to move, as though she were praying.

No, that was ridiculous. He'd met nature-worshippers,

but Peri surely wasn't one of them. As far as he'd been able to tell, neither she nor Paul was particularly religious: that was one of the reasons he'd looked forward to coming here, knowing they wouldn't judge him by what he did or didn't believe.

So…what exactly *was* she doing?

Timothy squinted out the window until Peri rose, brushed the mud from her knees, and began walking back towards the house. But she'd left something behind: a little parcel, sticking out from the base of the tree.

He had to know what was in it.

Timothy stood still a moment, eyes fixed on Peri's retreating figure. Then he spun around and ran back down the corridor to his bedroom. Pulling on his jacket, teeth gritted in anticipation of the cold, he slipped downstairs and eased out the front door, closing it quietly behind him.

Outside the air felt heavy, the smell of rain-soaked earth overpowering. A damp chill seeped through the soles of Timothy's shoes as he edged around the corner of the house and through the garden gate, keeping low so as not to be seen.

The garden looked empty: Peri must have gone back inside. Timothy waited a few more seconds, just to be sure. Then, moving so stealthily that even the sparrow hopping across the lawn didn't turn its head, he crept towards the oak.

'Timothy!'

Peri's voice rang out from behind him. He'd been caught, but there was no way Timothy was going to give up now. He lowered his head and started to run.

She came after him, but Timothy was faster. He sprinted across the wet lawn, then caught his foot on a root and fell sprawling. Dazed though he was, his eyes darted at once to where Peri had kneeled and left her offering just a minute before…

But the little package was gone.

'Timothy, what is wrong with you?' demanded Peri as she strode up to him. 'I told you to—'

'I saw something fly past me,' said Timothy, getting up and wiping his mud-smeared hands on his jeans. 'Upstairs, in the house. I thought it might be your bird, so I tried to chase it down, but then it flew out here and… I tripped before I could catch it.'

Peri's eyes narrowed. 'I didn't see any bird.'

There was nothing Timothy could say to that. He stood there looking at her, trying not to shiver as the icy wind bit through his jacket and raised a fresh layer of goosebumps on his skin.

'Look,' Peri went on after a moment, 'I don't know why you came out here, or what you thought you were going to find. So I'll just say this.' Her face hardened. 'Stay away from the Oak.'

Not *the oak tree* but *the Oak*, as clear as if she'd written the capital letter in the air between them. She wore the same ferocious expression Paul had painted in her portrait, and Timothy stepped back, wary. 'What do you mean?'

'I saw you poking at it yesterday, when you first got here,' she said. 'It's very old, and fragile, and you're big enough to know better. So you can just keep to the house from now on, and leave the Oak alone.'

Heat rushed into Timothy's face. Was that what she really thought – that he'd been trying to damage the old tree? Pick off the bark and carve his name into its skin like some ignorant lout with no respect for nature or other people's property?

'I'd never do anything to hurt it,' he protested, trying not to think of the fact that only yesterday, he had – albeit by accident. 'This is because of the suspension, isn't it? Just because I got into one fight at school, you think I'm some kind of troublemaker?'

Peri folded her arms and looked at him, her mouth a straight line. She didn't speak, but all at once Timothy understood.

'No, I get it,' he said with sudden bitterness. 'You don't want me here. That's why you never even asked me, isn't it? Five months at Greenhill, and I never heard from you or Paul once. And now that you're stuck with me you've been trying to make the best of a bad lot, but what you really wish is that I'd never come here in the first place.'

'Timothy, it's not—'

'Yes, it is. I can tell.' He was shaking now, though with

cold or anger he couldn't tell. He felt hollow inside, like an empty cage: his last hope of security had flown and there was nobody he could count on now, not even himself. 'Fine. I'll go. I'll stay out of your way. And I won't touch your precious Oak again.'

'Timothy!'

She sounded distressed, but Timothy was in no mood to listen. He turned his back on her and stalked off towards the house.

He didn't come down to supper when Peri called him, or answer her tentative knock at his door. But when he heard the drone of the stairlift, Timothy realised that he'd taken his rebellion too far. He opened the bedroom door to find Paul sitting in the corridor just outside, hands gripping the wheels of his chair as though preparing to ram the door down.

'Sorry,' said Timothy, before his cousin could speak.

'It's not me you should be sorry for,' said Paul curtly.

'I know. I'll apologise.'

'That you will.' Paul wheeled into the room, his cool gaze sweeping over the clothes scattered across the floor, the unmade bed. 'Peri's willing to make excuses for you, but she doesn't know your parents. They're good people – and I know they raised you better than this.'

Somehow Timothy could tell that when Paul said *this*, he didn't just mean what had happened between him and Peri. He looked down at his feet.

'It can't have been easy for them,' Paul went on, 'sending you away. Obviously they thought you'd get a better education here, but it can't have been cheap, either. I'm guessing Uncle Neil doesn't make a lot of money, church support or not.'

There was a dead bluebottle on the windowsill. Timothy brushed it off and leaned his forehead against the cold glass, suddenly weary. 'It wasn't just them. I wanted to come.'

It had seemed like an adventure, back then. But nothing had turned out the way he'd hoped. Academically, Greenhill was an excellent school, but the so-called Christian atmosphere didn't seem to have done much for Timothy's schoolmates. At best they'd kept an uncomfortable distance, not knowing how to talk to a boy who looked English but didn't care about any of the things the rest of them considered important, like the plots of Hollywood action movies or how to play the latest video games. At worst they'd mocked Timothy openly, finding fault with his clothes, his accent, and most of all, his love of Uganda.

Timothy's confidence in the transforming power of Christianity had begun to weaken, his doubts growing as he encountered scientific books and articles that argued against his faith. Then the Gospel Hall he'd been attending – the closest thing he could find to the Brethren chapel he'd been part of in Kampala – closed down after one of the elders was caught stealing from the missionary fund. When Timothy's isolation became unbearable he'd prayed fervently that Paul and Peri would invite him to Oakhaven, but they hadn't called or written once. By the time he'd seen the bus advertisement telling him that God probably didn't exist, Timothy was ready to believe it.

'So is it really that terrible for you, being here?' Paul persisted. 'Or is it just the school you hate?'

'Greenhill's all right,' said Timothy, his eyes following a pair of crows as they flapped past. 'I mean, the teachers are decent, and I've been getting good marks and that sort of thing. I just…don't fit in.'

'The battle cry of the McCormicks,' said Paul dryly. 'I see your genes have done you no favours there. But was it really necessary to get yourself suspended to prove the point?'

'What makes you think I—'

'Oh, come on, Tim. Even as a kid you were a calculating little beggar. Don't think I hadn't noticed you timed that stunt perfectly so you'd end up being sent here, instead of moping about in Tunbridge Wells with my mum and dad. What are you thinking, then? That if you make yourself odious enough at Greenhill your parents will have to pull you out and send you to a different school instead?'

Timothy shifted uncomfortably. 'It's not like that.' Well, maybe it was, but he hadn't planned that far ahead yet. All he'd been able to think of while he was at Greenhill was that somehow he had to get away from there before he went insane.

'What is it like, then?'

The words came automatically. 'You wouldn't understand.'

'Right. Because no one has ever felt the way you do.' Paul blew out a sigh. 'Fine then, I'll leave you to your beautiful misery. But if you're planning to sulk your way through the next three weeks, I may as well drive you into town right now and book you into the hostel. Peri's got enough on her mind at the moment – she shouldn't have to deal with your attitude on top of everything else.'

Humiliation scorched through Timothy. To be thrown out of Oakhaven, the one place in England he'd counted on always being welcome…it was the worst thing he could imagine right now. And why? Just because he'd touched some old tree, and dared to be curious about what Peri had been doing in the garden? What kind of sense did that make?

'Anyway,' remarked Paul over his shoulder as he pivoted the chair and rolled towards the door, 'if you can stop brooding long enough to eat, Peri's kept some supper for you. Otherwise, we'll see you tomorrow.'

Timothy waited until the hum of the stairlift receded before slamming the door and throwing himself down on the bed. Anger seethed inside him, and it took all his resolve not to snatch the alarm clock off the bedside table and hurl it across the room.

So that was all he had to look forward to at Oakhaven? Three weeks shut up in the house, with strange things happening all around him that he wasn't allowed to question, let alone investigate? There was no way Timothy could stand it.

May as well drive you into town right now and book you into the hostel...

He grabbed his rucksack and pulled out his wallet, leafing through its contents. The bank card was good for a couple of hundred pounds, plus he still had fifty, no, sixty left over from Christmas. If he was careful, it might just be enough to get by. And if he got stuck, he could always make some money by playing his guitar. In which case there'd be no need for him to come back here, except to pick up his suitcase...

Timothy shoved the wallet into his pocket, then dumped the schoolbooks out of his rucksack and started stuffing clothes in. Halfway through the process he paused to tear a page out of one of his workbooks and scrawl a hasty note:

Thanks for the food, sorry for the trouble.
See you in three weeks.
Timothy

He was just shoving the last pair of his socks into the rucksack when the light above his head winked out. Annoyed, he dropped the pack and opened the bedroom door – to find the lights in the corridor still glowing brightly.

A fuse must have blown, but he wasn't about to go downstairs and ask Peri to fix it. Timothy left the door open and returned to finish packing as best he could. But then the corridor lights flicked off as well, and in the distance he heard the thin chuckle of running water.

No worries, Timothy told himself, though his heart was skittering around in his chest. *You left the tap on by accident, that's all.* Feeling his way through the blackness, Timothy followed the noise to find a steady trickle coming from the bathroom tap. He turned it off – and at the same instant, the lights behind him blinked back on.

Timothy didn't believe in ghosts. But *something* was playing games with him, and the knowledge sent electric eels down his spine. Slowly he walked back to his room, braced to confront whoever – or whatever – might be waiting. But he had just reached the doorway when all went black again.

That was it. Timothy leaped into the darkened bedroom, zipped his rucksack and flung it over his shoulder; then he snatched up his guitar case in one hand and his shoes in the other, and fled.

It was an almost impossible effort to slow down and tread lightly on the staircase, but somehow Timothy did it, reaching the front door with barely a creak. As he wrestled his feet into his trainers he held his breath, sure that at any moment Paul or Peri would come out of the kitchen to challenge him; but no sound came from the far end of the house except the clatter of dishes and the blare of the evening news.

Timothy eased the door open and squeezed out onto the

step, clutching the guitar in front of him like a shield. Then he stepped cautiously over the wheelchair ramp, hurried through the front garden, and sprinted down the road towards the village.

The train station at Aynsbridge wasn't far, not for a seasoned walker: it took Timothy only forty minutes to get there. But by the time he struggled through the door with his guitar case he felt as though his arm were coming out of its socket, and he was glad he hadn't brought anything heavier with him.

He bought a ticket and sat down to wait, his leg jittering nervously, until the last stripe of sunlight bled into the horizon and the sign above him read LONDON BRIDGE: 1 min. As he walked outside the man sweeping the platform gave him a quizzical glance, and despite the chill Timothy felt sweat prickle along his hairline. Any minute now somebody would march up and demand to know what he was doing travelling so late on a school night, and where his parents were...

But this was England, where other people's children were other people's business, and no one spoke to him, or even moved in his direction. The train screeched into the station, and he jumped onto it. The doors hissed shut, the carriage jolted into motion, and just like that, Timothy Sinclair was away.

FOUR

A rack of brochures stood by the station exit. Timothy flipped through them, looking for hostels. There seemed to be quite a few within walking distance, but the closest was the Trans-National, a few streets away. Stuffing the pamphlet into his pocket, he picked up his guitar case and headed off.

A slimy rain began to fall as he walked, dripping down the collar of his jacket; taxis honked at him, and buses rumbled by. He passed clumps and straggles of pedestrians, all walking briskly and not sparing him so much as a glance. The guitar case dragged at his arm, and the straps of his rucksack chafed. Timothy was gazing blearily into the distance and thinking that the hostel had looked a lot nearer on the map when suddenly he tripped, staggering against a shop window. He looked down and saw with dull surprise that his shoelace had come untied.

Now that was odd. He'd done it up on the train, and he was sure he'd double-knotted it. Setting down his guitar case, he dropped to one knee to fix it – and someone bumped into him from behind.

'Oh, sorry!' said a light alto voice, and a hand came down on his shoulder. Timothy spun around to see a willowy girl with skin the colour of tea leaves and dark hair falling in braids to her shoulders. His heart felt weak, and his lips moved in soundless disbelief: *Miriam?*

No, of course it wasn't. This girl's nose was narrower and longer, her lips less full. 'It's OK,' he said, feeling his ears grow hot at his own mistake. 'I shouldn't have just stopped like that. Sorry.'

The girl laughed, a rich throaty sound. 'Well, if we're both sorry, then it can't be anyone's fault, can it?' Under the glow of the streetlamp her teeth flashed white. 'I'm just glad I didn't smash your guitar. Off to a gig?'

He had a fleeting thought of lying and saying yes, just to impress her. 'No,' he admitted. 'Just the hostel.' She looked only a couple of years older than he was, well-dressed and alone; it was probably safe to tell her that much. Besides, even if her accent was pure London, the friendliness in her voice reminded him of home.

'Which one, the Trans-National?'

He nodded.

'Ah.' She looked amused now, though he couldn't imagine why. 'Well, best of luck.' Without waiting for a response she walked off, her hips swaying lightly but her shoulders perfectly straight. It was the same way Miriam walked when she was carrying something on her head – a skill he'd never been able to duplicate, no matter how hard he tried – and Timothy watched her with a wistful lump in his throat until she raised a hand to her ear and began speaking into it:

'Rosie? It's Veronica. Listen...'

The sound of her voice faded as she crossed the street. Funny, he hadn't seen her take out a mobile... Timothy shook himself back to attention, finished tying his shoelace, and started off again.

When he reached the Trans-National, its doors were half-blocked by a cluster of young people in ragged jeans, smoking cigarettes and chatting in a babel of languages. Whoops and giggles rang in his ears as two of the boys shoved each other around in a mock fight. Timothy dodged past them and plunged inside.

'Sorry,' said the shaggy, heavily pierced clerk at the desk. 'Can't get a room here without proof of age. Driver's licence, that sort of thing. Got to be eighteen or over 'cause of the bar, see.'

Timothy slumped. Sixteen he could pass for, but not eighteen. 'Do you know another hostel I could try?' he said.

The clerk chewed on his lip ring, sizing Timothy up. 'There's the Old Victoria,' he said, pointing out the location on the map tacked to the desk. 'They'll probably take you.'

'Thanks,' said Timothy wearily, and squeezed back out

the door again. This time he bumped into one of the boys, who said in a gruff American accent, 'Watch it!'

'Aw, he's just a kid,' said the girl next to him. 'Leave him alone, Tyler.'

Tyler shot him a glare, but subsided. Timothy gave the American a wide berth, and was just stepping onto the pavement when a young woman with hair like a crested crane touched his shoulder. 'Try this place,' she said, pushing a card into his hand.

Timothy looked down, expecting a coupon for some local pub or tourist trap. Instead he saw a cream-coloured card with a single engraved word on the front: SANCTUARY. He turned it over and read:

FOR THE DISCRIMINATING TRAVELLER ON A BUDGET
SECURE, WELL-MAINTAINED, ATTRACTIVE HOSTEL
IN THE HEART OF LONDON
NO SMOKING, NO ALCOHOL, NO AGE LIMIT
PRESENT THIS CARD AT BOOKING FOR A 20% DISCOUNT

'So why aren't you staying there?' he asked, trying to keep his voice light so he wouldn't sound accusing, merely curious.

She gave him a sly grin and tapped the words *no alcohol*. 'But if I were underage or just wanted a place to sleep, I'd go to Sanctuary like a shot.'

Timothy started to pocket the card, then thought better of it and handed it back. 'It's OK,' he said.

'What, you don't trust me?' She looked affronted. 'I was just trying to help.'

'I know,' he said, 'but the Old Victoria is closer.'

He must have spoken louder than he'd realised, because someone in the crowd behind him laughed. 'Yeah – if you like ripped sheets and bedbugs.'

There were noises of general agreement, and the crane-haired girl dropped her cigarette and led Timothy a little way down the pavement. 'Here,' she said, pointing up the street. 'Go that way, take the second street on the left and walk for about…' She thought for a moment. 'Five minutes. It'll be on the right, just past the fish and chip shop. Used to be a church, so you can't miss it.'

A church. Timothy's heart sank a little, but after what the others had said about the Old Victoria, it seemed he didn't have much choice. 'Thanks,' he said, and set off.

Some time later, Timothy stood gazing up at a pillared entrance with the words GRACE BAPTIST CHURCH carved over the lintel. A scrap of greasy newspaper tumbled by and plastered itself against his shoe; he shook it off, and it whisked into the street and was gone.

He shouldn't have come here, Timothy realised with a flicker of apprehension. The street was too quiet, too dimly lit. Besides, the old church looked deserted: no light shone from its windows, and the battered wooden doors were closed. He was wondering if he should go back and look for the Old Victoria after all when the door swung open, flooding the step with honeyed light. From inside he heard laughter, and the faint, lilting notes of a guitar. 'You looking for Sanctuary?' said a cheerful voice.

Suddenly the place seemed transformed, no longer a haunted church but a haven of worldly welcome. 'Yeah, I am,' said Timothy, and hurried in.

Brushing past the smiling boy at the door, he found himself in a vestibule plastered with posters advertising bus tours to Stonehenge, offering discount coupons for a local café and announcing the opening of a new 24-hour launderette, international visitors welcomed. A wall rack that had once held gospel tracts was now stuffed with tourist brochures, while the shelves built for hymn books were full of visitors' muddy shoes. Reassured, Timothy made his way through a second set of doors and into the noisy bustle of the hostel's common room.

His eyes found the guitarist at once: a young man with a lean face and fox-coloured hair, eyes half-closed as his fingers plucked out a Spanish melody. He sat alone on a dilapidated sofa in one corner, while by his feet two bored-looking and nearly identical boys in leather jackets played chess. In the opposite corner a small crowd had gathered, of varying ages and ethnicities; he could see a pair of Japanese girls giggling over a laptop, while two Arabs and a lanky Ethiopian carried on a passionate, hand-waving argument in French.

The reception desk stood against the far wall, beneath a cracked stained-glass window. After giving his card to the hair-twirling girl on duty, Timothy got a locker key and a set of sheets, and she pointed him through a second set of doors to look for cubicle nine.

It didn't take him long to find it. There were four bunks in the room, none occupied, so he dropped his rucksack on the floor and started making up his bed for the night.

'There you are!' said a delighted voice from behind him, and Timothy jerked to attention, nearly cracking his head on the upper bunk.

It was the girl who looked like Miriam.

Why Veronica hadn't told him about Sanctuary the moment he'd admitted he was looking for a hostel, Timothy couldn't imagine – but on the other hand, there was something special about meeting her again. It made him feel almost as though there were some greater purpose at work, and he hadn't felt that way for a long time.

'Look who's turned up!' she announced as she tugged Timothy and his guitar back into the common room. 'Another musician!'

This was greeted by cheers, and Timothy was bemused. 'What's going on?' he whispered, but Veronica only laughed.

'I love music, that's all,' she said. 'Why don't you sit down and show Rob what you can do?'

Rob turned out to be the foxlike young man on the sofa,

who set his own guitar aside and regarded Timothy with shrewd dark eyes. 'How long have you been playing?' he asked.

'A few years,' said Timothy.

'And where are you from? I can't place the accent.'

'Uganda. But I've been here since September.'

'Ah,' said Rob, leaning back and slinging his arm across the back of the sofa. 'Well then, troubadour, why don't you play us a song?'

Half the people in the room seemed to be watching Timothy now. Veronica pulled a chair around and sat down across from him, eyes fixed eagerly on his face; even the black-haired twins set their chessboard aside, though they still looked bored and a little contemptuous. Timothy's cheeks heated, but he lifted his guitar from the case and tuned it, trying to pretend that he was just practising and that there was no pressure, no hurry. At last he lowered his head over the strings and began to play.

He'd meant to start with something everyone would recognise, like the Beatles or Elvis Presley. But Veronica still reminded him of Miriam, and before he knew it his fingers had started plucking out a Ugandan song instead. At first he played cautiously, unsure of his reception. But when he glanced up he saw Veronica smiling, and took courage.

His thumb tapped the guitar's hollow body, weaving percussion into the melody, and his confidence swelled as he saw the onlookers nodding and tapping their feet. Moving closer, they formed a loose circle around him, surrounding him with the warmth of their bodies and the rhythm of their hands, and when Rob picked up his own guitar and began thumbing a bass line it seemed so natural that Timothy didn't even falter.

He'd never played this well before, every fingering perfect, every note vibrating clear and true. But after the first couple of numbers, playing other people's songs wasn't enough for him any more: he wanted – no, *needed* – to improvise, and when he shifted into a different rhythm and a chord progression that was all his own, the crowd whistled and clapped as though they knew. Rob cocked his head to the side and cast him a swift glance, then joined him on the new melody.

A pair of bongo drums appeared from nowhere. A bleached-looking Nordic girl conjured up a flute from the depths of her bag. Soon half the room was playing, dancing, even humming along with the tune – *his* tune. Timothy felt an incredulous warmth in the pit of his belly. It had been months since he'd felt wanted and valued, instead of like an outsider. But these people were happy to be near him, and they seemed to love every song he played...it was intoxicating. Nothing mattered but the music now: he could forget where he was, who he was, and simply *be*.

Veronica slipped onto the sofa beside him, so close that he could smell the spice of her perfume. Timothy's heart quickened and his fingers flew across the strings as the melodies kept pouring out of him, each more brilliant than the last. Where were they all coming from? Would he even remember any of them tomorrow? He had no idea. All he knew was that he never wanted it to stop—

All at once Rob played a sour note, a discord so loud and obviously deliberate that it startled Timothy and the others silent. Then he thrust his guitar aside and stalked away.

Fatigue washed over Timothy as his exhilaration faded. He could feel the strain in his arms and shoulders, and his fingertips throbbed. How long had he been playing?

'Never mind him,' said Veronica, her eyes shining. She touched his shoulder, added playfully, 'Poor boy, we've worn you out. I'll walk you to your room.'

'You played so well tonight,' she said softly as Timothy fumbled the door open. 'And such wonderful music... I do believe Rob was jealous.'

It would have been flattering to think so, but Timothy wasn't sure. Rob hadn't looked envious when he'd stopped the music – he'd looked angry.

'Those songs you played,' Veronica went on. 'Were they from Uganda?'

'Some of them,' he said. 'And some...' He ducked his head self-consciously. 'I just made up.'

Her wide mouth spread in a smile. 'I thought so,' she said. 'I have met musicians of all kinds since I came to Sanctuary, but seldom ones as gifted as yourself. Players are easily found, but composers…those are rare.'

There was something odd about the way she was speaking, but Timothy was too tired to question it. He slumped down on the edge of his bed, stuck his key in the locker and pulled out his rucksack for the night.

He was unzipping the top of the pack when realisation struck: there was no one else in the room with them. He'd expected to have one or two roommates at least, but the cubicle was still empty, the other bunks and lockers bare. And when Veronica put her back to the door and gently pushed it shut, he felt a stir of misgiving.

'What are you doing?' he asked.

She walked towards him, still smiling. 'Such a sweet boy,' she said, and with that she bent swiftly and pressed her lips to his.

Her mouth was icy cold, and Timothy flinched away as though she had burned him. Veronica's brows arched. 'You're stronger than I thought,' she said. 'One might almost think you were…protected.'

Timothy rubbed his hand across his mouth, shaken. 'Stop it,' he said hoarsely, though part of him didn't want her to. 'Get away from me.'

'Oh, I will,' she said, sounding amused. 'Just as soon as I've taken all that lovely music you carry inside you. But don't worry, by the time I'm done, you won't even miss it.' And with that her long fingers curled around the back of his neck, nails stinging bloody crescents into his skin. Timothy yelped, but Veronica gripped him with inhuman strength, and though he struggled, he couldn't pull away…

'LEAVE HIM ALONE!'

Timothy's rucksack erupted, shooting socks and underwear in all directions. Suddenly there was another girl in the room with them, her hands shaping light and hurling it through the air. Veronica staggered back as the flash hit her, the brown tones melting away from her skin and her braids unfurling into a silky blonde crop that looked nothing like Miriam's at all. She cursed and fled, leaving the door open behind her.

Timothy sat up slowly, staring at the strange new girl. She was small but shapely, with a round face and brown curls tumbling about her shoulders. The light she had flung at Veronica still glowed on his retinas when he blinked. 'Who are you?' he demanded.

'My name is Linden,' she said, dropping to a crouch and looking up at him with earnest hazel eyes. 'But never mind that just now. Can you move? We have to get out of here.'

fIVE

It had been a long ride from Oakhaven. Hidden away in Timothy's pack, Linden could see nothing of the journey, and her heart had trembled at every unfamiliar noise she heard, every new smell that filtered in to her. This city was so *loud* – full of screeches and hisses and thumps, the blare of raucous music and the growling voices of more humans than she'd ever heard in her life. She had felt every jolt as Timothy walked, and when he'd swung the pack off his shoulders and let it drop onto the floor of the hostel, she'd had to clap her hands over her mouth to keep from shrieking. It was a relief to finally be free.

And yet it was also terrifying. She was still learning to use the magic the Queen had given her, and compared with the easy power of someone like Veronica her own skills seemed hopelessly puny. It had taken all her concentration to cast two glamours at once – one to make herself large and the other to startle the other faery away – and her head still ached from the effort. Nor had Linden ever taken human shape before, and standing so tall with no wings to balance her, she felt as though she might teeter over at any minute.

Meanwhile Timothy still sat motionless, staring at her. Of course he was in shock: he'd never seen her before, and here she'd popped up suddenly out of his rucksack. But she had no time to explain, not now.

'Please,' she said. 'We can't stay here, we have to get away before it's too late!' Snatching up his discarded pack, she stuffed his clothes back into it and tossed it against his chest. 'Come on!'

'But…where did you come from?' Timothy said slowly.

'I'll tell you everything, I promise, but just come!' She pulled at his wrists, but he still wouldn't move. How could she get him to obey? In desperation she looked around – and saw the guitar case sitting by the door.

'Hey!' he protested, as she snatched it up and ran with it.

Linden didn't look back, didn't hesitate. If he didn't come now, there was no hope for either of them. But the subtle herb-fragrance of her fellow faeries was everywhere in this place, and she could only pray that when she reached the end of the corridor she would find only humans there, and not Veronica or one of her allies.

She could hear Timothy pounding down the corridor behind her, shouting at her to stop; her plan had succeeded, but they were far from safe yet. Linden burst through the doorway and collided with a stranger on the other side, a young man with jutting cheekbones and feathery dark hair. He stumbled back, knocking into another boy who looked just like him, and she stammered out an apology before ducking past and looking about wildly for the exit.

Merciful Gardener, where was it? There seemed to be doors everywhere, and the scent of faery was stronger than ever. Would she never find her way out of this place? But then a whisper of cool air touched her cheek, and she caught a glimpse of starlight as another human came blowing and stamping in from outside. Linden plunged past him and threw her weight against the outer doors until the metal bar gave way and they flew open. Still dragging the guitar, she stumbled down the steps to the edge of the road and waited for Timothy to join her.

It was only a few seconds before he emerged, a tall figure silhouetted against the light. 'Give me back my guitar,' he warned, stalking down the stairs with his hand outstretched. 'Or I'll call the police.'

'You don't understand!' she pleaded with him, backing away. 'You have to come with me! Now!'

'Don't listen to her, Timothy,' said Veronica's throaty voice from the doorway. 'She's a thief and a liar.' Her face softened as she walked out onto the step. 'This has all been so confusing for you. I'm sorry. Why don't you come back inside with me, and we'll talk about it?'

Linden watched Timothy waver, his gaze shifting from her to Veronica and back again. The other faery's magical disguise was back in place, and her words were laced with enticement. Though Linden's head still throbbed from the spells she'd cast already, she knew what she had to do: she grabbed Timothy's hand, and willed him to see Veronica as she truly was.

One glimpse of the face behind the glamour, and he recoiled. No longer an enticing twin of the girl in his mother's photograph, but a pale, sharp-faced blonde whose beauty was far from human...

Linden handed the guitar case back to Timothy, a silent pledge of her good faith. If he didn't come with her now, he never would.

'Run,' she whispered. 'Please.'

He ran.

'We need a place to hide,' Linden said breathlessly as the two of them dashed down the street. 'Somewhere with lots of people, where she won't dare to try anything even if she finds us...'

Timothy barely heard her: his head was still reeling from all that had just happened to him. How could Veronica have made herself look like Miriam, when in reality the two girls were nothing alike? What had she meant about taking his music, and how had Linden shown up so suddenly to rescue him? The guitar case thumped against his leg as he sprinted along, shivering. He'd left his jacket back at Sanctuary, but there was no way he was going to turn around and get it now.

'I can't see her any more,' Linden said after a few minutes, slowing to a trot. 'Maybe we've lost her, or else she's given up—'

'This way,' Timothy panted, grabbing her arm and yanking her beneath the glow of a fast-food restaurant sign. Through the window he could make out a scattering of diners and a spotty-faced boy in uniform mopping the tile. Not exactly lots of people, but he decided it should be safe enough. Timothy tugged the door open and wrestled himself and his luggage inside.

He was leaning against the wall trying to catch his breath when he realised Linden was no longer with him. He turned to see her still standing on the pavement outside, her hands pressed helplessly to the glass.

'Well?' he mouthed at her, beckoning, but she seemed unable to open the door, or even find the handle. Frustrated, Timothy dropped his guitar and his rucksack and pushed it wide for her. 'Come on!'

Linden stumbled into the restaurant after him, looking ready to collapse. 'I couldn't get in by myself,' she gasped. 'Not until you invited me. That's never happened to me before – it must be because I've got magic now. But that means *she* won't be able to come in here unless someone invites her, either.'

He wished she wouldn't keep talking nonsense; it made him nervous. Timothy shoved his baggage beneath the table and slid into one of the high-backed booths, keeping his head low so he wouldn't be visible from the street. Hesitantly Linden padded to join him.

'No shoes,' said the boy with the mop, pointing to Linden. 'Can't serve you like that.'

'It's not her fault,' snapped Timothy. 'Give us a minute.'

'It's all right,' said Linden. She reached behind her back and pulled out a pair of slippers that hadn't been there a second before. 'I have some.'

She bent to put them on, while Timothy stared at her. The attendant shrugged, leaned his mop against the wall and ambled behind the counter. 'So what'll it be?'

Reluctantly Timothy got up and took out his wallet. He paid for two Cokes and a large order of chips, while Linden edged into the booth and sat there looking around uncertainly, as though she'd never seen a restaurant before. Their food arrived; Timothy carried the tray to the table and thumped it down between them. 'All right. It's time you told me who you are. Where you came from. What happened back there—'

'I told you, my name is Linden,' she said. 'I've been with you ever since you left Oakhaven.' She leaned forwards and added in a husky whisper, 'I'm a faery.'

'A *what*?'

'A faery,' she repeated. 'And so was that Veronica – only she's a bad one. Very bad.' She put a hand to her forehead as though it pained her, and the corners of her mouth pulled down. 'I'm sorry I didn't introduce myself to you back at the

75

house, but I didn't know if I could trust you yet. I was just working up the nerve when I realised you were going away, and then all I could think to do was hide in your pack and hope for the best.'

Timothy regarded her blankly for a moment. Then he jabbed the straw into his Coke and took a long, deliberate sip.

'You don't believe me!' Her face darkened with indignation. 'How can you be so stubborn when you saw for yourself back there—'

'Saw what?' It had all happened so fast, he couldn't be sure what he'd seen. Maybe Veronica had drugged him, and he'd been hallucinating. Maybe she and this girl were a team, trying to trick him into saying he believed in faeries as part of some hidden-camera television show.

'Oh, this is impossible,' huffed the girl. She folded her arms and sat back, her brows an angry line. 'How am I supposed to explain when you won't even believe the first thing I say?'

'Look,' said Timothy, trying to sound reasonable; there was no point upsetting her, especially if she was mentally ill. 'You got me away from…whatever Veronica was going to do to me, and I appreciate that. But Linden—' All at once he stopped. '*Linden*,' he breathed.

'What?'

'Paul and Peri. I overheard them talking about you last night, when they thought I was asleep. But if you really did come with me all the way from Oakhaven…' His mind flashed back to all the places he'd been since he left the house: the road to the village, the station, the train carriage. 'Why didn't I notice you before?'

Linden's lips pursed. She leaned out into the aisle and looked around, as though to reassure herself that no one was watching. Then, quick as a blink, she disappeared.

Timothy jumped, heart jarring against his ribcage, and then he heard a high-pitched voice coming from around knee level, 'Look under the table.'

Dry-mouthed, he leaned sideways and peered under the table's edge to see a tiny version of Linden sitting across from him, balanced on the edge of the plastic seat. Spread out behind her were a pair of delicate-looking, translucent...*wings?*

'Have you seen enough now?' she demanded.

Numbly, Timothy nodded.

'Is anybody looking at us?'

He shook his head.

Immediately Linden flashed back into view on the other side of the table, human-sized and wingless again. She looked tired, but triumphant. 'So now you *have* to believe me. Right?'

Timothy grabbed a handful of chips, just to have something to do while he struggled for composure. When he tried to speak again his voice sounded squeaky, and he had to clear his throat before he could get the words out: 'Do they know that you're a...er, I mean, Paul and Peri, if you know them, have they ever...'

'Of course they know,' said Linden. 'The woman you call Peri – she used to be a faery herself.'

That was it, he was going insane. Timothy pushed his chips away. 'I have to go.'

Linden caught his arm. 'It's the truth, I swear. She started out as our Hunter, back when she was just a little older than me, and we called her Knife…well, we still call her that actually, even though she's a human now and goes by her true name of Perianth instead. But anyway, she met Paul and they fell in love, and in the end Queen Amaryllis made her human so she could stay with him, but she had to promise to go on hunting food for us and protecting us from the crows as her part of the bargain. That's why she looked sad when you were talking about Uganda. She knows she can never travel, never even leave the Oakenwyld for more than an hour or two, so long as the rest of us need her.'

So she'd overheard their conversation at the dinner table as well? 'How long have you been spying on me?' Timothy demanded.

A flush crept into Linden's cheeks. 'Since you came to the house, off and on. I know I shouldn't have, but you were young like me, and I saw the way you looked at the Oak, and…' She played with her straw. 'I wanted to find out more about you. What things you liked or needed, if there was anything that I might be able to offer you as a bargain…I had to know whether there was any chance you might take me away with you, when you left.'

Oh. He understood now – or thought he did. 'The Oak is where you live?' he said. 'You and your Queen and...the rest of you?'

She nodded.

That explained a lot, thought Timothy. He went on, 'OK, so you wanted to see some more of the world. I get that. But what about your parents? Aren't they going to be upset that you just took off with me?'

'Parents.' She ran the word around her tongue as though it were unfamiliar. 'I don't have any parents.'

Whoops. He should have guessed she was an orphan, with those worn-looking clothes and tangled hair. That must be why Paul and Peri had been concerned about her. 'Sorry,' he said.

'Why should you be?' Now she looked confused. 'No one in the Oak has parents, because there aren't any male faeries. Knife is my foster mother – well, one of them, anyway. She looked after me when I first hatched.'

Hatched? thought Timothy in disbelief, but Linden was still talking: 'But that's not the point. I didn't come with you because I wanted to see the world. I came with you to try and find more faeries. Because my people have lost their magic, and we need to get it back.'

Over the next few minutes Linden did her best to make Timothy understand about Jasmine and the spell she had cast on the Oakenfolk, and how vital it was that their people's magic be restored. 'There are only a few of us left now,' she said, 'and if it weren't for Knife and the Queen there'd be even fewer. We're so afraid of being eaten by crows and foxes that most of us won't set foot outside the Oak unless we have to. But now there's even more for us to worry about, because the Queen is dying – and though she gave me a half-share of her power, I can't cast the glamours that protect the Oak nearly as well as she used to. We'll never be safe, or free, until *all* of us have our magic back.'

'So why don't you find this Jasmine and get her to undo the spell?' said Timothy around another mouthful of chips. Linden had tried one but didn't like it, so he was finishing off the box by himself – though how he could eat so much and still be so thin, she couldn't imagine.

'Because we can't,' Linden replied. 'It's been well over a hundred years since Queen Amaryllis turned Jasmine into a human and exiled her from the Oak, so she's long dead by now. And anyway, she'd never have done it. If she was mad enough to think it worth using up all our magic just to keep us away from humans, do you really think she'd be likely to change her mind?'

'Fair enough,' said Timothy. 'So you think the faeries here will help you?'

'I don't know,' Linden said. 'I'd hoped so, but after the way Veronica behaved to you, tricking you into seeing her as someone you trusted, and then trying to take your music…' The memory of the other faery bending over Timothy, that hungry light in her eyes, still made Linden shudder.

'I still don't get that part.' Timothy swirled his drink around with the straw. 'How could she steal music from me? Why would she want to?'

Linden sighed. 'You have to understand. We faeries aren't creative, like you humans are. On our own, we can't make art or music, or come up with new ideas – we have to learn all those things from you. But at the same time, having faeries close by makes humans more creative, so it works both ways. Or at least it's supposed to.'

'But?' prompted Timothy.

'Well, it's also supposed to happen gradually. But when Veronica dragged you off to play for her…it didn't. Even shut up in that locker, I could hear. I could tell.'

Timothy looked down at his reddened fingers. 'So she did that,' he said. 'She made me—'

'She *pushed* you,' said Linden. 'Forced all your musical ability to the surface, so she could take it for herself. I didn't even know that was possible.'

'I've never played like that in my whole life.'

She touched his arm, trying to reassure him. 'I won't let her do it again.'

Timothy did not reply. He sat back against the bench, his eyes unreadable. 'So now what?' he said.

'I have to try and find some *good* faeries,' Linden said. 'Ones who will listen to what I have to say, and care enough to want to help – or at least be willing to bargain.'

Timothy studied her a moment. Then he said, 'Well, good luck with that, I guess,' and began to slide out from behind the table.

'Wait!' she said. 'Where are you going?'

'To find another hostel. I'm tired.'

'But what if Veronica finds you again? And I need your help!'

'I don't know what for,' he said. 'I gave you a ride here, and you got me away from Veronica, so it looks like we're even. If you need to get back to the Oak, just buy a train ticket to Aynsbridge.'

'But I haven't any money—'

'Why would you need it? You've got this "glamour" thing: you can probably conjure up a few pounds.'

'I can't do that,' protested Linden. 'It would be stealing.' *Use your gifts wisely and in good conscience,* Amaryllis had told her, *not for selfish gain.* 'And anyway, I don't want to go back, not until I've found the help I need.' She clutched at Timothy's sleeve. 'Please don't go. There's so much I still don't know about your world. And I can help you too, if you give me the chance.'

For a moment Timothy still hesitated. Then he heaved a sigh and slumped back down onto the bench. 'Oh, all right,' he said. 'Sure you don't want some chips?'

'Closing up,' announced the boy with the mop, and quickly Timothy drained the rest of his Coke, willing the sugar and caffeine to spark through his exhaustion, and keep him going just a little while longer.

'Come on,' he said to Linden. 'We'd better find somewhere to sleep.'

'Let me go first,' she said, springing up from the booth. She peered out the window into the street, then said, 'I think it's clear.'

'Of course it is,' said Timothy, shoving the door open and dragging his guitar case through. 'She must have given up ages ago. I'm not *that* special.' But then a new thought occurred to him, and he turned back to Linden with a frown. 'But if she was looking for a musician…why didn't she take Rob instead?'

'Rob?' said Linden, and Timothy remembered: she'd never met Rob, she'd only heard him play at a distance.

'There was another guitar player at the hostel,' he said. 'Older than me, but still pretty young – and he was good. Excellent, even. Why me, and not him?'

'I don't know,' said Linden. 'I don't even know why she felt she had to— Ow!' She hopped to one side and turned her foot over to look at it, wincing. Timothy was about to ask what was wrong when he saw that the slippers she'd been wearing in the restaurant had vanished, and that a chip of glass was sticking out of her heel.

'What happened to your shoes?' he asked.

Linden picked the shard out gingerly and rubbed her thumb across the wound. 'They were just glamour,' she said, as a dark bead of blood welled out. 'I don't have the right kind of magic to make real shoes, and keeping up the illusion was giving me a headache. Besides, I usually go barefoot at home – how was I to know I'd be walking all over London tonight?'

Timothy swung his rucksack down onto the pavement and rummaged through it until he'd found the old T-shirt he usually slept in. 'Here,' he said, tearing a strip off the bottom and wrapping it around her foot. 'This should help – but watch where you're walking from now on.'

'That's kind of you,' said Linden, limping a few steps experimentally, 'but I have a better idea.' She gave herself a little shake and suddenly she was tiny again, wings unfolding from the deep V at the back of her jacket. 'Ah yes,' she sighed as she hummed into the air, 'that's much better.'

Timothy watched, amazed, as she hovered around him. So small, and she darted so quickly – no wonder he'd mistaken her for a little brown bird...

The night breeze nipped at him, forcing him back to attention. He pulled an extra sweatshirt out of his rucksack and tugged it on. It wasn't as warm as the jacket he'd left behind at Sanctuary, but the extra layer definitely helped. 'Right,' he said, picking up his guitar again. 'Let's go.'

Linden flitted to land on his shoulder and sat down, her faery form fitting easily into the space between his collarbone and his jaw. She was so small he hardly noticed the weight, but he could feel her solid warmth against his skin, undeniably real. Timothy let out a short, disbelieving laugh.

'What is it?' Her voice was a breath in his ear.

'It's just...my cousin's wife is a faery. I'm talking to a faery right now. And here I thought I was having a hard time just believing in God.'

'God?' Linden sounded curious. 'You mean the Great Gardener?'

The Lord God planted a garden eastward, in Eden... 'Yeah.'

'But you believe in me, don't you?'

Timothy snorted out another laugh, this one more genuine. 'It's not like I have a choice! How can I not believe when I can see you right there?'

'Oh,' said Linden, and was silent. Then she said, 'So you have to be able to see something to know it exists?'

Her puzzlement seemed genuine, but Timothy didn't feel like getting into a lecture on the scientific method just now. 'No,' he said, 'of course there's more to it than that. It's just that I thought I knew what was real and what wasn't, and now I don't know what to think any—'

Linden gasped, but the warning came too late. All at once the air thickened around Timothy and he stopped in mid-stride, unable to move. He could only watch helplessly as a familiar figure spun itself out of the shadows and walked down the pavement towards him, smiling.

'Hello, my sweet,' said Veronica.

SIX

In the glare of the streetlamp Veronica's hair was pale as tallow, her skin the colour of ashes. 'You kept me searching a long time for you, human boy,' she remarked. 'And yet, somehow...the look on your face makes it all worthwhile.'

Linden slid down behind Timothy's shoulder and crouched on the top of his pack, willing herself not to panic. Veronica's spell had bound Timothy, but left her free to move: perhaps that meant the other faery hadn't seen her? So if she stayed very still, maybe she'd have time to think of a plan...

'That drab little creature has left you unattended, has she?' said Veronica, trailing a finger down Timothy's cheek. Linden expected him to flinch, but he only stared past her unblinking: Veronica's spell had bound him so fast that he could not even speak. 'I would call that a foolish mistake...though she was a fool to begin with, thinking she could steal you away from me.'

She brought her other hand to Timothy's cheek, leaned

forward – and her gaze fell on Linden. With a hiss she jerked back. 'You! So tiny, and with wings, no less – what in the Empress's name—?'

Stiffly Linden pulled herself upright, trying not to put too much weight on her injured foot. 'Timothy is under my protection,' she said with all the dignity she could muster. 'You cannot have him.'

Veronica breathed a laugh. 'Little one, you amaze me. When I believed you had stolen the boy so you could take his music for yourself, I admired your impudence even as I swore to make you pay for it. But now you ask me to believe you were trying to protect him? A mere human, with nothing in his head but music and ignorance?' Her lips compressed. 'Come now, tell me the truth and I may yet spare your life.'

The menace in the other faery's voice made Linden tremble, but her outrage was stronger than her fear. 'I mean what I say,' she retorted, and then, summoning up all her courage and her faith in Knife's example she added, 'I will fight you if I have to.'

Veronica's sceptical look shaded into contempt. 'Then you must have lost what little wits you ever possessed. To blatantly display your faery nature by taking this ridiculous little form, and ally yourself with a human in defiance of the Empress's decree—'

'Empress?' Linden interrupted. 'Who is this Empress you keep talking about?'

'Not know the Empress?' Veronica's eyes narrowed. 'Do you mock me? Or are you testing my loyalty? If you think I could ever be tempted to show mercy to rebels and humans, then be assured that I will prove you wrong – right now.'

With a flick of her fingers she knocked Linden from Timothy's shoulder, sending her tumbling backwards into the air. Then she seized Timothy's face between her hands—

Linden cried out and flung herself forward, but there was no need. Something like a small bird flashed out from the darkness and struck Veronica across the back of the head; her eyes glazed over, and she slid to the pavement.

'Veronica?' whispered Linden, hovering above the fallen faery. The bird-thing had vanished as quickly as it had appeared, and Timothy still hadn't moved; she had no idea how to free him from the spell. But then a hooded figure stepped out from between the buildings, and she caught the unmistakeable scent of another faery. With surprisingly powerful-looking hands the stranger tore Veronica's spell to glittering tatters, until Timothy gasped and stumbled forward, free.

Linden's heart leaped. 'Don't go!' she called out as the stranger backed away. 'Please, I need to talk to you!'

The other faery hesitated, then made a beckoning gesture and vanished back into the darkness. Linden was about to follow – then noticed that Timothy was still standing there, apparently too dazed to walk. She gritted her teeth and willed herself large again, then grabbed Timothy's wrist and pulled him along with her.

The strange faery led them through the alley, past a row of metal bins overflowing with rubbish and walls scrawled with painted symbols Linden didn't recognise. All she could do was limp along with Timothy in tow, wincing as cold grime crunched beneath her feet, and praying she didn't step on anything else sharp.

The passageway led them onto another street, where they walked a few more paces before stopping in front of a wall covered with colourful scraps of paper and yet more scribbles of paint. Linden was just about to ask what they were looking at when the other faery raised a hand, and a hidden door opened in the wall.

Stepping inside, they climbed a narrow, creaking staircase to its very top, emerging at last into a single tiny room. The air inside smelled musty, and the ceiling bowed low over their heads, cracked and stained from years of slow leaking. The wallpaper had peeled away in strips, the carpet was black with mildew, and when their guide pressed the light switch the naked bulb sizzled fitfully in its socket.

'All right,' said Timothy, shaking himself free of Linden. He looked tired, but now his eyes were clear. 'So now that you've rescued us, do you mind telling us who you are?'

The stranger turned, pushing back the concealing hood. Linden stepped forward eagerly – and her throat closed up with shock.

The faery who had rescued them was a *male*.

*

Timothy was still so dizzy from the aftereffects of Veronica's spell, it was an effort at first to tell who he was looking at. But gradually his rescuer's features came into focus, and he knew. 'Rob!' he exclaimed.

Linden whirled on him. 'Rob? *This* is the musician you were talking about? But he's...' Words seemed to fail her as she looked back at the other faery, her gaze travelling up his figure to linger on his broad shoulders and the spare, angular bones of his face. 'I don't understand,' she faltered.

'I thought you were a friend of Veronica's,' said Timothy, unable to keep the accusation from his voice.

Rob seemed unfazed. 'Our people make no friends,' he said, 'only allies and enemies. But for now, I am your ally, and not hers. She won't find you here.'

For now. That didn't sound too reassuring to Timothy, especially after the way he'd seen Rob play his guitar back at Sanctuary. What if he'd rescued them from Veronica just to steal Timothy's music for himself?

'You mistrust me,' said Rob. His voice had fallen into formal cadences, with a rich, rolling accent that sounded centuries older than he looked. 'I do not blame you for it. But I give you my pledge – I mean you no harm.'

'But you're a *faery,*' said Linden in a plaintive voice. 'And you're male. How can that be?'

'I am as real as you,' Rob told her. 'But enough idle talk. Tell me, who are you and where have you come from?'

His eyes were on Linden now, so intent that she might have been the only other person in the room, and Timothy felt a flicker of irritation. 'What about giving us a chance to rest a bit first?' he said. 'Linden's hurt, and I want to look at her foot before—'

He broke off as Rob swung around and gave him a hard look. All at once Timothy became aware that there was a bed just a few feet behind him, and that he was even more tired than he'd thought. He backed up slowly until the mattress bumped against his legs, and then sat down.

'Timothy?' said Linden, sounding anxious, but her voice seemed to be coming from a great distance. And the bed felt so soft, the springs trembling invitingly beneath his weight...it wouldn't hurt to lie down just a moment, would it?

He slumped over, his head dropping onto the pillow. The world around him faded, and Timothy sank into a deep, dreamless sleep.

'You put a spell on him,' Linden accused Rob, as Timothy began to snore. It was all she could do to speak firmly, and not betray the nervousness she felt inside.

'Not quite,' said Rob, looking amused. 'I merely took away the chemicals in his body that were keeping him awake. You might even call it a healing.'

'Healing?' She was taken aback. 'But you did it so easily...I thought that healing spells were the very hardest magics to perform.' Or at least, that was what Valerian had told her, and surely the Oak's Healer ought to know about such things.

Rob shrugged. 'For you they would be, no doubt. Just as the glamours that you and Veronica create would be all but impossible for a male such as myself. But you should know that without me telling you. Sit down.'

Linden tensed. Was he going to put her to sleep the way he had Timothy?

'Or not, if you prefer,' Rob said with a touch of exasperation. 'But it will be difficult for me to heal your foot if you insist on standing on it.'

Embarrassed, Linden sidled over and sat down on the end of the bed where Timothy slept, lifting her bandaged foot for Rob's inspection. The male faery kneeled and cupped her heel in one hand, deftly unwinding the bandage with the other. He considered her injury a moment, then laid his fingers against the wound and said, 'Done.'

She could feel a tingling warmth where his hands rested, but no pain. Wondering, Linden pulled her foot back and turned it over. There was no sign of blood or bruising, only a tiny white scar.

'And now,' said Rob, 'you are in my debt twice over.'

'I am,' Linden admitted, colouring at the directness of his gaze. 'What would you ask of me in return?'

'Knowledge, no more. But I warn you, I have a great many questions – and if you lie to me, I will know.'

His tone was mild, but the warning in it was unmistakeable. Linden took a deep breath. 'I accept your bargain.'

'Why did you save the human boy from Veronica?'

An odd question, considering he'd just rescued the two of them from Veronica himself. 'She was going to take his music. What else could I have done?'

Rob stooped and lifted Timothy's guitar from its case. He ducked his head under the strap, sat down in the room's only chair and began to play, fingers wandering over the strings. 'You could have taken his music for yourself,' he said. 'Or let Veronica take it, and escaped from Sanctuary unharmed. Instead you defied the Empress's decree, and risked your own life, to rescue him. Why?'

Linden sat back a little, moving carefully so as not to disturb the sleeping Timothy. 'I never even thought of doing anything else,' she admitted. 'I mean…his music means so much to him. And what Veronica was doing – tried to do – was wrong.'

Rob's left hand slid down the guitar's neck, his right plucking soft chords as he spoke. 'Wrong?' he said. 'How so? He would never have known what she took from him, or remembered how it was done. When he awoke, he would only find that his skill at making music was not what it had been, and in time he would give it up and move on. Where is the harm?'

'But it's stealing,' protested Linden, shocked. 'You don't

take from people without giving them something in return.'

'People?' said Rob. 'Faeries, perhaps. But humans? What do we owe to them? They have abilities we lack and envy, but they would say the same of us. We could kill them or herd them like cattle if we chose, but instead we allow most of them to live without even suspecting our existence. Having granted the humans so great a favour already, why should we give them more? It is not as though they are our equals.'

He spoke without hesitation, but his tone was colourless, as though he were reciting a speech he had given too many times. Still, hearing him say those words made Linden feel queasy.

'Like cattle…' she echoed, and then with sudden passion, 'No. No, I don't believe that. The Great Gardener—'

She stopped, unsure. Did these city faeries even believe as she did? Or were they like Timothy, certain of nothing but doubt?

'Go on,' said Rob.

'When the Great Gardener planted the world,' Linden went on carefully, trying to remember the story just as Queen Amaryllis had told it to her years ago, 'the humans were appointed to rule it and tend it and look after all the other creatures. And the first faery, Lily – she was supposed to help them by watching over the garden and letting them know when the plants or animals needed care.

'The Great Gardener promised Lily that if she did her work faithfully, she would in time receive a mate of her own. But as the days passed, Lily grew impatient. She left the humans and flew off to see if there were any others like herself, and when she returned, the garden was in chaos and the humans were gone. So the Great Gardener punished her by taking away her creativity.'

'That hardly seems fair,' said Rob dryly. 'What about the humans?'

'I don't know their part of the story,' admitted Linden. 'But I'm sure they were punished too. The point is, humans and faeries were meant to work together. We need each other.'

Rob gave her a pitying look. 'A child's tale,' he said, 'left over from a time when our people were too ignorant to know better. I would not be surprised to find that the humans made it up themselves, to keep us in our place. But you are a young woman now, and surely you are too intelligent to believe such fables?'

Linden was flustered. To be treated as an adult was flattering, even more so when the speaker was a male of her own kind. And to be called intelligent pleased her as well. But the contempt in Rob's voice when he dismissed the beliefs that she had been raised with, things she felt in her heart to be true...

'If being intelligent means agreeing that faeries are the only people who matter,' she said, 'then no, I suppose I'm not. But if that's what you really believe, then why did you help us?'

Instead of answering, Rob bent his head over the guitar

and began a lilting, mournful melody. Linden watched his averted face a moment, then added more quietly, 'And who taught you to play?'

Rob's hands fell away from the strings. 'Enough,' he said in a harsh voice as he took off the instrument and laid it back in its case. 'It is my business to ask questions, not to answer them. Or have you already forgotten the terms of our bargain?'

Linden reddened. She was so used to talking freely with Knife and Paul and some of her fellow Oakenfolk, it was easy to forget that most faeries used conversation only as a tool – or a weapon. 'I'm sorry,' she said. 'Please go on.'

Rob was silent a moment. Then he said, 'I may regret asking this, but…are you one of the *Plant Rhys Ddwfn*?'

'Plawnt hreece thuvin?' repeated Linden, puzzled. 'What does that mean?'

'The Children of Rhys the Deep,' said Rob. 'And since you do not recognise the name, then clearly I was mistaken.' He swore under his breath. 'I should have known. That one of the Children would come to me – it was too easy. But where else could you have come from, to know nothing of the Empress, and be generous even to humans?'

'Do you want me to tell you?' asked Linden.

Rob slumped back into the chair. 'I suppose you may yet say something worth hearing,' he said, though his voice held little hope. 'Very well, go on.'

Linden sat up straighter. This might be her only chance

to explain why she had come to London, to make Rob understand the Oakenfolk's desperate situation and persuade him, if he could be persuaded, to help.

'My name is Linden,' she began, 'and I come from a place called the Oakenwyld…'

When she had finished her story, Rob sat for a long moment without speaking. Then he said in a voice that rasped with disbelief, 'You mean to tell me that you and your fellow Oakenfolk – every one of you – are female, and always have been? For five hundred years you have lived alone in your Oak, and never seen a single male of our kind?'

Linden nodded, relieved that he finally understood. 'Until I met you tonight,' she said, 'I had no idea that male faeries even existed.'

'And before this Jasmine you spoke of came along and cast her spell, your people used to have their children by *humans*?'

'Only now and then,' said Linden hastily, blushing. 'Most often we took girl children the humans didn't want, and turned them into faeries instead. But we can't do either of those things any more. Not without our magic.'

Rob shook his head. 'Impossible,' he murmured. 'After all these centuries…'

Linden's heart thumped painfully. Was he saying that it was too late to help the Oakenfolk? She was about to plead with him, but Rob cut in:

'And you truly believe that all you need do is ask, or offer some crude bargain, and the rest of us will rush to help you, just like that?'

'I – I don't know,' she said. Put like that, it did sound hopelessly naïve. 'But I had to try. There are only a few of us left alive now. And now that the spells that protect the Oak are weakening, soon it won't even be safe for us to live there any more—'

'Then why not ask your human *friends* to take you in? Surely there must be room for you all in that big House of theirs.'

'But that wouldn't be fair to them,' protested Linden. 'And it wouldn't be safe for us, either. One or two of us might be able to hide away in the House, but not all. And if the other humans found out, they'd try to capture us, study us—'

'Then perhaps you should have thought of that before you threw in your lot with the humans in the first place,' said Rob coldly as he got to his feet. 'Because I can tell you that the Empress rules the whole of this great island, and no faery under her command will ever give help to one of the Forsaken.'

'The…Forsaken?'

'I had believed you to be no more than a legend,' Rob went on in the same flat tone. 'Faeries who so loved humans that they would serve them like slaves, choosing even to wed with them and bear their children rather than be true to their own faery blood. Traitors and renegades, exiled from the rest of our people centuries ago. If the Empress knew that I had helped you, even in ignorance...' He pulled up his hood and moved towards the door.

'Wait!' Linden leaped off the bed and darted to intercept him. 'Where are you going? You're not going to tell her, are you? Please!'

Rob closed his eyes, as though he could not bear to look at her. 'No,' he said. 'But Veronica will not be so discreet – and she was not the only one who witnessed your rescue of the human boy. It will not be long before the Empress learns what you did this night, and draws her own conclusions. And then your life, and the boy's too, will be forfeit.'

Linden stood rooted, trembling with horror and fury. Then she burst out, 'Well, if that's the kind of law you live by here – if that's what your Empress calls justice – then it's no wonder my people decided they'd be better off with the humans!'

'Linden...' It was the first time Rob had spoken her name, but she was too upset to care. Hotly she went on:

'Maybe we are renegades, as you say, but at least we know enough to care about something besides ourselves. At least we still remember that we belong to the Great Gardener, and not to some Empress who goes around putting people to death at the flick of a wing! I'm sorry I wasn't one of your precious Children of Peace—'

'Rhys,' said Rob.

'—but if you ask me, it makes no difference. Because if they're known for being generous and kind to humans, I can't imagine that they'd be any more impressed with your attitude than I am!'

She finished the sentence with a glare, daring Rob to make some caustic retort. But unaccountably, his stern expression softened. He reached out and touched her hair, letting the brown curls tumble between his fingers.

'You are young,' he said. 'And altogether too innocent to survive in this hard world. But you have courage. And the human boy – he played well tonight.'

He glanced over at Timothy, still sprawled oblivious across the bed. 'Let him sleep a little while longer, then wake him and go to the nearest train station. My people are not fond of places where many humans gather; you should be safe there until you can find transport out of the city. Return to your Oak quickly, and remain there, and you may yet escape the Empress. I cannot promise you anything more.'

Linden caught his arm. 'But if we leave, how will I find the help we need? Surely not *all* the other faeries serve the Empress – if I just knew where to look—'

'That,' said Rob, 'was what I had hoped you would be able to tell me. So it seems we are both disappointed.' He shrugged away from her grasp, flung the door open, and was gone.

*

'Timothy. Wake up.' Linden was shaking him. 'We have to go.'

He groaned and rolled onto his back, blinking his sleep-gummed eyes against the light. 'What, already?'

'Yes, right away. Rob's gone, and...' She cast a nervous glance at the open door. 'We can't stay here much longer.'

Timothy swung his legs around and sat up, squinting at his watch: 5.47 am. Beyond the cracked window the sky was still dark, the streetlights glowing eerily through a haze of mist. He felt dislocated, as though he had wakened on some alien planet. 'OK,' he mumbled, 'just give me a few minutes.'

'There's no time to waste.' She dragged his rucksack and guitar case towards him. 'If any of the Empress's faeries find us, we're dead.'

Abruptly he was wide awake. 'What?'

'Just come,' begged Linden. 'I'll explain on the way.'

As they stepped onto the landing, Timothy nearly tripped over a pair of leather shoes sitting just outside the door. 'What the—' he said, but Linden had already snatched them up.

'Rob must have left them for me!' she exclaimed, slipping them on and bouncing a little. 'They fit perfectly.'

'How'd he know your size?' asked Timothy, but to his surprise, Linden only blushed and hurried down the stairs.

She told him the story as they walked, passing one street after another on their way towards the nearest train station.

The glamour she'd put on herself before they'd left the flat made her look like an ordinary human girl in a winter jacket and jeans, but it plainly wasn't keeping her warm: by the time she had finished speaking her cheeks were rosy with cold, and she was hugging herself in an effort not to shiver. Timothy fished his last sweatshirt out of his rucksack and handed it to her.

'Oh, I am grateful,' she breathed as she floundered into it, rolling up the sleeves that drooped over her hands. 'But you haven't said anything.' She looked up at him, eyes big with apprehension. 'Are you angry?'

Timothy shoved a hand through his hair. 'No, it's all marvellous,' he said bitterly. 'I'm glad you and Rob had such a nice chat. Lovely people, your folk.'

'I'm sorry.' She looked stricken. 'I never imagined it would be like this. I thought if I could only find more faeries, everything would be wonderful. But to meet them, and then hear that they all despise us and call us Forsaken...and even worse, that they're ruled by someone *evil*...'

'So now we've got no choice but to run back to Oakhaven.' Timothy stomped on a discarded drinks can and kicked it aside. 'It'd be one thing if I'd been gone a week, or been in an accident or something. But coming back to Paul and Peri's the morning after I left, because I was scared of a lot of homicidal faeries – that's just pathetic. They probably haven't even found my note yet.'

Linden said nothing. Her head was bent, her face

invisible behind her turbulence of hair.

'On the other hand,' he continued, 'it's the perfect excuse not to go back to Greenhill. Hello, Mum and Dad, England's fine, I met some faeries and now they want to kill me. Sure you don't want to send me to school in Canada instead?'

Linden gave a quavering laugh and then, to Timothy's horror, burst into tears. He grabbed her by the shoulders and turned her away from the road, hoping desperately that she'd calm down before someone stopped and demanded to know what was going on.

But though Linden put her hands over her face and sobbed until her body shook, none of the passing cars even slowed down. And once she'd wept herself into dry hiccups and wiped her eyes on her sleeve, Timothy was finally able to make out what she was saying:

'I've done everything wrong,' she choked. 'I thought I could help the Oakenfolk – I thought I was helping you – but all I've done is put all of us in worse danger than ever. What if the Empress sends her people after us? What if they find the Oak? Valerian was right. I wasn't ready for this. And what am I going to tell the Queen, when I see her?'

Timothy regarded her helplessly for a moment. Then with sudden decisiveness he took Linden by the elbow and marched her along with him until they reached the train station. He steered her inside and made her sit down on one of the benches, before taking both her hands in his and speaking in the low, firm voice he used to calm his little sister.

'All right, yes, it's a bad situation. For both of us. But we're still alive, and we've made it this far. That's good, isn't it?'

Reluctantly, Linden nodded.

'So we'll get you on the next train to Aynsbridge, and you can go back to the Oak and tell the others what happened. At least now you know that there are other faeries out there. Male faeries, even. That's got to be worth something.'

Linden rubbed at her reddened eyes. 'But if all the other faeries want nothing to do with us, and all we can do is sit in the Oak and wait to die—'

'Who says that? Maybe the faeries here in London won't help you, but you can always go to some other city – or another country, if you have to. All you have to do is hide in the Oak for a few days until the Empress gives up looking for you, and then try again. What about these Children of Rhys that Rob mentioned? They're faeries too, aren't they?'

'Yes, but we don't even know where to find the Children, let alone whether they'd be willing to help us. And we're running out of time.' Her expression was desolate. 'Even working together, Valerian and I can't protect the Oak the way the Queen used to. If we'd done the wards properly, you'd hardly have noticed the tree at all when you came – but instead, you walked right up and touched it. We might be able to hide from the Empress, but what good will that do us if we just end up being found by the humans instead?'

Timothy let her go and stood up, shoving his cold hands

back into his pockets. 'I don't know. But I can't see you've got any other choice.'

Linden was silent, her gaze on the floor. Then she said, 'You're not going to come with me, are you? You're going to keep running away.'

She didn't sound accusing, only resigned. Timothy hunched his shoulders uncomfortably. 'Look, it's not that I don't want to help you. I just don't know what use I could be, especially if the Empress and her people do come after us. You might be safe in your Oak if you can keep up those spells long enough, but all they'd have to do to find me at Oakhaven is look through the window. They might even figure out that Peri used to be one of your people, and decide to punish her too. Is that what you want?'

Linden looked stricken. 'No!'

'Right. So if you ask me, it's better for everyone if I don't go back to Oakhaven. Besides –' he tried to keep his voice light, but somehow the old bitterness crept in – 'Paul and Peri already made it pretty obvious they didn't want me around.'

'Only because they were afraid you'd find out about the Oak—'

'Because they don't trust me, that's why!' The words came out louder than he'd intended, and Linden flinched. With an effort Timothy controlled his temper and went on, 'By now they should know what kind of person I am. But apparently they think I'm the sort who'd smash up a five-hundred-year-old tree for the fun of it, or stuff faeries into specimen jars and sell them for pocket money, or—'

'Or hit someone and get yourself sent away from school?' said Linden.

That stopped him. Timothy's bruised mouth twisted in frustration, but he couldn't think of anything to say.

'I know you've been hurt,' Linden told him quietly. 'But you should know something else, too. Ever since the first time you came to Oakhaven, Knife – I mean Peri – has been telling me about you. She always said how clever and funny you were, and how much she enjoyed having you to stay. But she also warned me, whenever you came, that I mustn't come to the House until you'd gone. It's not just you, Timothy – she doesn't trust *anybody* with our secret. Because the secret's not hers to share.'

Timothy hesitated. Then he dropped down onto the bench beside her, staring at the floor.

'I can't go back,' he said heavily. 'Not yet. Just...I'm not ready.'

Linden didn't say anything for a long while, and he wondered if she was angry. But when she spoke, her voice was calm.

'Then you'll just have to come to the Oak with me.'

SEVEN

Timothy seemed so cynical and world-weary at times, Linden had almost forgotten he was only a little older than herself. But now the eagerness in his face made him look truly fifteen again. 'You mean it?' he said. 'But I'm...can you really do that?'

'I think so. It would just be a temporary change, of course, and I'll have to keep renewing the glamour so you don't go back to your proper size. But...' Linden's brows furrowed as she considered the problem from every angle. At last she said with more confidence, 'Yes. We'll have to try it. It's the only way.'

'I don't know,' said Timothy, though he sounded reluctant to admit it. 'Bringing a human into the Oak – isn't it going to get you in a lot of trouble? It might be easier if I just took a train to France or something.'

'I'll hide you from the others,' she said. 'At least until we've had a chance to talk to the Queen, and tell her our story. She's very wise: I'm sure she'll understand. Especially once she hears about the Empress wanting to kill you.'

And perhaps, if the Oakenfolk did Timothy this favour, he might even be willing to repay them by helping Linden search for more faeries. After all, two travellers were safer than one, and surely the Empress wouldn't keep hunting them forever?

Timothy looked out across the station, eyes distant as he considered her offer. Then he stood up, reaching for his guitar case.

'All right,' he said. 'Hop into my pack, and we'll go.'

By the time Timothy stepped off the train at Aynsbridge the sun was just visible over the treetops, like a white hole punched through the sky. The air smelled clean here, damp and earthy, and as he walked down the steps from the platform into the car park the breeze that chased him felt surprisingly mild. Still, he was glad for his extra layer of clothing, and he could only hope that the Oak would be warm.

'Linden?' he said. 'You can come out now,' but she didn't answer. Carefully Timothy slid the rucksack off his shoulders, lifted the flap to look – and there lay Linden, fast asleep. Her wings were folded against her back, and she had curled herself up in a nest made from one of his shirts.

So small, thought Timothy. Even now, it seemed impossible that the girl who had rescued him from Veronica could also be a faery tiny enough to stow away in his rucksack. Not to mention how strange it was that in the space of just one night, this same faery had somehow become a friend.

But Linden was so different from anyone else he'd met in the last few months that Timothy couldn't help liking her. She didn't judge him by the shoes he wore, or what music he enjoyed, or who his parents were; she hadn't insisted that he share her beliefs or live by certain rules to please her. She'd just accepted Timothy as he was – even more than that, she'd risked her life to help him. How could he not be grateful for that?

Timothy slipped his arms back through the straps of the rucksack and set off again, treading softly so as not to wake Linden. Aside from the occasional passing car the road before him was deserted, and he dared to hope that Rob had been right: they'd escaped the city before the Empress and her servants could find them, and if they could just make it to the Oak, they'd be safe.

Half an hour later, Linden was still asleep, and Timothy had left the village well behind. The familiar wood rose up on one side of the road as he walked; he came around the bend and there, in the near distance, stood Oakhaven.

Time to get off the road, before Paul or Peri saw him. Turning off just short of the stone bridge, Timothy followed the footpath along the river bank, dodging in and out among the trees until he reached the wood's northeast corner. He could see the Oak now, stark and majestic against the pallid sky – but in between lay open meadow. How would he get across it without being seen?

Timothy set down his guitar and lowered his pack to the ground. 'Linden, wake up.'

He heard a rustle, and then Linden emerged from beneath the flap, stretching and yawning. 'What is it?' she asked, and then 'Oh!' as she saw the Oak. She fluttered out of his pack and made herself human size again, grimacing as her shoes squelched into the muddy ground. 'All right then, let's go.'

'Wait,' said Timothy. 'I thought you were going to make me small.'

'I am. As soon as we get to the Oak.'

'As soon as Paul or Peri happens to look out the window and spot us walking across the field, you mean?'

Linden puffed out a frustrated breath. 'Oh, Timothy. Would it really be so terrible if they did? It wouldn't take long for the two of us to just tell them where we're going, and why. Is it really fair to leave them worrying about you?'

'They're not going to be worried,' he said firmly. 'I left them a note. They won't be expecting to see me for three weeks.'

'Well, they've certainly been worried about *me*. What am I going to say to them, if I can't even mention you?'

Timothy said nothing, and at last Linden heaved another sigh and said, 'All right. But it's going to be a long walk.'

She turned to face him, and Timothy's pulse started to

beat faster. He was actually about to go *inside* the Oak, explore that mysterious place that no other human had ever seen...

'Wait,' said Linden suddenly. 'Your guitar. What are we going to do with it?'

Timothy glanced down at the case still sitting by his feet. 'Can't I bring it?'

'It's going to be awfully awkward,' she said, giving it a dubious look. 'Especially getting it up the Spiral Stair. Can't we just leave it here?'

'In the cold and damp? No, thank you—'

Linden winced. 'Please don't.'

'What?'

'The...the last thing. Don't just say –' her voice dropped to a whisper – '*thanks* like that. Especially if you don't mean it.'

Timothy frowned, but she seemed serious. 'Why?'

'Because it's a special word to us. Sacred, even. To thank someone means you're so grateful for something they've done, you consider yourself to be in that person's debt forever – and believe me, we faeries don't take that idea lightly.'

'Oh.' Timothy was subdued. 'Sorry.'

'Anyway,' Linden went on more briskly, 'let me think. Oh, yes, I know.' And with that she whisked the guitar off the ground and hurried away with it. A few minutes later she came back again, empty-handed and looking pleased with herself.

'What did you do with it?' Timothy asked.

'Put it back in your room. I made it small, flew up to your window with it, and sneaked it under the bed. It should be all right there, shouldn't it?'

'Excellent,' said Timothy admiringly. 'Th— I mean, I appreciate it.'

Linden gave a little, almost shy smile. 'It's all right. Now...' She reached out and put her hands on his shoulders, as though she meant to push him down to faery size by force. Timothy's skin prickled, a thrill running through his whole body; then dizziness swept over him, and he clutched at Linden's arms as his knees buckled—

The tingling faded. Linden let go, and Timothy opened his eyes.

It was breathtaking, and a little daunting, to see the field stretching out in front of him, like some withered alien jungle. The Oak still rose in the near distance, but now it looked huger than ever, a colossal pillar bisecting the sky.

'Come on,' said Linden. 'Hurry,' and she flitted off. Timothy thrashed after her, wincing as the wet grass whipped at his arms and legs. In minutes his jeans had soaked through and his trainers were heavy with mud, but the Oak seemed little closer than it had been before. His heart sank as he realised how much further they still had to go.

'I don't suppose...you could make me...some

wings...too?' he panted to Linden.

'That would mean turning you into something different than you are,' she called back. 'I can make you smaller for a while, but that's all.'

Somewhere in the wood behind them, a crow gave its raucous cry. Timothy froze. 'Did you...back in the restaurant, when you were telling me about the Oakenfolk...didn't you say that crows...'

'Eat faeries, yes,' said Linden. 'Which is why we've got to hurry. And keep your eyes open for burrows you could hide in, just in case.'

The idea of crawling into a muddy hole didn't much appeal to Timothy, but neither did being eaten. No wonder Linden's people preferred to stay inside the Oak. 'Right,' said Timothy faintly, and kept walking.

By the time they arrived at the foot of the Oak Timothy's legs felt numb, his teeth were chattering, and half his weight in mud seemed to be stuck to the bottom of his shoes. He had to stop and scrape them clean before he could move freely again. But as Linden led him down a rough ladder to a shadowy, root-framed door, he felt the old excitement resurface. He'd made it, they were really here—

'What is it?' he asked, seeing the look of distress on Linden's face.

She held a finger to her lips, then replied in a near-whisper, 'The wards that protect us from humans are down again. And so is the glamour I put on the Oak to hide our doors and windows. You didn't notice?'

Timothy shook his head. He'd been so focused on getting inside the Oak, he hadn't even paid attention to the outside.

'Well, maybe it's not as obvious as I thought,' said Linden, but without much conviction. She leaned all her weight against the door; with a grudging creak it swung wide, and the two of them walked in.

They emerged into a vast, cavernous space, where dim light filtered down from window-slits high above. To their left, a round tunnel stretched into darkness, while in front of them stood a door whose tarnished brass plate read LIBRARY. And to their right rose a spiral staircase wide enough for three faeries to climb side by side, its smooth-worn steps twining upwards as high as Timothy could see.

'We'll have to go as quietly as we can, and hope we don't bump into anyone,' Linden whispered. 'It makes my head hurt to keep up too many different glamours at the same time, so I won't make us invisible unless I have to – but it's a long way up to the Queen's chambers.'

Timothy nodded his understanding, and the two of them began climbing the Stair together.

They trudged up past one landing, then another, all ringed with closed doors that looked virtually identical. He saw no paint or pictures on the walls, no carpeting, not even a single piece of furniture to distinguish one landing from another. The staircase itself was a fantastic piece of engineering, but on the whole, the inside of the Oak seemed to be a place built for function rather than beauty.

Still, to think of all this, carved into the heart of a single tree – he ran his hand wonderingly along the rail, feeling the age-polished wood. In all his childhood daydreams he'd never imagined anything like it.

'Someone's coming,' hissed Linden. She pulled him back against the inside curve of the stairs, and sparkling heat rippled over him as she cast a glamour to hide the two of them from view.

Now he could hear the sound of bare feet padding down the stairs, see the glow of a lantern bobbing towards them. As the other faery passed he caught a glimpse of a square face and bluntly cut dark hair, saw the wings that sprang from between her shoulder blades. She paused to sniff the air, frowning, and Timothy held his breath – but then the faery stomped on down the steps and was gone.

Who was that? mouthed Timothy, when Linden nudged him to start climbing again.

'Thorn,' she whispered back. 'She's a friend…well, mostly. I'd love to introduce you, but trust me, this would be a very bad time.'

Timothy could believe it. From the scowl on Thorn's face, he could just imagine the kind of tongue-lashing she'd be capable of giving out. Especially if she knew that Linden had brought a human into the Oak…

Meanwhile, the Stair kept spiralling upwards. Timothy

had played football so often back in Uganda, and even since he'd come to Greenhill, that his leg muscles were in pretty good shape; but as the two of them climbed through turn after turn, the gentle burn in his calves grew to a fiery ache. He was just about to beg Linden to stop and give him a chance to rest when she stepped up onto another landing, and he realised they'd reached the top at last.

An intricately carved archway stood in front of them, hung with red curtains as soft as velvet. This was more like it, thought Timothy, limping after Linden as they passed through into a panelled corridor gently lit by brass lamps. A bit more like a high-class hotel than faeryland, but at least some thought had gone into decorating it – even if all the furnishings looked at least a hundred years old and the draperies were worn through in several places.

They were almost at the end of the corridor when a voice spoke up primly from behind them:

'Her Majesty is not to be disturbed.'

Linden made a startled noise and spun around, putting herself between the newcomer and Timothy. She pushed him back into the shadows, her invisibility spell prickling over him again.

'But Bluebell,' she said as the other faery advanced, 'I have to talk to her right now. It's important.'

Bluebell swept up to them, her long skirts almost

brushing the floor. The last time Timothy had seen a dress like that was in a museum. 'There were two of you here a moment ago,' said the other faery suspiciously. 'And what is that smell? Have you been with the humans again?'

'The Queen will want to see me,' Linden insisted. 'I know she will. Just ask Valerian.'

Bluebell gave a disdainful sniff. 'I find it hard to believe that the judgment of a mere Healer should matter more than the word of Her Majesty's own personal attendant. I tell you, the Queen is resting. If the message you have for her is so important, then you can deliver it to me.'

'So you can repeat it to Mallow?' retorted Linden with a fierceness that surprised Timothy. 'No, I will not. What I have to say is for Her Majesty's ears alone, and if you won't show me in, then I'll just have to announce myself.' And with that she reached out and rapped on the nearest door.

Bluebell gasped. 'How dare you! You impudent—' But the door opened almost immediately, revealing a tall, grey-robed faery with brown hair hanging loose about her shoulders.

'I am very sorry,' she said, lowering her sombre gaze upon them. 'But I fear that you have come too late.'

She stepped back, holding the door open. Inside, Timothy saw a splendidly furnished bedchamber, complete with a four-poster fit for a dying Queen to lie in – but now the covers lay smooth on both sides, with a hollow ridge down the middle, and the pillows by the headboard were empty.

'You mean…' whispered Linden, and the tall faery put a hand on her shoulder.

'I'm afraid so, child. Queen Amaryllis is dead.'

EIGHT

Linden felt frozen all over, numb with shock and grief. She had pinned all her hopes on this meeting with the Queen, trusting that once Amaryllis heard their story, all would be well. She would forgive Linden for running off to the city, she would welcome Timothy to the Oak, and they could all sit down and discuss what to do next. But instead Amaryllis had died, never knowing where Linden had gone and why, or even whether she was still alive.

Bluebell pushed past her and stumbled into the chamber, sobbing. 'Oh, My Lady,' she wept as she dropped to her knees beside the empty bed. 'What will we do without you?'

'We will mourn her, and honour her memory,' said Valerian. 'And then we will go on, as she would have wished us to do. Linden?'

The low pulse in her temples reminded her that Timothy was still by her side, invisible, uncertain, waiting. There was a stone in her throat and a bruising ache deep in her chest, but Linden knew her duty. She pulled herself up, brushing at her wet cheeks, and said, 'Yes, Your Majesty?'

'*What?*' Bluebell whirled on them, eyes hollow with rage. 'You speak treason, girl! *I* am the Queen now – I, by right of seventy years' service!'

'Indeed, you served Amaryllis faithfully,' said Valerian, 'and you will be well rewarded for it. But as this testament written and signed by the Queen's own hand will prove –' she reached into the dressing table and drew out a sealed parchment – 'she did not choose you as her successor. She chose me.'

'Lies!' sputtered Bluebell. 'The notion is absurd! Who are you to rule over the rest of us? You know nothing about matters of state!'

'Nor do you,' Valerian reminded her gently. 'For all the fine clothes she gave you, Bluebell, you were Amaryllis's servant, not her councillor.'

Bluebell's lips pinched together. 'I knew nothing good could come of you being here,' she said. 'Whispering in Her Majesty's ear, poisoning her against me. Conspiring with your human-loving *friends* –' she spat out the phrase as though it were a blasphemy – 'to put yourself on the throne. But we'll see about that!' She flounced out of the door again, adding over her shoulder, 'You're not Queen yet!'

Valerian remained silent until they heard the distant sound of Bluebell's door slamming shut. Then she said, 'Well. That was unfortunate.'

'You were right.' Linden bit her lip in distress. 'What you told me before, about not being able to trust her...but she never used to be like *that*. What's got into her?'

'This is Mallow's work, I fear,' said Valerian. 'Bluebell is vain, and easily flattered – and just as easily controlled. But let that be, for now.' She took Linden by the shoulders. 'Where have you been? Knife came to us yesterday, half-mad with worry for you, and then we heard that the boy had disappeared as well—'

Timothy gave a little cough at that, and Linden coloured. She shut the door, then turned back to Valerian and said apologetically, 'I know. Because I went with him, and now...'

She concentrated, and the ache in her head eased a little as the invisibility glamour dissolved. Timothy stood awkwardly on the carpet in his muddy shoes, his hands in his pockets and the rucksack sagging off one shoulder.

'Er, hello,' he said.

Valerian stared at him a moment, then turned on Linden. 'What in the name of the Great Gardener possessed you?' she demanded. 'To reveal our secrets to—' Then she stopped and took a deep breath, as though collecting herself. 'But no, I speak too soon. You came to tell the Queen something of great importance, and it would be folly to judge you before hearing what you have to say. Very well, go on.'

Relief spread through Linden. She would miss Queen

Amaryllis terribly, but with someone as wise as Valerian taking her place, perhaps things wouldn't be so bad. 'It's a long story,' she said. 'Perhaps we should call some of the others to hear it, too?'

'I don't want to be rude,' whispered Timothy in Linden's ear, 'but is there anything to eat around here? I'm starving.'

They were sitting at the table in the late Queen's study, waiting for Valerian to return from summoning three other faeries – the Council, she'd called them – to hear their story.

'I'm hungry, too,' murmured Linden, and then in a louder voice as Valerian came back in, 'Val— I mean, Your Majesty, do you think we might have something to eat?'

'Periwinkle is bringing refreshments, I believe,' said Valerian, sitting down at the end of the table. And sure enough, it was only a short time before the door opened again and a little red-haired faery bustled in with a tray almost as big as herself.

'Thorn and Campion are on their way,' she said breathlessly as she set it down. Then her eyes fell on Linden and Timothy, and she clapped both hands to her mouth with a little squeak. 'Oh! But you're— I mean he's—'

Quickly Linden rose and embraced the other faery, who burst into tears and clung to her. 'How *could* you go off like that and just *disappear* and not tell me or Knife or *anyone*, don't you know we thought you were *dead*!'

'I'm so sorry, Wink,' Linden said. 'Please forgive me.'

'Of course she will,' said a gruff voice from the doorway, and Timothy recognised Thorn, the faery who had passed him and Linden on the Stair. 'Though if you ask me, she shouldn't. Of all the fly-witted things to do—' Her eyes fell on Timothy. 'Great Gardener! Who or what is *that?*'

'I apologise for the shock, Thorn,' said Valerian's calm voice from the back of the room, 'but I thought it best to summon you here first and explain later. Ah, Campion, there you are. Would you mind shutting the door behind you?'

Timothy had been through some bizarre experiences in the last couple of days, but this had to be one of the oddest: sitting at a table with five faeries – all of whom had noticeably pointed ears and long translucent wings – while they took turns looking at him as though *he* were the strange one.

'I am grateful to you all for coming here at such short notice,' said Valerian. 'The news of Her Majesty's passing will soon spread throughout the Oak, and this may be our last opportunity to meet together for some time. Linden has brought us a human visitor, as I am sure you could not help but notice: I realise that this act is unprecedented, but there was reason for it, as you will soon hear. Linden?'

As Linden stood up and began telling their story, Timothy took a sip of his drink and nearly choked, it was so bitter. The cakes Wink had brought were dry and heavy, with hardly any sweetness to them, and only a generous dollop of honey helped them go down. He would have done anything for a plate of starchy *matoke* with some fish or beef sauce to flavour it, as he used to eat back in Uganda…

'WHAT?' yelled Thorn, and Timothy jumped, spilling his cup down the table. Wink grabbed a napkin and began mopping up the puddle, and Timothy was stammering an apology when he saw that Wink was smiling.

'I knew it!' she told him in hushed tones, as though they shared some wonderful secret. 'I knew they were real, no matter what anyone said! I even thought you might be a faery yourself at first, only you don't have wings…'

Oh. Now Timothy understood why Thorn had shouted: Linden had just told the Council that male faeries existed. He'd been so focused on filling the emptiness in his stomach, he'd stopped paying attention to anything else.

He forced himself to concentrate as Linden explained what she'd learned from her conversation with Rob: how the Oakenfolk were considered Forsaken by the other faeries, that neither Rob nor any others under the faery Empress's command would help them, and last of all that the Empress would execute any faeries or humans who defied her. She finished by telling how she and Timothy had fled the city for fear of the Empress, then dropped back into her chair, rubbing her forehead and looking spent.

'So all the other faeries hate us because they think we're too friendly with humans?' said Wink in bewildered tones, and Thorn remarked acidly, 'Now there's an irony.'

'This Empress…' Campion toyed with her pencil,

frowning. 'She must be clever as well as powerful, to have so many faeries under her control. I wonder how she managed it? Especially if she's been avoiding humans all this time, and they're where our cleverest ideas come from.'

'Well, she hasn't been *avoiding* them, obviously,' said Thorn. 'Seems to me that she and her people find humans useful enough, or they wouldn't be living right in the midst of them.'

Linden nodded. 'But human beings are just cattle, as far as the Empress and her people are concerned. They've become so selfish and proud, they won't even consider that it's wrong to deceive humans and take their creativity by force.'

'Yes, but doesn't it sound as though this Rob you met knew better?' Wink said. 'If he went to the trouble of saving you and Timothy...'

'I thought so too, at first,' Linden replied sadly, 'but it turned out he was just hoping I was one of these Children of Rhys he's been looking for. I don't think we can count on him to help us again.'

The Council faeries all looked sober at this, and the room fell silent. Timothy waited for someone to come up with another idea or at least a question, but no one did. At last, frustrated, he spoke:

'Don't tell me you're all giving up already? All right, so you can't count on the Empress and her people. But they can't be the only faeries in the world. What about trying to find the Children of Rhys yourselves?'

'Timothy, I already told you—' began Linden, but Valerian held up her hand.

'No, let him speak; I can see by his face he has more to say, and I would not dismiss his words without hearing them.' She turned to Timothy. 'Please, go on.'

'You're assuming that if Rob couldn't find the Children, you can't either,' Timothy said. 'But I'm not sure that's true. You've been cut off from the other faeries for hundreds of years, so obviously they know a lot of things about the world that you don't. But your people seem to know some things that the Empress and her faeries have forgotten, too. Don't you have any legends, or history books, or something that might tell you about the Children of Rhys?'

Campion pushed back her chair and rose. 'There's nothing about them in the archives downstairs, I know that much. But perhaps there's something here...' She began inspecting the bookshelves that lined the room, her head cocked to one side.

'Well thought,' said Valerian, inclining her head to Timothy. 'If I had any doubt of Linden's wisdom in bringing you to us, I have none now. Yet if we can find nothing in the Oak's records to tell us of the Children, what then?'

There was no mockery in her tone, no condescension; she really seemed to believe he might have an answer, and after a moment's thought Timothy found that he did.

'Then I'll sneak back into town,' he said, 'and look them up in the library.'

Linden looked at Timothy with surprise: she hadn't expected him to volunteer his services – especially at such risk to himself. Had he decided to join her on her quest to find more faeries after all?

Thorn made a sceptical noise. 'How's that going to help? You can't think some human writer is going to know more about our own people than we do?'

Timothy opened his mouth, but Campion spoke first. 'Why not?' she said to Thorn. 'You've never read the human legends about faeries, but I have, and you'd be surprised how often they were right about things we Oakenfolk had muddled up or forgotten. And,' she added with a touch of smugness, 'there were male faeries in some of those stories, too.'

'All right, fair enough,' Thorn replied. 'But Rob didn't know how to find these Children either, and he's been living in the middle of a big human city for years. So if he couldn't find out anything—'

'Unless,' said Timothy, 'he made the same mistake you're making.'

'Oh, really. And what's that?'

'Underestimating humans.' Timothy leaned forward across the table, his grey-green eyes intent. 'If the Empress and her faeries believe they're so superior to my people, of course they wouldn't expect us to have any information that they don't. And there's another thing I noticed, though I didn't think much about it at the time: Rob's place didn't have a television or a radio or even a telephone, let alone a computer. He's probably consulted every faery book he could find, but I'll bet you anything he's never searched the internet.'

Thorn looked blank, and Linden was wondering how to explain when Campion broke in excitedly: 'That's a special sort of library in a box, isn't it, where you can get information from all over the world. Don't Knife and Paul have it?'

Timothy looked discomfited, and Linden could guess why: he'd been counting on the faeries not knowing that particular detail. How could he explain to them that he'd rather walk all the way to the village and risk being caught by the Empress than go back to the House even for a few minutes?

'Yes, but Timothy can't go back to their place right now,' she said. 'It would be too easy for the Empress and her people to find him there.'

Wink nodded, but Thorn looked unimpressed. 'And you think he'll be any safer here?' she retorted. 'If the Empress's lot can find Timothy in the House, there's no reason they can't find him in the Oak just as easily. Especially with our wards in such a sorry mess.'

Linden gave Timothy an apologetic look. 'They're right, you know.'

'I'm not going back to Oakhaven,' he muttered back. 'If your people don't want me here then I'll leave – but I'll just end up buying a ticket to Dover instead.'

Linden could think of nothing to say to that, and there was an awkward silence. At last Valerian rose and addressed Timothy in her calm, measured voice:

'Today you have given us both insight and hope, and for that we are in your debt. You have proven yourself a true friend of the Oak, and if we can do you any service, we will be glad to know of it. Nevertheless, we cannot allow you to remain here.'

Linden began to protest, but Valerian held up a hand.

'You meant well, I know. But think, child. You are exhausted, and the effort of casting so many spells has drained you even further. The moment you fall asleep, the glamour that has made Timothy our size will stop working. And what will become of us all then?'

The blood drained from Linden's face, and her stomach flopped like a landed minnow. How could she have been so stupid? She'd been prepared to ignore the pain of her headache and keep casting whatever spells might be necessary to keep Timothy safe, but she couldn't stay awake forever...

'Indeed,' said Valerian gently. 'So please, would you escort our guest to the door?'

'I've a better idea,' said Thorn, shoving her own chair back from the table as Linden struggled to rise. 'The way *she* looks, she'll probably faint halfway down the Spiral Stair, and then just think what a fine mess of owl pellets we'll be in.' She stalked around the table and kicked the leg of Timothy's chair. 'Get up, human. You're coming with me.'

Timothy shot Linden a desperate glance. 'I can't go back to Paul and Peri's.'

'Then don't,' said Thorn with a shrug. 'East or west or down a foxhole, it's all the same to me. Just as long as it's *out.*' She turned to Linden. 'I'll whistle when he's safely on his way, and you can take the glamour off him. All right?'

'All right,' said Linden dubiously. How Thorn intended to get Timothy out of the Oak without anyone seeing, she couldn't imagine. But if Queen Valerian thought it would be all right – and by her silence it seemed she did – then who was Linden to argue?

Reluctantly Timothy got up from his chair. He followed Thorn towards the door, then stopped and turned back. 'Er...there's just one thing.'

All the faeries looked at him.

'What you said before, about being in my debt...Would you mind not telling Peri...I mean, Knife...that I've been here?'

The Oakenfolk exchanged surprised glances, and Wink positively glared at him. 'What sort of bargain is that?' she demanded, but Thorn interrupted her.

'It's not like he's asking for the moon on a platter, is he? Just because you don't like it doesn't mean it's not a fair bargain. Go on, promise.'

Wink folded her arms and said petulantly, 'Oh, all right.'

'Campion?'

'You have my word,' said the other faery, and Valerian gave Thorn an unfathomable look before adding, 'And mine. Although it seems a poor way to repay Knife for all her service to us.'

'There,' said Thorn to Timothy. 'Satisfied?'

Timothy nodded. He gave Linden a tight farewell smile, and followed Thorn out.

Linden's shoulders slumped, and she stared down at her crumb-littered plate. She had so hoped that Timothy would stay, that he might even come with her to find the Children of Rhys. But now he was going away, and who knew when – or whether – she'd ever see him again?

'I don't have magic, remember,' Thorn muttered to Timothy as he shuffled along at her side, barely able to see past the hood of the cloak she'd thrown over him. 'So if we bump into anybody else on the way, you let me do the talking, and if I tell you to run, you run.'

'Run where?' objected Timothy. 'We're nine floors up. And I don't have wings, remember?'

'Cheeky one, aren't you?' said Thorn. 'Just pick the nearest landing, up or down. If you can find a door that isn't locked, go through it and don't come out until I tell you. There's so few of us left now, odds are there won't be anyone on the other side.' She made a derisive noise. 'A human in the Oak. Don't know what Linden was thinking.'

'Speaking of Linden—' Timothy began, but Thorn hissed him silent. He grimaced and fell into step behind her as they trudged towards the Oak's ground floor.

When they reached the bottom of the Stair, Thorn marched straight for the exit, but Timothy lingered, gazing up into the great tree's vast, hollow heart. This would probably be the last chance he had to look at this incredible place, and he didn't want to forget any of it.

'Come *on*,' Thorn whispered at him, tugging open the same door that Timothy and Linden had used to get in. Reluctantly he obeyed – only to have her grab him by the scruff of the neck and practically toss him outside.

'Up the ladder! Go!' she ordered, and Timothy scrambled upwards, tripping on the topmost rung and tumbling onto the wet grass.

Thorn climbed up after him, then put two fingers in her mouth and let out a piercing whistle. 'Well,' she said with satisfaction, 'that's taken care of you – and none too soon, either.' She spread her wings and flashed away across the lawn.

Distractedly Timothy wondered where she was going – and then, to his horror, he realised. He leaped to his feet, shouting, 'Wait! Don't! You promised!'

But she had already given the signal, and his protest came too late. Panicked, Timothy tried to flee, but he had only taken a couple of steps when the glamour Linden had put on him dissolved, and he shot up to his usual size. Dazed, he reeled back against the Oak as the glass doors at the back of the house burst open and Peri rushed out, shouting, 'Timothy!'

Thorn flew past him with a chortle, and disappeared among the roots of the Oak. 'I know,' said Timothy resignedly, as Peri shook him and then seized him in a furious embrace. 'I'm in a lot of trouble.'

NINE

'You lied to him!' Linden accused when Thorn came back into the Queen's study. 'And you tricked me!'

'No, I didn't,' replied the older faery smugly, sitting down and propping her feet up on the table. 'I made you lot promise not to tell Knife – but did you ever hear me say that *I* wouldn't?'

She was right, Linden realised. Part of her was glad that Timothy was back with Knife and Paul, but what Thorn had done still made her uneasy, and she wondered if Timothy would ever trust a faery again.

'Linden,' said Valerian, and she looked up as the Queen continued: 'The knowledge that you gained from your adventure with Timothy is of great value to us all, and I am glad that you returned safely to tell us of it. But even so –' her voice became stern – 'you also acted foolishly in leaving the Oak without permission, and it is only by the Gardener's mercy that you are still alive. What I said to you before,

I will say again: you are still too young and unskilled in magic to undertake such a dangerous task.'

She rose to her feet, her gaze holding Linden's. 'As Queen Amaryllis's appointed successor, I forbid you to leave the Oak again until I give you my permission to do so.'

Linden's cheeks flamed, and she hung her head. 'Yes, Your Majesty.'

'I also forbid you to have any more contact with Timothy. This is not his quest, and we have no right to involve him in it. Already he dares not return to London because of what you have done; we can only pray that he suffers no worse consequences. Do you understand? You must let him go, for his sake.'

A knot of pain formed in Linden's throat. She slumped forward and buried her face in her arms, overwhelmed with misery.

'It's all right,' said Wink soothingly, stroking Linden's hair. 'Knife and Paul will take good care of— What is it?'

This last was to Thorn, who had gone very still and held up a hand for silence. Soundlessly the dark-haired fairy eased herself out of her chair, padded to the door, and with one swift motion yanked it open – but no one was there.

'Blight,' she muttered as she slammed the door again and stalked back to her seat. 'The little weasel must have heard me coming.'

Campion looked up sharply from her stack of books. 'Bluebell? How long was she listening?'

'She must have followed me up the Stair when I came back,' said Thorn. 'And I was too busy congratulating myself on having outwitted the boy to notice her listening at the keyhole – but I'd know that prissy sniff of hers anywhere. Wither and gall!' She thumped her fist into her palm.

'All is not lost,' said Valerian. 'If she only heard the last part of our conversation, then she knows nothing except that Linden is being punished for leaving the Oak and for making contact with Timothy. The matters we discussed earlier will remain safe with us, as they should be. Campion, have you found anything?'

'The problem is,' said the Librarian abstractedly, turning another page, 'even the best of our records only go back four hundred years, well after our people broke off from the other faeries – or were exiled from them, I suppose. And when I talk about *best*, I mean the Queen's own version of our history, which she had to rewrite from memory after the Sundering; Jasmine had destroyed or censored everything else. There just isn't much here to work with.'

Valerian looked grave. 'Then the human legends are our last remaining hope. We can only pray that Timothy is able to find the information we need.'

'If Knife doesn't strangle him first,' said Thorn, and Wink rapped her over the head with the teapot. 'Ow!'

'Serves you right, you mean thing,' said the little redhead.

*

'Sit down,' ordered Peri, pointing to the armchair, and Timothy sat. Apprehensive as he was, he could hardly take his eyes off her now that he knew she had once been a faery: the clues were all there in her lithe movements, the angles of her bones and those wild dark eyes. Not to mention about a hundred other things she'd done and said since he'd first met her...

'Why are you here?' she demanded.

He hadn't expected her to start into him quite like that. Most people would have said *Where have you been?* or *Why did you leave?* or *Don't you know how terribly worried we were?*

'I...didn't have a choice,' he said awkwardly.

'Nonsense. Your note said you'd be gone for three weeks; you obviously thought you'd have no trouble finding a place to stay. But now here you are again – so what went wrong?'

'I met Linden.'

Peri's whole face changed, anger washed away by incredulous hope. She sank onto the footstool and whispered, 'Linden? Thorn never mentioned...She's alive? She was with *you*?'

Timothy nodded. 'She told me everything. About the Oakenfolk, and how they lost their magic – and about you, too...Knife.'

For a moment Peri sat frozen; then she leaped up and ran down the corridor, shouting, 'Paul! *Paul!*'

Here we go again, thought Timothy.

'Children of Rhys,' muttered Paul some time later, wheeling up to the computer desk. 'Sounds Welsh if you ask me…' He squinted at the monitor, then made an exasperated noise and said, 'Oh, don't give me that rubbish.'

'What is it?' asked Peri. She'd followed Paul and Timothy into the studio but was keeping well back, eyeing the computer like a potential threat.

Paul peered down at the light on the modem, which was flashing red, then switched it off with an irritated sigh. 'It's on the blink again. I can try restarting, but I have a bad feeling it's not going to work.'

Timothy should have been disappointed, but he was too busy stifling a yawn. He'd told Paul and Peri his story over an enormous breakfast, which had gone a long way towards making him feel human again, and a hot shower and clean clothes had helped too. But now that his stomach was full and the ice in his bones had melted, he was finding it difficult to stay awake.

'No good,' said Paul a moment later, pushing back from the computer.

Peri looked frustrated. 'But we need to find out about these Children right away. If there's any chance of finding them, and convincing them to help the Oakenfolk—'

'There'll be internet access at the library,' said Timothy.

Paul gave him a curious look. 'You seem to be pretty committed to this, for someone who didn't even know faeries existed until yesterday. Are you sure you want to get involved?'

'I'm already involved,' said Timothy. 'So I might as well make myself useful, right?'

Paul and Peri exchanged glances. 'Fair enough,' said Paul, 'but from now on, you don't go anywhere without Peri or me. We all understand what's at stake, so there's no more need for drama, or keeping secrets. Whatever we do, we do together.'

Timothy couldn't argue with that. Especially since Paul and Peri had known about the Oakenfolk's plight, and been trying to help them, for a lot longer than he had. He nodded – and to his surprise, Peri put an arm around his shoulders and gave him a comradely squeeze. She didn't say *I'm sorry we let you down* or *I should have trusted you* or any of the things he'd thought he wanted to hear her say, but somehow that simple gesture made everything all right between them, just the same.

'I'll drive you to the library,' she said.

Sunlight was burning through the last of the rainclouds as Timothy and Peri left the house, and the temperature felt even milder than before. Overnight, a small clump of crocuses had forced their way through the soil of the front garden, and were blooming resolutely in the corner. As they crunched across the gravel towards the waiting car, Timothy zipped up his borrowed jacket and decided that

England wasn't so bad after all…but he still missed his home in Uganda, and probably always would.

'Was it hard for you?' he asked Peri. 'Leaving the Oak, I mean?'

Peri slid into the driver's seat and put the key in the ignition; with a determined twist she turned it, and the engine rumbled to life. 'Yes and no,' she said as Timothy climbed in beside her. 'I had Paul, of course: that helped. And I knew the Oak was still there, even if I couldn't live in it any more. But even though I'd learned enough about your world to get by, I wasn't prepared for how different it would be.'

'I suppose it would be pretty disappointing in some ways,' said Timothy. 'Boring, even.'

'Boring?' She flicked him a glance. 'You've no idea how tedious life in the Oak can be. But disappointing…I suppose it was. I'd been friends with Paul for over a year by then, and we already knew we loved each other, but his parents didn't know me at all, and it wasn't easy to win them over. They sent me to stay in town for a few days, alone, while they tried to figure out where I'd come from and what to do with me…it was horrible. And even after Paul persuaded them to let me move into the House, I had so much to learn, and I kept making mistakes. There were times we both wondered if we'd done the right thing – but it was done, and we had to make the best of it.'

She backed the grey Vauxhall out of the drive and onto

the road, speeding up once they'd crossed the stone bridge. Hedge-tangled walls rose around them as the wood fell away, making it difficult to see more than a few metres ahead. It must have been fun for Paul teaching her how to drive, thought Timothy.

'It did get easier, though, right?' he asked.

'Not for a long while. I just got better at—' Suddenly her foot came down on the brake, and Timothy rocked forward, the seat belt cutting into his shoulder.

'What?' he exclaimed, but then he saw it: a small brown and red bird, fluttering back and forth across the road as though to block their path.

'I've never seen a robin behave like that before,' said Peri, frowning as she drove closer. 'Is it injured? Or protecting a nest?'

Timothy started to answer, then yelled and flung his arms over his face as the bird launched itself straight at the windscreen. Peri wrenched the wheel, skidding the car across the road; they crashed into a hedgerow and stopped abruptly, broken twigs and dried-up berries pattering over them.

'Peri?' asked Timothy, and then in alarm, 'Peri!'

She sat motionless, slumped against the steering wheel. He couldn't see any blood on her face, but when he grabbed her shoulder she felt stiff as glass, and he couldn't make her move.

A bird-shaped shadow flickered past the car's front

window, then dropped down beside Timothy's door and swelled, ominously, into a tall human shape. Then came the voice, level and commanding, impossible to disobey:

'Get out of the car.'

TEN

Timothy shoved the car door open and stepped out onto the road, his shoulders squared defiantly. 'If you've hurt Peri, I swear—'

'She is not injured.' Rob pushed back the hood of his sweatshirt and shook out his damp red hair. 'Only suspended in time.' His eyes narrowed. 'Why are you looking at me like that?'

'I was just trying to figure out where the other six feet of you came from, *Robin*.' Timothy spoke in his boldest tone, trying not to let the faery see that he was afraid. 'That's quite a trick, changing shape like that.'

'Enough,' said Rob. 'I did not come here to indulge your human curiosity. Tell me: where will I find Linden?'

'Why?'

'Because the message I bring is urgent, and it is for her sake that I came. Where is she?'

Timothy folded his arms. 'I'm not telling you anything

until you tell me why you're here.' After all, from what he'd learned of faeries, they didn't usually do things for others out of the kindness of their hearts. If Rob had flown all the way here just to talk to Linden, then he must be expecting an equally big favour from her in return. And what if she couldn't afford to give him what he was asking?

Rob made an impatient noise. 'I do not bargain with humans. Tell me, or—' He raised a hand and Timothy tensed, not knowing whether to expect a threat, a spell or a physical blow. But then Rob let his arm drop and said flatly, 'Very well, I will take the risk. Do you remember the twin brothers who were playing chess when you came to Sanctuary last night?'

Lean frames, strong bones, cold black eyes. He'd seen them a second time as he was chasing Linden out the door. 'I think so,' said Timothy.

'They are known as the Blackwings,' Rob told him. 'Byrne and Corbin are expert hunters, clever and ruthless and ambitious for the Empress's favour – and in their raven forms they can fly further and more swiftly than I. The Empress has commanded them to bring you and Linden to her alive, but rest assured that if they catch you, you will find that small consolation.'

Cold ants swarmed up Timothy's spine. 'You mean…they know where to find us? But how?'

Rob pulled a scrap of fabric from the pocket of his sweatshirt, shook it out – and there, suddenly, was the jacket

Timothy had left behind at Sanctuary. 'I tracked you here with this,' he said, tossing it back to him. 'Fortunate for you that I found it before the Blackwings did; for all I know they are still back in the city, looking for some similar means to hunt you down. But it will not be long before they find something they can use: a drop of Linden's blood on the pavement perhaps, or a single hair from your head. And with that, they can follow you anywhere.'

Timothy's hands clenched around the jacket. 'So how do we stop them?'

'You cannot,' said Rob. 'But if you cease wasting my time and show me where to find Linden, then I will tell you what you can do instead…'

Linden sat up, rubbing sleep from her eyes. After a bath and an hour's rest in her own bed she felt a little better, but she had hoped to sleep longer, and now it was impossible. Why was there so much noise going on outside her door? All those shouting voices and running feet – the last time she'd heard such a commotion, it was when she'd accidentally left the East Gate open and a mouse got in.

'Oh, Linden!' Wink burst through her door, wings and hands flapping in excited unison. 'You won't believe this!' She whisked around her, brushing wrinkles from Linden's skirts, straightening her tunic, helping her into her leather waistcoat and buttoning it tight. She combed Linden's brown curls with her fingers, then propelled her out the door, announcing, 'Here she is!'

Linden stumbled, and stopped short. There on the landing stood Rob, surrounded by a crowd of awestruck, excitedly chattering Oakenfolk. At this small size, with those angular bones and the points of his ears showing through his russet hair, there could be no doubting he was a true faery. And yet...what was he doing here?

She ought to have been afraid, but somehow she couldn't be: she had told him about the Oak, after all. And despite all the harsh things he had said about the Oakenfolk being Forsaken, he had still given her shoes to wear afterwards. Linden opened her mouth and, stupidly, said the first thing that came into her head: 'You don't have any wings.'

'Being male, I should think not,' said Rob. 'But rest assured that I can fly as well as you,' and with that his form blurred, and the faeries around him all jumped back as a full-sized robin appeared in his place.

'You must pardon us,' said Valerian, and Linden looked around to see her coming down the Spiral Stair. Even in her plain grey robes, with not a single jewel or a spark of glamour to adorn her, she had a regal dignity. 'It is our shame to have forgotten nearly all we once knew of our own heritage. And you are the first male of our kind that any of us Oakenfolk have ever seen.'

The robin ruffled his feathers, and became Rob again. He moved towards Valerian – but then a shrill voice rang out from the back of the crowd:

'It is not *your* place to speak to him, Healer!'

Inwardly Linden cringed as Bluebell came marching up onto the landing from the other side, her skirt gathered primly in one hand. Her hair was piled high atop her head, and the glittering circlet woven into it could only have come from the Archives – a treasure to which she had no right. She glanced imperiously at the faeries blocking her path, but nobody moved until Mallow barked, 'Make way for the new Queen!'

Reluctantly the others shuffled aside and Bluebell swept through. 'On behalf of my people I welcome you, stranger,' she said. 'And I trust you will forgive their unseemly curiosity—'

'Stop talking rubbish, Bluebell,' said Thorn. 'You aren't any Queen of mine, and if you interrupt Valerian again, I'll stuff you in a sack and sit on you.'

'Thorn,' said Valerian quietly, 'there is no need.'

Rob stepped up to Valerian and bowed. 'Your Majesty,' he said. 'I have an important message to deliver. May I speak with you and Linden alone?'

Bluebell opened and closed her mouth, like a baby bird deprived of its worm. Then she spun around, thrust her way back to the Stair, and disappeared. Only Mallow remained, her gaze fixed on Rob with a mixture of loathing and hunger. 'You're making a mistake,' she told him huskily. 'Valerian's not a proper Queen – she's not even a proper faery. She's just a Healer who's got above herself, and a half-human one at that.'

Her last words hit home: Rob stiffened. But he did not move from Valerian's side, and Linden gave him a grateful smile.

'It's good to see you again,' she told him. 'But how did you find us here?'

Rob glanced back at the crowd of Oakenfolk. 'I think,' he said, 'that story would be better told in private. Is there somewhere else we can go?'

'Children...of...Rhys,' muttered Timothy as he typed it into the library computer. Since he didn't have a card he'd had to fill out an application to use the terminal, and they'd only allowed him half an hour. But if the Blackwings were on their way, he couldn't afford to spend more than a few minutes here anyway. He needed an answer *now*.

Peri sat beside him with tight lips and folded arms, still furious after what Rob had done to them on the road. The car had been only a little scratched, but she'd hated having magic used against her that way. And once they started driving again, and Timothy explained what Rob had told him about the Blackwings and the Empress – he'd never seen Peri look so savage. No wonder the faeries called her Knife.

'Well?' she demanded.

Timothy did not reply: he was busy scanning the page he'd just found, which claimed to be an online dictionary of faery folk. Sure enough, there was an entry about the

Children of Rhys, but it was only a couple of lines and didn't tell him anything he didn't know already. Except…he studied the screen a moment, then went back to the search engine and typed in the Welsh version of the name: *Plant Rhys Ddwfn.*

Now *that* was more like it. The first link he found was an excerpt from a book of Welsh legends, and there was a whole story about a farmer named Gruffydd who had found the Children with the help of some magic herbs…Timothy read the page from top to bottom, then got up quickly and went to the library's help desk, leaving Peri frowning at the computer.

'Could I send a few pages to the printer?' he asked. 'We're in a hurry.'

'Please make yourself comfortable,' said Valerian as she ushered Linden and Rob into the Healer's quarters. She gestured to the sofa, but Rob remained standing, looking around the room with an expression Linden had never seen on his face before: there was wonder in it, and even a hint of envy.

Of course, thought Linden. Compared to the squalid, barely-furnished apartment Rob had shown them last night, or the shabby disorder of the hostel, Valerian's rooms must have seemed like paradise. The chairs were not only sturdily built but attractive; Thorn had learned a great deal from studying Paul's books on design. Wink had taken scraps of fabric from the House, and sewn draperies and cushions in serene patterns of blue. Twig-framed pictures of medicinal plants hung on the wall, drawn by Knife with a very fine pen, and by the door a glass jar held dried herbs that Valerian had arranged herself.

'I apologise for being unable to receive you in the Queen's chambers,' said Valerian, evidently misunderstanding Rob's reaction. 'But her quarters seem to be under dispute at the moment.'

'Yet you have magic,' Rob said as he sat down, 'and this Bluebell does not. Why not bend her and her supporters to your will – or at least punish them as their disloyalty deserves? Do you want your subjects to perceive you as weak?'

'I want my people to accept me willingly as their Queen,' replied Valerian, 'not bow to my rule out of fear. I may not be able to persuade them all to follow me. But if most of them do, that will suffice.'

'Easily said when your enemies have little power,' countered Rob. 'But if your plan to restore the Oakenfolk's magic succeeds, then they will soon have as much magic as you do. What if they attempt to overthrow you and take the throne by force? Will you not regret your mercy then?'

'Perhaps,' said Valerian, unruffled by Rob's challenging tone. 'But I would rather risk losing my throne than claim it as a tyrant.' She rose from the sofa and opened the window, inviting fresh air into the dusty-smelling room. 'You must be parched after your journey; may I bring you a drink of water, or some berry wine?'

Rob looked startled. He glanced at Linden, and she could read the question in his eyes: *Is this a mockery? Or is your Queen truly offering to serve me?*

'You should try the wine,' Linden reassured him. 'Queen Valerian makes it herself, and it's very good.'

'Then I will do so,' said Rob. He took the cup that Valerian handed him and sipped it, then set it aside and said, 'But I am not here as an idle visitor. A few moments ago I met the human boy on the road, and what I told him then, I tell you now: you are all in grave danger.'

Valerian caught her breath. 'The Empress?'

'Indeed. As I feared, Veronica has gone to her and told all she knows, and now the Empress has sworn to capture Linden and Timothy and make an example of them. She has sent two of her deadliest hunters – the Blackwing brothers, who take the form of ravens – to track them down, and if you do not act quickly, they will find the rest of you as well.'

Valerian's brow furrowed with anxiety. 'Can we not hide the children? Or send them elsewhere to safety?'

Rob shook his head. 'There is no safe place for them anywhere. Every faery under the Empress's rule – and there are hundreds of us scattered throughout this land – knows what Timothy and Linden look like, and we have all been told to report the instant either one of them is seen.'

'How?' Valerian demanded. 'How could one faery become powerful enough to control so many?'

'The Empress began her rule long before I was born,' said Rob, 'but I know this much. She asked her first followers to share with her a single drop of their blood in token of their loyalty. Then, using an ancient magic, she used that blood to bind them to her service. She sent her servants to recruit other faeries by the same means, and those in turn enlisted more, until all but a few of our people belonged to her – and those who resisted did so at the cost of their lives. So how can any of us stand against her now, when she has tasted our blood and knows all our true names?'

Linden was horrified. To know a faery's true name was to have absolute power over her, which was why most faeries lived their whole lives and died without ever sharing that secret. To think of the Empress ferreting out those precious names with dark magic, and using them to control faeries like Rob against their will – it made Linden want to be sick.

'I have served the Empress all my life,' Rob continued, 'but not by choice, and I know others who would also be glad to escape her rule. Still, as long as she holds our names we dare not rebel openly against her. Yet among the Children of Rhys, it is said, there is a white stone that gives a new name to any faery who holds it. If someone could find that stone and bring it to us, we would be free.'

His musician's hands spread in a pleading gesture. 'For

years I have sought the Children of Rhys, but all my attempts to find them have failed. Even if I knew where to look for them, I could not leave the city for more than a few hours without arousing suspicion. But Linden is outside the Empress's power—'

'And so you would send her out into the world to hunt for the Children of Rhys on your behalf?' said Valerian incredulously. 'A girl of fifteen, with nothing but glamour to protect her, and these Blackwing brothers pursuing her all the while?' She rose from her chair. 'No. This is madness. There must be another way.'

'There is no refuge for Linden here,' insisted Rob. 'With the little magic you have, you cannot hold the Oak against the Blackwings, not even for a moment. You must send Linden away if the rest of your people are to survive – and is it not better to send her out with a purpose, than with no direction at all?'

'But if Linden leaves us, the Oak will still be at risk,' objected Valerian. 'We need her to sustain the glamour that hides our doors and windows from human eyes – her spells may be weak and unpractised, but they are all the protection we have.'

'I can help you with that,' said Rob. 'I have no skill with illusion, but if you close your shutters I can command this tree to grow a fresh layer of bark across them, until only a slit remains. You will have air and a little light, and no human will guess your Oak is inhabited – at least, not so long as you draw your curtains and guard your lamps carefully after nightfall.'

Linden held her breath, watching Valerian. The new Queen's head was bowed, her eyes shut. At last she said, 'Even the Sight cannot counsel me otherwise. I accept your offer. Linden will go.'

Fearful excitement fluttered through Linden. She had another chance to help the Oakenfolk – and now, it seemed, Rob and his people as well.

'Yet one thing still troubles me,' Valerian went on. 'If the Blackwings are so swift, so powerful, and so ruthless – how can Linden and Timothy hope to escape them even for a little while, let alone stay ahead of them long enough to find the Children of Rhys?'

'I know!' said Linden. 'We can take the train!' After all, it had worked for her and Timothy before, and even the strongest ravens could only fly so fast or so far...

Valerian looked at Rob.

'It is possible,' said Rob. 'My people dislike train stations, for the scent of so many humans together is unpleasant to us, and we have our own methods of journeying from one place to another. Most faeries loyal to the Empress would scorn to travel in such a way – and that pride may prove to be their weakness.'

The Queen sighed. 'I can only pray that you are right,' she said. 'But so be it. Linden, go quickly now, and say your farewells, and pack what you need for the journey. As soon as Timothy and Knife return, you must go.' She took Linden by the shoulders and stooped to kiss her brow, adding softly, 'And may the Great Gardener watch over you.'

The sun was high over the rooftops of Oakhaven by the time Timothy and Peri returned. Peri backed the car into the drive, so they could get away quickly if need be, and the two of them sprinted into the house shouting: 'Good news!'

Paul wheeled quickly to meet them in the corridor. 'It worked? You actually found out about the Children of Rhys on the *internet*?'

Timothy nodded, and held up the pages he'd printed at the library. 'I've got a legend that tells where the Children are, and how to find them. I don't know how much truth there is to the story, but it's the best chance we've got...' He looked over at Peri, who nodded and said, 'Off you go. Hurry.'

'Where's he going?' asked Paul as Timothy raced up the stairs. He was nearly at the top when he heard Peri reply in a rueful tone, 'Well, that would be the *bad* news.'

Even so, there was one good thing about knowing his life was in danger, thought Timothy as he stuffed some more clothes in his rucksack. If nothing else, it had made him very wide awake.

Reluctantly he shoved his guitar a little further under the bed – he wished he could take it with him, but it would only get in the way. He was heading down the stairs again when a tentative knock sounded at the back of the house. Timothy hurried down the hallway just as Peri unlatched the glass door and Linden burst inside, human-sized and quivering with nervous excitement.

'I'm so sorry I worried you – I know I should have left a note—'

'Never mind that,' said Peri, quickly returning Linden's embrace. 'I'm just glad you're—' She broke off, frowning. 'What's that bird doing out there?'

'It's Rob,' said Linden. 'He came with me from the Oak, but he can't come in unless you invite him. Would you?'

'Of course,' said Peri sweetly, but there was a dangerous gleam in her eye. She flung the door open and addressed the robin on the veranda, 'Greetings, Rob of London. I am Perianth, also known as Knife, Queen's Hunter and chief protector of the Oak. I may be human now, but I was born as much a faery as you are, and if you dare to use magic on me without my permission again, I will *shoot* you.' She stepped back, holding the door wide. 'Now that's settled, will you come in?'

Timothy had never seen a bird look embarrassed before, let alone contrite, but this one did. He fluttered over the threshold, unfolded himself into six feet of lanky height, and stood meekly by Linden's side.

'Well?' asked Paul.

Rob looked down at his feet, and all at once Timothy

realised that the male faery was younger than he'd thought. It was only Rob's formal way of speaking, and that ageless look all grown faeries seemed to share, that had fooled him. 'Cold iron,' Rob said in a subdued voice. 'If you have a piece small enough for Timothy to carry, it will weaken any spells that the Blackwings try to cast over him.'

'Good suggestion,' Paul remarked. 'But if it affects faery magic, won't it weaken Linden too?'

'It will make it hard for her to cast spells on Timothy, yes. And she must take care not to touch the iron herself, or she will not be able to use her magic for some time afterwards. But believe me, the benefit of carrying such a talisman will be far greater than any risk.'

'Right,' said Paul, turning to Peri. 'There's a key in the old trunk upstairs that should do the trick.' Then as she started off he added, 'And while you're up there, bring down my suitcase, will you? I need to pack.'

'Suitcase?' exclaimed Timothy. 'Where are you going?'

'Good question,' Peri said, turning to face her husband with her hands on her hips. 'I thought we agreed that *I'm* going with them.'

'No doubt they'd be glad if you did,' said Paul. 'But the Oakenfolk need you here. Besides, I'm Timothy's guardian, so if anybody's going to drive him to the back end of Wales, it ought to be me.'

Linden's eyes lit with sudden hope. 'Wales? You mean you've found out where the Children of Rhys are?'

But then Rob spoke up. 'Your intentions are noble, human, and I cannot fault your courage. But a single car, once identified, is easily tracked – and as Timothy and your mate can tell you, easily intercepted as well. Also, the Blackwings must take Linden and Timothy alive to earn the Empress's reward, but they have no such command concerning you. I do not advise it.'

Peri dropped into the chair next to Paul, her face a portrait of frustration. 'But *someone* has to go with you,' she said to Timothy and Linden. 'It's dangerous, and you're far too young.'

'It's a good thing no one told you that when you were fourteen, and fighting crows twice your size with the blade of my old craft knife,' said Paul. 'Somehow I don't think it would have gone over very well.' But a corner of his mouth turned up as he said it, and he put his arm around her shoulder and kissed her cheek with a tenderness that held no reproach.

Peri relaxed a little. 'Yes, but—'

She was interrupted by a frantic pattering at the door. They all looked around to see Thorn crouched on the veranda, hammering at the glass with both fists.

Instantly Peri leaped up and threw the door open. The faery flashed inside, shouting, 'Close it! Close it now!'

'What's going on?' Peri asked as Thorn dropped to the mantelpiece, one hand pressed to her heaving ribs.

'Saw them – from the top of the Oak,' gasped Thorn.

'Two of them – too big for crows. Flying in from the northwest.'

Rob went very still, and his eyes became distant, as though he was listening. 'She is right,' he said at last. 'The Blackwings have found us.'

ELEVEN

There was a moment of dreadful silence. Then:

'I'll hold them off,' said Peri. 'The rest of you, get ready to move.' She took a step towards the door, but Rob intercepted her.

'This is folly,' he said. 'What can you do against them? Whatever you may have been once, you are a mere human now, and you have no magic.'

'Maybe not,' agreed Peri, and her mouth curled in a bleak smile. 'But I do have a gun.' And with that she sprinted off down the corridor, leaving Rob staring after her.

Paul spun his chair to face Linden and Timothy. 'Right, this is what we're going to do. Knife will keep the Blackwings distracted at the back of the house, while we sneak out the front. Then I'll drive you to the train station.'

He didn't even notice that he'd called her *Knife*, Timothy thought, and a shiver went through him at the strangeness of it. But Paul was still talking: 'Linden, do you think you can cast some kind of glamour to hide us?'

'I can try,' said Linden in a small voice. The excitement that had lit her eyes earlier had vanished; she looked tense now, and very pale.

'The glamour you need is simple,' Rob assured her. 'If you hold a picture in your mind of the front of this house as you wish it to seem, it will appear so to the Blackwings until you are safely away. The only thing that might enable them to see through your illusion is if they hear you leaving – but I can cast a spell of silence to prevent that.'

'But what will you do when we've gone?' Linden asked anxiously. 'How will you get away?'

Rob's mouth quirked, as though her concern amused him. 'I will be safe enough here in this house until the Blackwings have gone. They will not sense my presence, never fear; I have my own tricks, and am a match for either of them.'

'Assuming that fat head of yours will still fit out the door when they're gone,' said Thorn sardonically from her perch above the fireplace, but Timothy could see that she was shaken. She rose and dusted off her breeches, adding, 'I'd best get back to the Oak before that blighted pair of carrion-eaters arrives. Linden, you watch yourself – and the boy, too.' And with that she heaved open the window and disappeared.

'Timothy!' shouted Peri's voice from the floor above, and Timothy raced down the corridor to answer. He reached the bottom of the stairs just in time to catch the glimmering object she tossed down to him – an old-fashioned iron key.

'Thanks,' he said as he slid it into his pocket, only realising his mistake when he saw her flinch. 'Sorry.'

'No matter,' she replied. 'Old habits, that's all.' She galloped down the rest of the stairs and pulled Timothy into a rough embrace before reaching out to do the same with Linden, who had just hurried up with the others. She stooped to kiss Paul, gave Rob a curt nod, and strode towards the back door with rifle in hand.

'Will she be all right?' Linden asked Rob. 'Will they hurt her?'

'They have no knowledge of your history, or hers,' said Rob. 'To them she will appear no more than another ignorant human shooting at them for sport: as long as they do not suspect that she is knowingly defending you, she should be safe. But enough talk. The way is clear. Go.'

Rob's spell of silence seemed to be working, because as Linden crept out the front door and onto the gravel drive with Timothy and Paul behind her, none of them made a sound. The car doors opened without creaking, and shut just as noiselessly; and when Paul transferred from his wheelchair into the driver's seat and turned the key, only a slight vibration assured Linden that the engine had started at all.

She closed her eyes and pictured the front of the House

just as Rob had told her, with an empty car sitting in the drive and no humans or faeries in sight, even though in reality Paul was already easing the car out onto the road. The effort made her temples pound, though not as badly as she'd feared; after a moment she even dared to look back, and see what the Blackwings were doing.

If she craned her neck she could just make out Knife standing tensed by the side of the House, watching the ravens as they circled high above. The air between their wings shimmered, and ripples of power expanded across the Oakenwyld, breaking against the House and the great tree.

'They're searching for us,' she whispered.

Suddenly the two birds wheeled in midair and veered towards them. 'They've spotted us!' gasped Linden, and Paul's hand moved sharply on the controls, urging the car to greater speed. But the road was winding, and it would be all too easy for their faery pursuers to cut them off—

Then Knife burst through the gate into the front garden, swung up her rifle, and fired.

It was a spectacular shot. Black feathers exploded into the sky, and the lead raven shrieked and straggled downwards. Immediately his brother dived after him, and the two birds plunged into the shadows of the wood.

'Yes!' exulted Timothy from the front seat, but Linden slumped down beside Paul's folded wheelchair and closed her eyes, shuddering. Knife had indeed saved them – but at what cost? She had only winged the raven, not killed him.

And if his brother could heal his wound as Rob had healed hers last night, it might not be long before the two of them rose up to take their revenge...

Timothy must have been thinking the same thing, because when he spoke again he sounded less confident, as though he were trying to reassure himself. 'She'll be all right. Even if they do suspect she was helping us, they won't do anything to her. They can't afford to waste the time.'

Paul did not answer. His expression was grim, his eyes fixed on the road. In silence they sped away, leaving the Oakenwyld and its lone defender behind them.

Timothy had assumed Paul would take them to the station at Aynsbridge, but his cousin had a different plan. 'You'll get away faster from Oxted,' he said, 'and it'll make it harder for the Blackwings to catch up with you. When I drop you off, just go to the information desk and tell them you want to get to Cardigan as fast as possible; they'll tell you where to go from there.'

'Cardigan?' asked Linden from the back seat. 'Is that where we're going?'

'Somewhere around there.' Timothy pulled the pages out of his jacket pocket, unfolded them and handed them back to her. 'There's a map of Wales there. See where I've circled Cardigan, on the coast? And the next couple of pages are the information I found about the Children of Rhys.'

'*The Plant Rhys Ddwfn, or Children of Rhys the Deep,*' read

Linden aloud. '*A small fair folk dwelling upon the Green Isles of the Sea...came often to market at Cardigan, and paid the farmers generously in silver...*' Her lips formed a soft O of comprehension.

'Right, so that's why I thought Cardigan would be the place to start looking,' said Timothy. 'But the last page is the best of all – it's a story about this farmer named Gruffydd who actually met the Children of Rhys.'

He waited as Linden read over the legend, which told how the farmer had been walking through St David's churchyard when he noticed some beautiful green islands out at sea. He decided to sail out to the islands in his boat, but as soon as he left the church, they disappeared. Gruffydd had gone back and forth in confusion a few times before realising that he needed to pull up some of the strange plants that grew in the churchyard and take them with him in his boat. He did so, and when he reached the islands, the Children of Rhys greeted him warmly and gave him rich gifts.

'So if we're going to find the Children,' said Linden slowly as she finished reading, 'we have to find this churchyard and these magical plants first?'

'I know it sounds far-fetched,' said Timothy. Then his mouth twisted wryly and he added, 'Or considering that I'm talking to a faery, maybe not. But it sounds to me like the church isn't far from Cardigan, so it can't hurt to look, right?'

Linden nodded, though she still looked uncertain, and

Timothy couldn't blame her. How much confidence could they have in a story that was now hundreds of years old?

'There's something else about the Children you should know,' she said, and went on to tell him about the conversation she and Valerian had with Rob in the Oak – including what the Empress had done to gain power over all the faeries, and how the Stone of Naming was the only way to free them. 'But these legends don't say anything about the Stone,' she finished, looking down at the pages again. 'I hope Rob wasn't mistaken…'

'So do I,' Timothy said grimly.

A few minutes later Paul dropped them off at the station, pressed a wad of notes into Timothy's hand, and roared off back down the road to Oakhaven. And now Timothy stood on the platform with Linden in his rucksack and Paul's money in his wallet, watching the sign that read LONDON BRIDGE: 5 min.

He hadn't wanted to go back to London at all, especially not to the same station they'd arrived at before, but the woman at the desk said there was no help for it. 'Only way to get where you're going at this hour, love,' she'd explained as she was printing off his tickets. 'And you've got a long enough journey ahead of you as it is.'

It was early afternoon now, the commuter rush long past, and when Timothy boarded the train he found it more than half empty. Still, he had difficulty finding a seat where he could talk to Linden without being overheard.

'It's going to take us until nightfall to get to Wales,' he told her when she emerged, dishevelled and blinking, from the depths of the pack. 'And the train only goes as far as Aberystwyth, so we'll have to stop there overnight and take a coach to Cardigan in the morning. But before that we're going to have to spend something like an hour in London, getting to the station where we'll catch our next train. And that's what I'm worried about.'

'Do you think the Blackwings will catch up with us?' Linden asked.

'I doubt they can fly that fast. But they're not our only problem, remember? All the Empress's faeries will be looking for us. Especially if the Blackwings tell them we're coming.'

Linden sucked in her breath. 'Can they really do that?'

'I don't know. But just after I met Veronica the first time, I saw her talk into her hand as she was walking away. Back then I thought that she must be using a mobile phone, and I'd just missed seeing her take it out of her bag...but now I think she was using magic. That must be how she arranged for that other faery to meet me at the Trans-National, and give me that card for Sanctuary—'

He broke off to see the woman passenger on the other side of the aisle frowning at him: she obviously thought Timothy was talking to himself. Embarrassed, he bent over and pretended to be searching for something in his pack, lowering his voice to a whisper as he went on: 'The point is, if they *do* have some way to talk to each other over a distance, then there's a good chance the faeries in London know we're coming, so we'll have to be on our guard. Can you tell when another faery is around?'

Linden shook her small head. 'Valerian has that power, I think, and obviously Rob does too, but not me. I can smell them, though, if they're close by. Will that be good enough?'

'It'll have to be,' said Timothy.

'May I come out now?' said Linden as loudly as she dared, wondering if Timothy could even hear her amid all the noise of the station. 'It's hot in here.'

'Just wait until I'm through the turnstiles,' Timothy muttered over his shoulder. 'Then I'll find somewhere to let you out.'

Reminding herself to be patient, Linden drew a deep breath through her nose, concentrating on all the smells filtering in to her: sweat and skin, metal and rubber, coffee and spices, all heavily overlaid with the dusty canvas of the pack and the faint soap-and-musk that was Timothy. But in all of that, not a trace of the wild, tingling scent of her fellow faeries.

'All right, you can come out now,' said Timothy at last, and Linden wriggled out of the pack and dropped to the floor beside him, making herself human size again. By now she hardly had to concentrate at all to make herself grow, and being big felt almost as natural as being small: the spell didn't even give her a headache any more.

'I think Rob was right,' she confided to Timothy as she stepped out from the shadows, 'the Empress's people don't like these places. Maybe they don't even know we—'

Timothy caught her by the arm and jerked her back as a huge man in baggy clothes strode past. 'Watch where you're going,' he said. 'In a crowd like this, you can't count on other people to watch out for you.'

Linden blinked and looked around, noticing her surroundings for the first time. Behind her, a set of moving staircases rose and fell with mesmerising smoothness. Beside her was the darkened alcove where Timothy had let her out of his pack. And stretching before her – a wide, windowless tunnel, swarming with more people than Linden had seen or even imagined in her life.

They came in every skin colour, every possible size and shape. Their clothes and hair were such a riot of styles, textures and hues that she felt hopelessly drab, like a wren among goldfinches. But strongest of all was the wave of sheer *humanness* that washed towards her, that thick meaty smell pungent with chemicals and salt.

'Come on,' said Timothy, tugging at her, and Linden obeyed, gulping shallow breaths to calm her nausea. She clung tight to Timothy's hand, and together they plunged through the crowd to the end of the tunnel.

They had just emerged onto a platform whose sign read NORTHERN LINE when the ground rumbled beneath her feet. Linden clapped her hands to her ears, her hair whipping in all directions, as a giant metal snake came crashing out of the darkness and hissed to a stop in front of them, disgorging more humans onto the platform. Linden's knees wobbled, and she couldn't move until Timothy took hold of her and practically dragged her inside.

'Sit down before you faint, will you?' he muttered in her ear as he led her to the back of the carriage. Linden sank into an empty seat and put her head in her hands. The human smell wasn't quite as strong here, she realised with dim relief…but then a thread of winter-pine scent wafted towards her, and she sat up abruptly, dread prickling the back of her neck.

There was a faery on the train with them.

'We have to get off,' she started to tell Timothy. 'It isn't—'

But then time stopped, and she couldn't say anything at all.

There was no sound, no movement, not even a breath of air. The passengers around Timothy were as still as photographs; outside, even the platform had ceased to bustle. Feeling as though he were swimming in wet cement, Timothy forced his head around to look at Linden and saw her frozen like all the others, one hand uplifted and her mouth open in a cry of warning that had come half a second too late.

And yet he could still move, however sluggishly. Why? He crept his hand into his front pocket, and as his fingers brushed past his train tickets and touched the iron key the heaviness in his muscles fell away. His first impulse was to jump up, leap out the door, and dash for the station exit – but Linden was still trapped, and how could he use the key to free her without robbing her of all her magic as well?

The faery rose from his seat at the far end of the carriage and walked towards them, teeth gleaming in a feral smile. A male, slight and wiry, with blond hair worn poet-length but no softness in his face at all. He stopped in front of Timothy, then raised his fingers as though touching a hidden earpiece and spoke into his palm:

'It's Martin. I've found them—'

There was only one thing Timothy could think to do. He leaped out of his seat and tackled the faery, slamming him back against the carriage wall.

Martin went limp, slithering out of Timothy's grasp. He dropped to the aisle, rolled away, and bounded to his feet again; then he snatched a pen from the pocket of a nearby passenger, and with a flash it became a silver knife in his hand.

'Catch this, human boy,' he said silkily, and lunged forward. Timothy dodged, but not quite fast enough. The knife drew fire across his ribs, and he gasped – but at the same moment he flung out the hand that held the iron key, and the faery ran straight into it.

The iron jerked in his palm, flaring with sudden heat: Martin gave a harsh cry and dropped to the floor. At the same instant the carriage woke up, doors hissing shut and passengers settling into their seats as though nothing had happened. Quickly Timothy kicked the knife away from Martin's limp hand – but it was a pen again now, harmless.

'Cleverly done,' panted the faery, getting up slowly and shaking the hair out of his eyes. 'But what good will your secret weapon do you, now it is no longer a secret?'

He had barely finished the sentence when the train jolted forward, throwing them both off-balance. Martin lifted a hand as though to grasp the rail, then suddenly feinted and jabbed his fingers into Timothy's wounded side. Timothy staggered, choking off a cry, and with a mocking slap on the back and a tug at his pocket the faery shoved him away and ran.

Timothy rebounded against the wall and crumpled into a seat, his ribs flaming with agony. He was scarcely aware of Linden's hands fluttering over him, her panicked whisper as she begged him to forgive her, it had all happened so fast and she hadn't known what to do and she was so, so sorry…

'Here, you can't do that!' bellowed a man further up the carriage, and Timothy looked up dazedly to see Martin grab the doors and prise them apart with impossible strength. He braced them open with his feet as the train slowed, then sprang forward and landed on the very corner of the platform, sure-footed as an antelope. Within seconds he had vanished into the crowd.

The train ground to a stop halfway out of the station. Grumbles and clucks of protest rose from the other passengers as a terse voice over the loudspeaker announced that there would be a delay. But no one appeared to have noticed that Timothy was injured, and through his haze of pain he wondered why – until he saw the look of concentration on Linden's face.

'I'm trying to put a glamour around us,' she said between her teeth, 'so I can look at your wound without anyone seeing. But it's *hard*.'

Slowly Timothy opened his hand. He'd been gripping the key so tightly that it had left a red imprint on his palm; now he let it drop onto the seat beside them, and Linden relaxed.

'That's better,' she said. She crouched in front of Timothy and pulled up his shirt. Her touch was feather-light, but when her fingers probed the wound, he flinched.

'It's messy,' she said after a moment, 'but not too deep. Do you have anything we could use for a bandage?'

Several minutes passed while the underground train remained motionless, and Linden was beginning to despair when it finally shuddered to life again. She leaned into the circle of Timothy's arm, pressing a crumpled rag against his side, as the lights of the platform slid away and they plunged into the blackness ahead.

'You were so brave,' she said softly, trying to give him something to think about besides the pain. 'It's not your fault he escaped.'

'I don't even care about that,' Timothy mumbled, his

head lolling back against the window. 'I just hope we don't miss the train to Birmingham.'

'I thought we were going to Aber...somewhere in Wales.'

'We are, but we have to change trains at Birmingham New Street first.'

Linden's heart began to thump. 'How much time do we have?'

'I can't remember,' said Timothy wearily. 'Let me look at my tickets.' She moved aside as he straightened out one leg, slid his hand into his front pocket – and stiffened.

'What is it?' she asked.

Timothy didn't answer: instead he leaned onto his other side with a pained grimace, and felt in his back pocket. Then he said an ugly-sounding word she didn't recognise, and slumped down in the seat again.

'What?' Linden repeated, more alarmed than ever.

Timothy's mouth twisted bitterly. 'The tickets are there, all right. But my wallet, with my ID and my cards and all our money in it – it's gone.'

TWELVE

They couldn't turn back. They couldn't call for help – even if they managed to beg or scrape together enough coins for a pay phone, what could Paul and Peri do? Besides, they had no time to spare; they had to keep moving if they wanted to catch the next train. Timothy just hoped they could make it out of the city before any more of the Empress's servants found them.

Linden sat close to him, holding the cloth pad to his wounded side; she'd put on a brave face, but he could feel her trembling. She must realise, as he did, that having no money meant no food, no lodging, no coach fare to Cardigan the next morning – and no way to find the Children of Rhys before the Blackwings caught up with them. But if the only alternative was to give up and surrender to the Empress...

Timothy sat stiffly, every breath a stab of pain, while the minutes dragged by and the stations passed one by one. At last the recorded voice above them said kindly, '*The next station is Euston*,' and as the train began to slow Timothy steeled himself to get up.

'It's still bleeding,' said Linden in a worried tone, lifting the rag away from his side and peering underneath.

'Never mind,' he said between his teeth. 'Let's just go.'

Together they limped off the train, skirting the edge of the fast-moving crowd as they followed the signs towards the overground part of the station. When they reached the foot of the escalators they shuffled back into the shadows and Linden made herself small again – but this time instead of climbing into Timothy's pack, she burrowed up under his jacket to keep holding his makeshift bandage in place. Grateful, he shifted the rucksack to his good side and stepped gingerly onto the moving stairs.

They glided slowly out of the underground, up a second set of escalators and then a third, emerging at last onto a busy concourse lined with shops. Timothy feared to look at the monitors hanging on the wall, in case their train had already left – but no, it had been delayed, there was still time. He shoved his ticket through the turnstile to the overground trains and loped towards the platforms as fast as the pain in his side would let him.

'Wait!' cried a small voice from beneath his jacket, and Timothy stopped, blood pounding through his ears. That warning tone told him everything he needed to know: Linden had scented another faery nearby.

'Where?' he breathed, looking around wildly. Was it the too-sleek businesswoman striding up on his right? Or the boy leaning against the wall ahead, who looked about seventeen but was suspiciously spot-free? Timothy inched the iron key out of his pocket and gripped it between his fingers, bracing himself for another fight.

An elusive floral scent teased his nostrils, and he twisted around – *ouch* – to see a young woman with glossy black hair and a face like a harvest moon regarding him thoughtfully.

His heart stopped.

'I have waited in this human place a long time,' the faery said in lilting tones as she walked a slow circle around him, 'watching for you, as I was bidden. And yet...' Her fingers brushed his shoulder, warm even through the jacket he wore. 'I never saw you.' And with that she gave a conspiratorial smile, and vanished back into the crowd.

Dazed with relief, Timothy was still gazing stupidly at the place where she had stood when a voice echoed from the speakers above: '*The train to Birmingham New Street is now boarding from platform seven.*'

Timothy hefted the rucksack, gritted his teeth, and ran.

'Rob said there were other faeries who didn't like the Empress,' Linden whispered to Timothy as she settled into the seat beside him, human size once more. They'd caught the train just in time; already it had slipped free of the station and was picking up speed. 'But I didn't expect one of them to help us just like that. Did Rob send her a message, I wonder? The same way Veronica talked to that other faery before?' She looked at her open palm. 'I wish I knew how to do that.'

'Maybe you can,' said Timothy, but his voice sounded thin, and his eyes were half-closed. 'Has it stopped bleeding yet?'

Linden peeled the makeshift bandage away from his side. 'It's not quite as bad now,' she said, though privately she was glad she'd spent enough time with Knife not to be squeamish. She folded the sodden rag over and pressed it back against the wound, then moved Timothy's elbow down to keep it in place. 'I'll see if I can make a better bandage—'

'Ticket inspector coming,' gasped Timothy, and Linden ducked down, hastily casting a glamour to hide herself and Timothy's wound from view. She could only be glad that the backs of the seats were high, and there was no one sitting across the aisle to notice her disappear. She held her breath until the man had looked at Timothy's ticket and moved on to the next carriage, then willed herself visible again.

'Will he come back?' she asked.

Timothy shook his head fractionally, his eyes shut tight now. 'Not until we stop at the next station.'

'Good,' said Linden. She pulled the remnants of Timothy's T-shirt out of his pack – she'd used part of it earlier to stanch the wound, but there was still a good bit left – and began ripping it up to make bandages. Passengers in the seats ahead of them stirred at the sound, and Linden's face grew hot, but she kept working until she'd torn off several long strips of the soft material. Carefully she knotted them together, then made Timothy sit forward and pull up his shirt while she wrapped the makeshift bandage around his waist.

'Is that better?' she asked.

He took a slow breath, and a little colour eased into his face. 'Yeah.'

Linden sank back into her seat, wiping her blood-smeared hands. Until now she'd been so focused on tending Timothy's wound that she could think of little else, but now the enormity of their situation pressed in on her again. 'I'm so sorry, Timothy,' she said miserably. 'I dragged you into this, and everything's gone wrong, and it's all my fault.'

Timothy made a creaking noise that might have been a laugh. 'Right. You forced me to come to London with you, and then you beat me up and stole my wallet.'

'That's not what I—'

'Linden, shut up a minute, will you? It's true this wasn't how I imagined things would turn out. But it's still better than being stuck back at Greenhill and hating every minute of it. At least I feel like I'm *doing* something here. Something that might actually matter.'

That quietened her. She slid down a little, picking at

a ragged edge on her thumbnail, and said in a small voice, 'But if we don't have any money, then how are we going to—'

'I don't know, all right? Maybe *you* could try thinking of something.'

His voice sounded harsh, and Linden shrank back, disconcerted. What had she done wrong?

'I'm going to rest for a while,' he said flatly. 'Wake me if anything happens.' And with that he turned his face away.

The city was falling behind them now, ugly square buildings and heaps of rusted metal giving way to grassy banks and stretches of open countryside. Linden pressed her cheek to the window and watched, the hurt inside her fading to fascination as the train passed one village after another – dreary places, all built of the same red brick with roofs of mouldy-looking slate, but it made her realise just how many people must be living in those towns, and how enormous and complicated the human world was compared to the Oak.

But as their journey lengthened, even Linden's enthusiasm began to wane. She hadn't eaten a proper meal all day, and by the time their train finally stopped in Birmingham, her stomach felt bruised with hunger. Then they had thirty minutes to wait for their next train, so all they could do was wander around the station and watch other people eat. When they passed the sandwich shop

Timothy gave her an exasperated look; but when she asked him what was wrong, he only shook his head.

She felt a little better when they boarded the train to Aberystwyth. Not only because the Empress's servants still hadn't caught up with them, but by that time she and Timothy had found a water fountain and drunk enough to make their stomachs feel bloated, if not exactly full. And as Linden gazed out the window and watched the scenery change from the gentle flats of the English Midlands to the mountainous grandeur of Wales, the sight filled her with such awe that she could think of nothing else.

But eventually the spectacular view blurred into fog, then vanished as the sky grew dark. Exhaustion crept up on Linden, and at last she wilted onto Timothy's shoulder and fell asleep.

'Linden. Wake up.'

It felt as though only seconds had passed since she had laid her head down. Her stomach held nothing but a gnawing hollowness, and she felt dirty all over. 'Unh?' she mumbled, sitting up and knuckling her eyes.

'I said, wake up. We're here.' Timothy climbed out of his seat, wincing as he bent to pick up his rucksack. 'Come on.'

They stepped out into a cold, spitting rain. An icy wind swirled along the platform, smelling faintly of salt, and Linden shivered. 'Where do we go now?' she asked.

'It's too late to get a coach to Cardigan tonight,' Timothy said. 'Even if we had the money. So I guess we just wander around and look for a dry place to sleep. Unless you have a better idea?'

Linden shook her head.

'Didn't think so.' He sounded angry again. 'All right then.' He limped towards the archway at the end of the platform, and Linden hurried to follow.

The streets of the town were deserted, its shops and most of the restaurants already closed. Linden and Timothy walked for what seemed ages, passing one blank-faced building after another, the rain soaking into them all the while. Every few minutes they paused in a doorway to escape the biting wind, but the chill and the dampness followed them everywhere.

Teeth chattering, they ducked into a fish and chip shop to warm themselves. Timothy studied the map of Aberystwyth hanging on the wall, while Linden read the notices posted beside the door. But they couldn't see anywhere that they could sleep – not without money, anyway – and when the woman behind the counter noticed they weren't buying anything, she shooed them out into the street again.

Now they were tromping along with the sea wind at their backs, hugging themselves and shivering. Linden was almost certain they'd been this way already, but the scowl on Timothy's face made her afraid to say anything, until—

'All right,' snapped Timothy, rounding on her. Rain dripped from the ends of his hair, and his eyes were as cold as stone. 'I've had enough of this. Are you being insanely stubborn, or just stupid?'

Linden recoiled. 'I...I don't know what you mean.'

'We've been walking around this miserable town for nearly an hour, and we haven't found one decent place to spend the night. Think, Linden! *I* figured out we needed to go to Wales, and how to get there. *I* paid for the train tickets. *I* got stabbed trying to protect you, and had my wallet stolen by one of *your* people. And after all that, you expect me to conjure up food and shelter for us out of nowhere, too? You're the one with the magic – *you* do something!'

Humiliation burned in Linden, the first warmth she'd felt since they left the train. 'I don't expect anything,' she said, her voice thick and hoarse. 'I'm grateful for all you've done – more grateful than I can say. But how can I help? I can't make bread out of stones, or conjure up a place for us to sleep—'

'No, but you could at least make it *look* like we have the money to pay for those things. Yes, I know,' he interrupted as she began to protest, 'that would be stealing. Well, maybe it is, but right now I don't care, and neither should you. If we get hypothermia and end up in hospital, how's that going to help the Oakenfolk, or Peri, or anybody?' She didn't reply, and he added caustically, 'Or are you hoping that if we just suffer long enough, the Great Gardener's going to rain down free hotel vouchers and fairy cakes from heaven?'

Linden swallowed back a sick sourness in her throat. 'Don't.'

'Well, somebody's got to say it. You can't just keep throwing yourself into things and hoping for a miracle, Linden! This is the real world, and life doesn't work that way.' He pressed a hand against his injured side, looking tired and wretched and too old for his years. 'Nobody's going to magically appear to save us. The only one who can help us right now is you.'

Doubt snaked into Linden, coiling deep inside her. She didn't want to believe what Timothy was telling her, but what if he was right? So many people were counting on them, and they were staking their lives on this journey. With so much at risk, could she really afford to listen to her conscience?

Desperate, she closed her eyes. *Help me, Great Gardener!* she prayed. *Show me what to do!*

But no answer came, only another blast of sea-wind that whipped her wet skirts against her numb and trembling legs. Linden's head drooped, and she drew a shaky breath.

'All right. I'm sorry. I'll do it.'

THIRTEEN

Timothy's emotions were a discord of relief, fury and disappointment. Part of him was amazed that Linden had given in so easily; the other part was annoyed she hadn't done it earlier. She was gazing at him with pathetic hopefulness, no doubt expecting him to apologise, or at least forgive her. But the wound in his side still stabbed him every time he moved; exhaustion dragged at his shoulders like a burden, and his hunger was so intense he felt weak. So in the end he said nothing, only gave a curt nod and started walking.

If they turned right at the next corner, it would take them back towards the train station. He'd seen a pub there, full of university students laughing over their pints and tossing chips at one another with the ease of people who'd never been hungry. Inside it would be warm, and he'd order a huge sandwich, or maybe even a steak…

'Wait,' said Linden suddenly, her voice thick with tears and cold. 'I hear music.'

Timothy ignored her and walked on a few more steps, then realised that Linden was no longer with him. He turned to see her gazing at a squat, rough-plastered building across the street.

'I don't care,' he said irritably. 'Come on.'

'They're singing,' she replied in a wondering tone. 'I've heard Paul sing, a little...but they're all singing *together*. I've never heard anything like that before.'

Timothy was on the verge of losing patience and dragging her away when he remembered what she'd told him about faeries learning creativity from humans. Maybe his interest in music was starting to rub off on her? She certainly seemed absorbed in what she was hearing, although he couldn't hear a thing himself...

'Hey!' he called as she drifted away, but she was already crossing the street and walking up the path towards the little building. She pressed her ear to its wooden door, then eased it open and poked her head inside.

Curiosity was one thing, but this had gone too far. Timothy stomped after her and was about to pull her back when he finally heard the music that had drawn her there:

Yet it must be; Thy love had not its rest
Were Thy redeemed not with Thee fully blest...

The words shocked through him. That wasn't a popular hymn. In fact, he was pretty sure that there was only one small group in Christendom that sang it. Timothy backed up from the door and swung around to look at the sign posted on the church's left side. It said, in worn black letters:

ABERYSTWYTH GOSPEL HALL
Breaking of Bread 11.00 Sun.
Gospel Meeting 7.00 Sun.
Prayer 8.00 Wed.

'Oh, look!' exclaimed Linden, and before he could stop her, she darted inside. Timothy hissed at her to come out, but she didn't answer, so at last he ground his teeth and followed.

Inside it was warm, and Timothy found himself competing for space in the narrow entry hall with a coat rack holding twice as many hangers as coats, a table stacked with tiny blue hymn books, a stand of old-fashioned gospel tracts, and a large corkboard on which someone had painted a map of the world, with photographs pinned up all over it.

Linden was standing right in front of the African continent, prising one of the pictures off the board. Timothy was about to demand whether she had lost her mind, when she turned and held it up to him, and then he could only stare.

'It's you!' Linden said excitedly, waving the photo. 'Is this your family? Why do they have your picture here?'

She was halfway through the sentence when the hymn ended, and in the reverent silence her words echoed through the vestibule and into the sanctuary like a shout. The people in the congregation looked around with varying expressions of surprise and alarm, and after an awkward moment one woman got up from her seat and bustled over.

'What can I do for you, love?' she said in a hushed voice, blinking as she took in Linden's sodden clothing and bedraggled hair. 'Have you lost your way?'

'Not exactly,' said Linden before Timothy could answer. 'But we have lost all our money, and we're very tired and cold, and then I heard you all singing and it sounded wonderful, and when I looked in here I saw this.' She held up the photograph, which showed Timothy and his sister Lydia with their parents standing under a jackfruit tree. It was labelled *Neil and Priscilla Sinclair – Uganda*.

The woman's expression had become wary when Linden mentioned money, but now she looked from the picture to Timothy, and her round face lit with delight. 'Well, isn't that wonderful!' she exclaimed. 'You must come in and join us!'

'That's kind of you, but we really...' Timothy began, but Linden had already followed the woman into the main hall and was gazing about the room in fascination. Her eyes lingered on the scattered congregants in their chairs, most of them elderly, the women all wearing hats. She watched with interest as a thin man with a gently drooping face got up and began reading out requests for prayer, and when everyone bowed their heads and a voice boomed out from the other side of the aisle, 'OUR GRACIOUS HEAVENLY FATHER...' she jumped and stifled a giggle. But she clearly had no intention of leaving, so at last Timothy shuffled to a seat in the back row and resigned himself to wait until the meeting was over.

After the third or fourth prayer he must have dozed off, because when he lifted his head again people were getting up from their seats, and the woman beside Linden was talking in a voice loud enough to carry to the back of the hall:

'Poor lamb, you look done in. What a dreadful experience for you. How did it happen?'

'Someone picked my pocket,' said Timothy quickly, stifling a yelp of pain as he got up and hurried to join them. 'There was nothing the police could do. But it's all right, we'll manage.' He nudged Linden. 'Ready to go?'

'Go where, I'd like to know?' asked the woman with mild indignation, and patted Linden's knee. 'You sit right here, love, while I talk to my husband. We'll set you right.'

She hurried over to the droop-faced man who'd read the prayer requests, and talked rapidly to him while he listened in sober silence. The two of them came back together, and the man said to Timothy, 'Neil Sinclair's son, eh? I'm Owen Jenkins. Our chapel's been supporting your parents these past...how long would it be, Gwladys?'

'Must be going on eight years now,' said his wife, taking off her knitted cap and passing a hand over her frizzy curls.

'Visited us on furlough, showed us lots of lovely pictures of the work they were doing in Uganda. Such a nice couple.'

That must have been after his parents left him at Oakhaven the first time, Timothy realised in surprise. He knew they'd done a lot of travelling, but he'd never guessed they'd been all the way out here.

'So,' Mr Jenkins continued with a shrewd look from Timothy to Linden, 'who's this young lady?'

He couldn't pass her off as his sister Lydia; the picture on the board was too recent for that, and the two girls looked nothing alike. 'My cousin,' Timothy said quickly. 'I've been in the UK since September – for school, I mean – and when Linden wanted to visit some friends of hers in Cardigan, her parents asked if I'd go along. But when my wallet was stolen we got delayed looking for it, and when we finally got here we'd missed the last coach, and, well…'

The story was thin at best, but it was all he could think of on short notice. He could only hope that Gwladys and her husband didn't ask too many questions.

'What a shame!' exclaimed Gwladys, and then in a stage whisper to her husband, 'It's so late, dear. Don't you think…?'

'Yes, certainly,' said Mr Jenkins. 'You'll come home with us, then. Our children are grown, so we've a spare room for both of you. Have you eaten? Would you like to call your friends in Cardigan and tell them you're all right?'

Having grown up in the Brethren church, Timothy was

used to such invitations, but Linden's eyes became huge. She blurted, 'Do you mean it? You'd do that for us, even though we can't repay you? Oh, you are so kind!'

The woman looked surprised, but gratified. 'None of that, my dear,' she said. 'We're pleased to do it. Now, we'll just have to wait until my Owen locks up, and then we'll nip out to the car and take you home.'

Within an hour Linden was sitting at the Jenkins's kitchen table, warm and dry in a robe that had once belonged to Gwladys's youngest daughter, while Timothy pressed buttons on the telephone at random and pretended to talk to their friends in Cardigan. By the time Linden had eaten her first slice of toast with blackberry jam, he had finished the call and started on his ham and cheese sandwich. But he still did not look happy.

'What's the matter?' she whispered across the table to him, when Gwladys padded off to make up their beds for the night. 'This is wonderful!'

'Yes, well, you would think so, wouldn't you?' said Timothy in acid tones. 'You're not the one trading on your parents' reputation and making yourself a hypocrite.'

Linden flushed as she had when he challenged her on the street, but this time with anger. 'Not as much of a hypocrite as you wanted to make of me!' she retorted. 'I told Rob that taking things from people without paying for them was wrong, but if I'd listened to you—'

'Oh, don't talk rubbish,' said Timothy. 'It's not the same thing. I wasn't telling you to be selfish or lazy or take advantage of people just because you could. This was an emergency.'

'Well, it's not an emergency any more. So why can't you be glad that we've got food and a place to stay, instead of sulking because it didn't happen the way you wanted?'

Timothy didn't answer, but took another savage bite of his sandwich. Linden watched him a moment, then tried again more gently:

'I don't think you're being a hypocrite. You never told them you believed the same things they do. And do you really think they'd be any less kind to you if they knew the truth?'

Timothy raised his head, his mouth a bitter line. 'Actually, yes.'

'Well, I don't,' said Linden firmly. 'Or at least, I don't see why they should. I think you're just being miserable and assuming the worst about everybody.'

'And I think *you've* led a sheltered life and have no idea what you're talking about,' Timothy snapped back.

Linden took a deep breath. *He's in pain*, she reminded herself. *He's exhausted. And you're tired, too.* 'Think whatever you like,' she said, pushing away her empty plate and brushing the crumbs from her lap. 'I'm going to bed.'

On her way through the parlour she nearly bumped into Mr Jenkins, who looked so grave that she feared he'd overheard. But all he said was, 'Sleep well.'

'Oh,' she said, flustered, and then, 'Yes,' and ducked him a little curtsy before following the sound of Gwladys's humming to a bedroom papered with red roses.

'There you are, my dear,' said the woman, turning down the sheets. 'Here's some towels for you, and the toilet's the second door on your left. We'll give you a good breakfast in the morning, and then Owen'll run you into town and put you on your coach to Cardigan.'

Linden couldn't bring herself to say 'thank you' in the casual way that humans did, but she clasped Gwladys's plump, wrinkled hands in her own and gave her an impulsive kiss on the cheek, which seemed to please the woman just as much.

'You're a sweet child,' she said. 'I didn't think they made 'em like you any more. Mind, I'd not seen clothes like yours for quite some years either. Hand-sewn, and looks like hand-woven cloth, too – did your mother make them?'

Linden nodded, embarrassed by the half-truth, but not knowing how else to respond.

'Well, isn't that something,' said Gwladys. She gave Linden a pat on the shoulder, added, 'I'll just finish up your laundry for tomorrow. Let me know if there's anything else you need,' and waddled out.

Linden slipped out of her borrowed robe and climbed into the bed. The sheets felt deliciously smooth, and the blankets were a comforting weight against her skin. She was just closing her eyes when an unpleasant thought jolted her – the Blackwings! What if they caught up with her and Timothy in the night?

But no, it would surely take them longer than that to fly so far, and in any case, they couldn't get into the house without an invitation. The knowledge comforted her, and she relaxed again. Though she had a nagging feeling that there was something else important she'd forgotten...but before she could remember what it was, Linden had fallen asleep.

Timothy was still in the kitchen, finishing the last of his sandwich, when Owen Jenkins shuffled in, all long limbs and stooped shoulders, and pulled out a chair at the other end of the table.

'Well, then,' he said. 'Everything all right?'

Timothy swallowed with an effort. 'Yes, thanks.'

'Hm,' said Mr Jenkins, and drummed his fingers on his knee. Then he said, 'You're a good deal like your father, by the look of you. Fine man, Neil Sinclair – enjoyed the talks we had together, when he was here.'

Timothy gave a faint smile, but inside he was squirming. He could just guess what Owen Jenkins was like, because he'd met the type before: sincere and good-hearted, devoted to his faith, but with no real knowledge of the world outside his own tiny Brethren circle. He'd probably grown up in the church, spent most of his spare time reading the Bible, and never had a serious doubt in his whole life...

'Take a lot to make me forget him,' mused the man. 'Gwlad invited him and your mum to our house for Sunday dinner, and we ended up having a fine discussion about genetics – your dad and I that is, and a couple of my students from the University.'

Timothy choked. 'You're a *professor*?'

'Well, not now,' said Owen Jenkins. 'I retired from the Biology Department some five years ago.'

'But…don't you…I mean, wasn't it hard to…' Timothy was flabbergasted. At last he cleared his throat and said weakly, 'But you go to a Gospel Hall.'

'You think I shouldn't? Not the right place for a scientific type? Best resign from the church eldership then,' and he gave a wheezing laugh.

Embarrassed, Timothy fell silent.

'Now, I won't say there aren't a lot of foolish and ignorant believers in the world,' said Owen Jenkins after a moment. 'And I even know some fine godly Brethren who decided not to pursue higher learning, for fear it would make them proud. But I wanted to find out everything I could about God's creation.'

'But what you learned…didn't any of it bother you? I mean, some of the things I've heard scientists say about God and the Bible…'

'…sound convincing, no doubt,' agreed the older man. 'But you'd be surprised how much of that talk isn't really *science* at all. I won't say that now and then I don't come across some piece of data that doesn't fit quite comfortably with what I believe. But then I've talked to atheists who've had the same problem. There's not a belief in the world can save you from doubt.'

Timothy gave a reluctant nod. 'I guess I just…some beliefs make more sense to me than others. I don't want to ever hide from the truth, you know? I want to know how things really are.'

Owen Jenkins leaned forward earnestly. 'Not a thing wrong with that,' he said. 'To look at the world as it is, study it with the mind God's given you, and believe: that's faith. But to hide from hard facts, or hide them from others, because you're afraid of where they might lead you…' He sat back again. 'That's just ignorance.'

'So if I'm questioning my beliefs…you think that's actually good?'

Owen Jenkins peered at him from beneath his bushy brows. 'Better than never questioning them? I'd say so. But you can't go on questioning forever. Sometime you're going to have to stake your reputation, maybe even your life, on what you believe. And when that moment comes…then you'll know where you really stand.'

Timothy picked at the crumbs on his plate, unable to think of a reply. He was afraid that the other man would say *I'll be praying for you*, or some equally condescending remark, but he didn't. He only shuffled his chair back, said gently, 'Have a good night, lad,' and left.

For a few more minutes Timothy sat at the table alone. Then he sighed and got up, wincing as the movement pulled at his injured side. Maybe he should dab some warm water and soap on it, try to clean it out before it got infected. He might be able to find some gauze and proper bandages if he hunted around a bit...

He was making his way through the sitting room when he caught sight of a bookshelf, and curiosity made him stop to look at it. A set of Matthew Henry's commentaries on the Bible, some devotionals and missionary biographies, the complete works of James Herriot and a few volumes of Dickens: no surprises there. Further down, however, he found books on gardening, home remedies, and travel, including one entitled *A Wayfarer's Guide to Wales*. He had just pulled it off the shelf and was leafing through it when Gwladys Jenkins spoke up unexpectedly from behind him.

'Like that, do you? Some lovely walks in there.'

Timothy started guiltily, nearly dropping the book before remembering that he had nothing to hide. 'Er...yes,' he said. 'I just...we're going to Cardigan tomorrow, and I thought...'

'Oh, of course, you'll want to do some sightseeing.' She shifted her laundry basket to the other hip and leaned forward to peer at the book over his shoulder. 'What sorts of things are you interested in? I was brought up near Cardigan myself, so I know all about those parts.'

His heart quickened. 'Do you know a church named St David's?'

'St David's! My goodness, love, that's not in Cardigan, that's all the way down in Pembrokeshire.' She took the book from his hands, flipped quickly through the pages and handed it back to him. 'There it is on the map, see? A great old cathedral, it is, hundreds of years old. Right at the tip of Cardigan Bay.'

She was right, Timothy realised with dismay. There were so many references to Cardigan in the legends about the Children of Rhys, he'd just assumed St David's church must be in or near Cardigan as well...but he'd been wrong. If only he hadn't been in such a rush back at the library! He'd made a terrible mistake, and now he and Linden were hours from where they needed to be.

Timothy closed the book and slid it back onto the shelf. 'Thanks,' he said weakly.

'But you never mind,' said Gwladys Jenkins, 'just ask those friends of yours about it, and see if they won't drive you down there anyway.' She patted his arm. 'Now come along, and I'll show you to your room.'

FOURTEEN

'The coach to Cardigan leaves from the train station,' said Owen Jenkins as he drove them back into Aberystwyth the next morning. 'So that's where I'll let you off, and you can get your ticket there.'

'That's very kind of you,' said Linden. She dared a challenging glance at Timothy as she spoke – they'd barely exchanged a word since last night's argument. But he was looking out the window, and didn't seem to care.

As they came down the hill into the town, Linden caught her breath in surprise. In the darkness the place had seemed dreary and unwelcoming, with its narrow streets and tall, flat-faced houses that offered little shelter from the rain. But by daylight, the buildings of Aberystwyth were a paintbox of vibrant colours: forget-me-not blue and the deep pink of foxgloves, daffodil and mint and primrose. And rolling towards those brightly plastered buildings was a white-capped mass of water that stretched away into the distance until Linden's eyes ached from straining to see the end of it – Cardigan Bay, and beyond it the open sea.

When they reached the centre of town their host stopped the car, and they all got out. The streets were full of life now, people hurrying here and there, vehicles of all sizes stopping and starting and honking at one another. Linden watched the traffic with interest until she heard Professor Jenkins say to Timothy, 'Here's a few pounds to see you on your way. And if you look in your rucksacks, I think you'll find Gwlad's packed you both a bit of lunch.'

Linden beamed at him. 'I'll never forget what you've done for us,' she said. 'I don't know what we'd have done without you.'

'Thank you, sir,' said Timothy, and shook Owen Jenkins's hand. The older man nodded at them both with just a hint of a smile, then got back into his car and drove away.

'So?' said Linden, trying not to look at Timothy in case he snapped at her and they started quarrelling again. 'What now?'

'We find the coach to Cardigan,' said Timothy. 'And when we get there, we take another one to Fishguard, and a third one from there to St David's. I'll let you know when it's safe to come out.'

He was right to expect her to hide in his pack, Linden knew. They needed to make their money last if they wanted to find the Children of Rhys – or even just stay ahead of the

Blackwings. But it irritated her that he hadn't even *asked*.

'Fine,' she said shortly, and they set off across the street towards the station.

As the coach rumbled along the coastal road half an hour later, Timothy caught glimpses of Cardigan Bay in the distance: lead-coloured waves, rocky cliffsides, and here and there a wavering line of wet sand. Over the ocean the clouds hung so low that they looked like islands, and it was hard to tell where the sea ended and the sky began.

Doubt stabbed into him, sharper than the pain in his side. He hugged the rucksack on his lap – there was nowhere else to put it, the bus was so full – and wondered if they really had any hope of finding the Children of Rhys. What if the legend he'd read about the faery islands and the herbs that made them visible was no more than some storyteller's wild imagination? How did Rob or any of them know that the Children existed at all, let alone that they had this magical naming stone?

And what if he never got to make that phone call to his parents and tell them the truth about why he'd got himself suspended from Greenhill, because the Blackwings caught up with him first?

He took the key out of his pocket and clutched it, but the cold iron gave him no comfort. All at once he wanted very badly to talk to someone – no, not just anyone, he wanted to talk to Linden, and tell her he was sorry. But with a stout woman sitting in the seat right next to him, he could hardly start whispering to his rucksack. All he could do was wait.

And wait some more, because the stop at Cardigan was on a busy street, and he only had a few minutes to catch the coach to their next destination. Which turned out to be almost as crowded as the last one, so again he was forced to remain silent, knowing Linden was only a few centimetres away and yet she might as well have been in Uganda for all the good it did either of them...

The inside of Timothy's pack smelled unpleasantly of damp, not to mention the dirty socks and T-shirt he'd stuffed into it that morning, and it galled Linden that she couldn't see a thing that was going on. This journey felt ten times longer to her than yesterday's had been. Still, at least she was warm and dry, with a full stomach – and after last night, she would never take any of those things for granted again.

She had lost all sense of time or direction and was half-asleep from sheer boredom when she felt a soft bump and the mouth of the pack opened, letting in a gust of cool, deliciously fresh air. Timothy was gazing down at her, his mouth crooked in a rueful smile.

'Sorry,' he said. 'About everything.'

She'd been savouring her resentment all morning, but now it evaporated in the sheer relief of knowing they'd reached their destination at last. 'It's all right,' she said. 'I'm sorry, too.'

'Wait a minute,' Timothy cautioned in an undertone. 'Just until these people walk past us...all right, they've gone. You can come out.'

It was so *easy* for Linden to change size now; the hard thing was remembering that it had ever been difficult in the first place. 'Oh!' she said as her head rose to the height of Timothy's shoulder, 'I forgot to tell you! Last night I was so tired that I went to sleep at this size instead of remembering to make myself small, and I was still big when I woke up in the morning! Isn't that—' But then she saw what lay ahead of them and broke off, her lips parted in wonder.

They stood at the top of a cobbled street, beside a wall of uneven dove-grey stones. The lane ended in a soaring gateway flanked by square towers, and looking through it Linden could see the spires of St David's Cathedral.

It was old, older than the Oak by far, she could tell. To think that human hands had built this enormous church and preserved it over the long centuries amazed her, but even more exciting was the hope of what they might find within its grounds – the magical herbs that would lead them to the Children of Rhys.

As they passed beneath the gate and into the churchyard, Timothy let out a low, disheartened whistle. 'This place is huge,' he said. 'We could be here until the Blackwings catch up with us.'

'Then we had better start looking, hadn't we?' Linden shielded her eyes with her hand as she surveyed the distant horizon. 'But shouldn't we be able to see the ocean from here? It all looks like sky to me.'

'It's too cloudy,' said Timothy. 'Or maybe the legend was wrong. I don't know.' He seemed defeated already, his hands in his pockets and his shoulders slumped beneath the rucksack's weight.

Linden looked behind her and saw a low-walled garden with a stone cottage behind it. Perhaps it hadn't been part of the original churchyard, but it might give her a better view...and she climbed up onto the tiny lawn, treading carefully to avoid the shoots of young daffodils that were just beginning to nudge through the grass.

At first she saw nothing beyond the cathedral but a haze of leafless trees and the rocky shoulder of a faraway hill. She stood on tiptoe, straining with all her senses...and gradually the island appeared to her, shining out from the mists.

It seemed almost to float, independent of the sea, and the grass that velveted its slopes was not the uncertain yellow-green of early spring but the deep emerald of midsummer. A little wood grew on one side of the island, and its leaves too were green, as though winter had never touched them.

'Timothy!' she shouted down to him. 'I see it!'

He scrambled up to join her, one hand pressed to his injured side. 'Where?'

'Right there,' she said eagerly, pointing ahead. 'A minute ago there was nothing, and then...'

Timothy squinted into the distance. 'I don't see anything.

Here, move over and let me stand where you are.'

Linden stepped to one side and he took her place, but his frown remained. 'I can't see anything,' he said. 'Are you sure it wasn't just the clouds?'

'I'm certain,' she said. 'I can still see it now.'

Timothy let his hand drop back to his side. 'Of course you can,' he said, sounding disgusted. 'You're a faery yourself, and you knew what you were looking for – their glamour couldn't fool you. You could probably have spotted that island from the window of the coach, if only I'd given you the chance.' He kicked the turf, stomped a few paces – and stopped.

'Did you only see *one* island?' he said. He sounded dazed, almost dreamy, and he was looking off at a different angle, beyond the cathedral tower.

Linden followed the line of his gaze, and let out a slow exhalation of surprise. He was right: there were two islands. But if he could see them as well…

She bent to examine the turf at Timothy's feet. What she'd taken for daffodil shoots were actually a smooth-leaved plant she'd never seen before. When she broke off one of the leaves the juice that welled out had a sweet, fruity scent, but it left no stickiness upon her fingers.

'I think we've found Gruffydd's magic herbs,' she said, smiling up at him.

With the iron key in his pocket, a clump of strange plants in his rucksack, and his injured side clumsily patched together with bandages and gauze, Timothy felt like he'd just come back from a visit to the witch doctor – but he couldn't deny that the magical herbs seemed to do exactly as the legend claimed. Eyes fixed on the distant islands, he and Linden made their careful way down the slope of the churchyard, past the ruins of the Bishop's palace, and out beyond the stone walls of the cathedral close. Within minutes they had found a footpath that would lead them towards the sea.

'How are we going to get out to the island?' Linden panted as they hurried along. It was past noon, the sun high above them, but the air was still cold enough to make Timothy's lungs ache. He had to catch his own breath before he could reply: 'We'll have to hire a boat, I guess.'

Preferably one with a motor, or at least a good pair of oars. He hadn't a clue how to sail, but Paul had taken him rowing on his last visit to Oakhaven, and he'd learned a few things then. Never mind that he'd probably rip his side open on the first stroke, or how likely it was that some current would grab hold of the boat and whisk the two of them straight out to sea...

The path grew rockier as they walked along, the countryside more open and wild. Soon they had left St David's behind, and were edging around the side of a steep and rugged hill. Timothy paused to get his bearings, and when he looked out at the choppy waters of Cardigan Bay he could now see three distinct green islands.

'We need to go over more this way,' he called back to Linden, but she had lagged behind, and he could no longer see her. He was cupping his hands to his mouth to shout again when he saw her flashing towards him at faery size, her wings buzzing frantically.

'They've found us!' she gasped, circling around him. 'The Blackwings – they're here!'

Timothy looked up to see two familiar ragged shapes flapping across the sky towards them. The first raven's wings beat the air with smooth, powerful strokes, but the other's flight was halting, as though it had been injured...

He broke into a run, leaping from rock to rock with blind urgency as he angled down the gravelly slope towards the sea. The green islands looked so close – he knew he hadn't a prayer of reaching them, but there was nowhere else to go except back and he wasn't ready to give up, not like this, not yet—

The world pitched over and he hit the ground hard, skidding his palms raw on the stony ground. His side flared with agony as he rolled over, sickeningly certain the Blackwings had caught him in their spell – but then he saw his shoe trapped between two rocks, wedged there by nothing more sinister than his own carelessness. He wrenched his foot free, ignoring the throbbing pain in his ankle, then scrambled around and prised the shoe loose so he could put it back on.

'Hurry!' screamed Linden, her voice so high he could

barely hear it. She was just a speck in the distance now: he'd never catch up with her. But the ravens were almost upon him, weaving through the air, a shimmering web of magic coalescing between their wings. Timothy limped down the hillside as quickly as he could, eyes raking the slope for some sign of cover. He'd seen a lopsided heap of stones on the far side of the hill, ruins of some ancient monument. If only he could find something like that, he might be able to hide – but though his gaze swept the ground in every direction, there was no sign of shelter.

A tingling heat raced up his back, and all his hair stood on end. Timothy knew at once that he'd been touched by magic – but as the electric feeling died, he realised that the iron key in his pocket was still protecting him.

Relieved, he scrambled around the side of the hill and back onto the footpath. The ravens wheeled above him, regrouping for another try...no, wait. There was only one of them now. Where was the other? He looked around – and a great black shape leaped into him, snarling.

Timothy tumbled flat onto his back, rigid with horror as he stared up into the glowering eyes of an enormous hound. It bared its teeth, and hot breath steamed over his face, reeking of carrion. Then a word rumbled up from its throat, slurring over the dog's lips and tongue but horribly comprehensible just the same:

'Checkmate.'

He couldn't see Linden anywhere. Not that it mattered:

there was nothing she could do. *You didn't warn us they could be dogs too, Rob.*

The dog reared up, heavy paws lifting from his shoulders – and suddenly he felt a booted foot on his chest instead. 'I know about the iron you carry,' said a cool voice, and he looked up into the faery's hard, contemptuous eyes. 'Attempt to touch it, and I will snap your neck.'

The remaining raven flapped down onto the path, folded its wings – and became another male faery, like a slightly flawed copy of the first. He flexed his stiff arm and winced, then slapped his brother on the shoulder and broke into a grin. 'Good hunting, Corbin.'

'The hunt is not over yet,' said the taller Blackwing, his eyes still on Timothy. 'The little rebel escaped – but in that small form, she cannot fly far. We will take her soon enough.'

'How did you...find us?' gasped Timothy. The Blackwings didn't know about the Children of Rhys; if he kept them talking long enough then Linden might be able to fly to one of the magical islands, out of their reach. 'Thought we'd thrown you off the scent.'

'We track by magic, not some human stench,' said Corbin with contempt. 'With a hair from the girl's head in our possession, all we needed to catch you was patience and time.' Then he leaned down and said softly, 'But where, I wonder, were you headed? And what did you hope to find there?'

Timothy faked a fit of coughing, buying himself a few

precious seconds to think. 'We were looking for some...magical plants. They're...supposed to grow around here. Because Linden's Queen...she's dying.'

Corbin made a scornful noise. 'And for this you chose to throw in your lot with the Forsaken, and risk your very life? Only a fool would believe such a tale.'

'She promised me...gold...if I helped,' Timothy wheezed. 'As much as I wanted.'

Behind them, the injured Blackwing laughed. 'Gold! Say rather a handful of acorns and a few withered leaves, for that is all you would have in the end.'

'Indeed,' said Corbin, and the pressure on Timothy's chest eased a little. 'And where is your faery companion now? Flying away from you as fast as her wings will carry her. So much for your hopes of reward.' He stepped back, nodding at his brother. 'Byrne, guard him. I will catch the girl.' And with that he shifted back into raven form and flapped off down the hillside.

Until then Timothy had lain limp on the rocky ground, offering no resistance. But all the while he and Corbin were talking, he'd been inching his fingers towards his pocket. Now he risked everything on a sudden snatch at the key – but he'd only just pulled it out when Byrne kicked his elbow, and the key went flying. As Timothy's only weapon clattered against the rocks and tumbled out of sight, the faery grabbed him and wrenched him to his feet.

'That was foolish, boy,' he breathed, his dark eyes

gleaming. 'Very foolish.' He hooked his fingers, and Timothy jerked back—

'Let him go!' shrilled Linden's voice from behind them, and the male faery whirled, his grip on Timothy loosening. Timothy's ankle still throbbed and his side felt as though it were splitting open, but he planted his feet and shoved Byrne as hard as he could.

The Blackwing swayed, lost his footing and toppled down the hillside. 'Come on!' Linden shouted at Timothy, and he lurched after her, mouthing *Ow* with every step.

From somewhere behind him came a raven's croaking call, then an answering cry from the far side of the hill. But Linden darted straight towards the ocean, and Timothy forced himself to ignore the pain and just run, run, run down the lessening slope until at last the pebbles and dry scrub gave way to green grass, and he could see the waves smashing against the rocks far below.

'What do I do now?' he yelled at Linden, as the frigid sea-wind whipped his hair into his eyes. 'I can't fly!'

'This way!' she shouted back, pointing to a narrow trail that slanted down from the cliff's edge. At its foot lay a smudge of sandy beach, a scant half-moon of a cove, where two tall stones stuck out of the water like the ruins of some ancient Roman gate. 'Can't you feel it? It's magic!'

So this was where Linden had gone, when the Blackwings thought she'd deserted him. She could have flown straight to the Children of Rhys for help, but instead she'd scouted out this cove, and then returned to the hillside to rescue Timothy and bring him there. As plans went it was noble, impractical, and built mostly on faith – in short, just like her.

But all these thoughts flashed through his mind in an instant, as Timothy scrambled onto the trail and began to pick his way downwards as fast as he could go. Still, between his twisted ankle and his bleeding side he had a hard time of it, and he knew that at any second the ravens would swoop down upon him…

'Where are they?' demanded Byrne's voice from the top of the cliff.

Timothy froze.

'They cannot have vanished into the air,' replied Corbin's cooler tones. 'No doubt the girl has merely cast a glamour to throw us off their trail. But the finding spell will—' He stopped, and when he spoke again his voice was flat: 'Impossible.'

'You can't find them? Let me try.' A pause, and then: 'Her magic must be stronger than we thought. But the boy will still have footprints and a scent, no matter what glamour she puts on him. You fly that way, I'll go back around the hill…'

Flattened against the cliff face, Timothy listened in disbelief as the sound of the Blackwings' voices faded away. They'd tracked him and Linden all the way out here, only to lose them at the last moment – but how?

Linden was waiting for him at the bottom of the path, human size once more. The waves washed foam around her feet, and the breeze lifted her brown curls in all directions. 'Look up!' she called excitedly. 'Look at the sky!'

Timothy shot a wary glance upwards – and saw only empty, cloudless blue. Even the wind that had been tugging at his jacket had subsided, and there was no sign of the Blackwings anywhere.

'The glamour around this cove is incredibly strong,' Linden said. 'I don't think the Blackwings could even see it – or us either, once we'd started down here. We must be very close to the Children of Rhys.'

Legs wobbly with the effort of clambering down the path, Timothy edged the last few feet and stumbled onto the sand beside her. He dusted the grit and lichen off his hands, then straightened up and looked out at the sea. The mist over the ocean had cleared, and the sun shone summer-bright; he had a perfect view of the first of the magical islands, framed between the two ancient stones that rose up from the water. But it was still just as far away as ever – and they had no boat.

'What now?' he said.

Linden gazed out at the island, and her expression became distant. She raised her hand and touched her ear, cupping her palm against her cheek as they had seen Martin do on the train. 'Children of Rhys,' she said. 'We have come a long way to seek your help. Please, speak to us.'

Long seconds passed, but the only sound was the waves crashing into the nearby cliffs. Linden's face creased with disappointment, and she let her hand fall. 'I really thought,' she began – but before she could finish the sentence the air between the standing stones shimmered, and a little boat slid out of nothingness to glide across the waves towards them. It drew up on the beach at Linden's feet, empty and waiting.

'You have called the *Plant Rhys Ddwfn*,' said a melodious Welsh-accented voice that seemed to come from everywhere and nowhere: it could have been a man's light tenor or a woman's contralto, it was impossible to tell. 'And we have answered. But we cannot allow strangers to set foot upon our islands unless we are certain that they are trustworthy. Will you turn away, or seek to pass the test?'

As a child in Sunday School Timothy had tried to imagine how the 'still, small voice' of God had sounded when the prophet Elijah heard it in the wilderness. Now he felt as though he knew. 'What test?' he asked, and the words sounded impossibly loud and coarse in his own ears.

'The questions are these,' came the reply. 'Do you honour the wishes of your ancestors, and obey those who have rule over you? Are you honest in all your dealings, forsaking treachery or deceitfulness? Are your hands clean of violence, and your heart free of envy and selfish ambition? If so, you are welcome among us. If not, you must forbear.'

Timothy was taken aback. He had been expecting some test of skill or intelligence, not a boiled-down version of the

Ten Commandments. There was no way he could answer all of those questions honestly and still hope to win the Children of Rhys's approval – but if he lied to them, would they know?

'I honour my foster mothers and my Queen,' said Linden. Her voice shook a little, but her expression was resolute. 'Though I have not always obeyed them perfectly. I have kept my bargains with my neighbours and not deceived them. I have harmed no one, and I come to you not for my own sake, but for the sake of my people.'

There was a pause, and then the voice said, 'You may come.'

Linden relaxed, and broke into a smile. She stepped into the little boat and sat down.

'Speak, human,' said the voice.

Timothy licked his dry lips, not knowing what to say. He remembered the stunned look on Luke Barfield's round face when he realised that Timothy had just hit him. He thought of how he'd lied to the Dean by writing that fake email to his parents, not wanting to admit to what he'd really done, or why. He'd yelled at Peri when she was just trying to protect the Oakenfolk, tried to bully Linden into using glamour against her conscience, resented the Jenkinses' hospitality even as he'd stuffed his face with their food and slept in the bed they'd made up for him...

He said roughly to Linden, 'You go on. I'll wait here.'

'The tide is rising,' said the disembodied voice. 'You

cannot remain in this place. If you will not answer our questions, then you must return the way you came, and there meet whatever fate awaits you.'

Meaning the Blackwing brothers. Timothy swallowed and said, 'I can't pass your test. I've lied – and dishonoured my parents – and hit people who didn't deserve it. So I guess…' He looked back at the cliff-side trail, and sickness burned the back of his throat. 'I'll have to leave.'

FIFTEEN

'Wait!' Linden scrambled out of the boat and ran to Timothy, catching his arm before he could turn away. She spoke urgently to the air: 'He's told you the truth, about the things he's done. But he's also been loyal and kind and brave. And now he's willing to go back up there all alone and surrender himself to our enemies for my sake – doesn't that count for something, too?'

There was a lengthy pause, filled only by the murmur of the wind and waves. Linden tightened her grip on Timothy, afraid that she had offended the Children and that now they would both be turned away. But at last the voice spoke again:

'Human, by your own admission you have violated the laws of our forefather Rhys. But for the sake of your faery companion, we will let you pass – if you repent of your wrongdoing, and pledge to be honest and true hereafter. Do you so promise?'

Timothy looked stunned, and for several long seconds he didn't speak. But at last he said hoarsely, 'I'll try.'

'Then you may come.'

Hesitantly Timothy followed Linden to the boat and climbed in. It slipped back into the water as though pushed by some invisible hand, and soon they were bobbing across the waves towards the pillared gate.

Linden had never been in a boat before, and the sensation delighted her. The ocean breeze fluttered her hair, and cold spray washed her face as she leaned forwards, gaze fixed eagerly on the island ahead. The boat crested a wave, rocked downwards as it passed between the two stones – and then in a flash they came aground again, white sand furrowing up on both sides of the boat as it glided onto an unfamiliar shore.

'In the name of Rhys Ddwfn I greet you,' said a voice that sounded familiar, but now unmistakeably male. 'I am Garan ap Gwylan.'

Linden clasped her head, still dizzy with the sudden shift from the cove to the island. Then her vision cleared and she saw him: a male faery considerably bigger than her fellow Oakenfolk but barely half as tall as Timothy – about the height of a human child. His hair was the colour of peeled willow, held back from his forehead by a circlet of twisted gold and falling loose and straight to his shoulders. But there was nothing childlike or feminine about the clean, proud bones of his face, or the muscles of his bare arms as he stretched out his hand to help Linden from her seat.

'Come with me,' he said. 'I will take you to meet the Elders of my people.'

Ever since the Children of Rhys had given their verdict, Timothy had been silent, his eyes downcast; but now he flicked a half-smile at Linden, and nodded for her to go ahead. She took Garan's hand and climbed out; Timothy followed, and the three of them set off down the beach together.

'Was it you who spoke to us, back there?' she asked Garan. It felt somehow rude to be addressing the top of his head, so she shrank back to Oakenfolk size and flew alongside him.

'I spoke with my people's voice and not my own,' he said, 'but yes, it was my turn as Speaker. I have waited many years for this day.' He gave her a sidelong glance with his sea-coloured eyes. 'May I ask what you are called, so that I may introduce you to the Elders?'

'I'm Linden,' she said. She waited for Timothy to speak, but he didn't, so she went on, 'And my human friend is Timothy.'

'It is an honour to meet you,' said Garan, making them both a short bow with his hand to his heart. 'Never in my lifetime have strangers come to our island. What news do you bring to us from the outside world?'

His gaze held a keen, almost hungry interest, and Linden felt suddenly self-conscious. 'It's a long story,' she said. 'Perhaps we should save it for the Elders.'

'As you wish it,' Garan said, but he looked disappointed.

'Tell me,' he added after a pause, 'do you find that small form comfortable? It gives me no offence if you prefer human shape; I am told that many of our people on the mainland do. I choose it myself, from time to time.' And in a blink he made himself as tall as Timothy, striding a few long paces across the sand before dropping back to his former height.

'Actually, this is my natural size,' said Linden, a little defensively. Did no other faeries look like the Oakenfolk any more? Veronica had appeared startled and even disgusted that she would make herself so small, and now Garan seemed to think it strange, too...

Garan laughed. 'How can that be? You are a faery, with magic in your blood: one size is no more *natural* to you than another. Perhaps you have become accustomed to being small, but with a little practice you could make yourself the height I am now, or half that, or twice as tall again, as easily as winking.'

Linden was startled. She had always known that before the Sundering the Oakenfolk used to make themselves human size at will, so it had seemed obvious to follow their example. But she had never even thought to try any of the sizes in between...

Well, there was one way to know for sure. She dropped to the ground, shut her eyes in concentration – and opened them again to find Garan looking at her. *Straight* at her, because she'd made herself exactly his height. Linden let out a laugh; it was the oddest feeling, being large and not large at the same time. But it hadn't been difficult at all.

'You see?' said Garan, smiling. They had reached the edge of the beach now; he took her hand and helped her climb up a low staircase of rocks, then stepped out in front to lead the way.

Onshore the wind had blown cold beneath a grey sky dappled with clouds: but here the sky was as blue as chicory, and the sun that beat down on them was warm. It might have been May or June, instead of February. They had only walked a few paces into the long, herb-seasoned grass when Linden paused to shrug off her coat and fold it away into her pack. Timothy hesitated, then did likewise – but he moved stiffly, and as he peeled the jacket away Linden saw the dark stain that had spread along his side. 'You're bleeding!' she said, alarmed.

'Bleeding?' asked Garan. 'You are injured, then? May I look?'

It was the first time he had addressed Timothy directly, but the concern in his voice sounded genuine. Timothy gave an uncomfortable shrug. 'It's not that bad,' he said. 'But sure, if you want.'

'He was hurt trying to protect me,' Linden said quickly as Garan moved past her, afraid that the other faery would see the obvious knife wound and come to the wrong conclusion. 'We were attacked on the way, and he fought to keep us both from being captured. That's what I meant when I said he was brave.'

Garan lifted Timothy's shirt and examined the ugly, weeping slash across his side. At last he laid his palm against it, ignoring Timothy's flinch, and when he took his hand away there was nothing beneath but a crust of dried blood and a pink line of newly healed skin.

'You will need your strength when you stand before the Elders,' he said. 'And I am always glad for a chance to use my healing gifts – in this place, the need for such skill is rare.'

An exciting thought sparked in Linden's mind. 'Can you heal any kind of injury?' she asked eagerly. 'If you met a human who couldn't use his legs, for instance…'

'If the injury was new and not too grave, I might be able to heal him,' said Garan. 'But if several months have passed, or if the injured part were badly crushed or severed, I would not dare to attempt it. There is only so much that even magic can do.'

Linden's hope faded to disappointment. For a moment she had dared to imagine how happy Paul would be if he could walk again. But if Garan was right, then it was far too late to help him.

Timothy was still staring at his newly healed side. He poked the scar and let out a short laugh, then turned to Garan and said 'Th— I mean, that's fantastic! I appreciate it.' He straightened his shoulders, looking more confident and happy than she had seen him in days. 'So what you said before, about not getting to heal people very often – I take it you don't see much fighting here?'

'No, indeed,' said Garan. 'We left all that behind a thousand years ago, when my ancestors first came to these islands. For years they had served their tribal chieftains faithfully, even surrendering their true names to them as proof of their devotion. But in time their lords grew greedy and ambitious for power, forcing their people into battle for no just cause. So when Rhys came to them from beyond the Sea with the Stone of Naming in his hand, my ancestors gladly gave up the names that enslaved them and took new ones, so that they might choose for themselves whom they would serve. And then they left their old homes and settled upon these islands, pledging themselves to a new life of harmony and peace.'

The Stone of Naming, thought Linden in wonder. Rob had been right – it was the very thing he and his fellow rebels needed to fight against the Empress. But if the Stone was so important to the Children of Rhys's history, would they be willing to give it up?

'How many of your people are there?' she asked Garan.

'We do not keep count of our numbers,' he replied. 'For though our people marry in their youth and live long lives they seldom have more than one or two children, and Rhys promised my forefathers that as long as we honoured his laws, there would be enough room on these islands for us all.' His mouth bent wryly. 'And so it has proved, though there are times I could wish for fewer voices in council.'

'How about this, then,' said Timothy. 'How many of these islands do you have?' He had stopped again and was peering out across the sea, his eyes shielded with his hand. 'Because I'm counting at least four…no, five…it's a wonder you aren't knee-deep in shipwrecks by now.'

'There are twelve in all,' Garan said. 'The *Gwerdonnau Llion*, what you would call the Green Isles of the Ocean. But no sailor sets foot here except by our leave. Here, we exist in a realm apart from human time, and unwary vessels sail right through us.'

'But you buy your goods onshore,' Timothy pointed out, 'or at least you used to. So you must visit the human world now and then.'

'You are well-informed about our people, for a human,' said Garan, his brows rising. 'Has the tale of Gruffydd truly survived among you for so long? So many years have passed since strangers came to our lands – if not for you, I could believe the whole world had forgotten the Children of Rhys.

'Yes, we do trade often with the humans upon the shore,' he continued, 'but only in disguise, and we do not linger there longer than need demands. And since our traders are chosen by lot, I have yet to visit your shores myself.' His eyes grew wistful. 'Perhaps I shall have that chance, one day. But we dally too much, and we should not keep the Elders waiting.'

He turned and led them onwards through the grass, until at last they reached the edge of the wood that Linden had seen from the shore. Two trees stood a little in front of the rest, their slender trunks perfectly symmetrical and their intertwined branches forming an arch overhead.

'Enter into our court, and be welcome,' said Garan, gesturing for them to go ahead of him. But when Linden looked between the trees she could see only darkness, and it made her uneasy.

'You go first,' she said. 'Please.'

'It is not my place,' protested Garan. 'The Elders will think I dishonour you.'

'I'll go,' said Timothy, and stepped forward. The shadows swallowed him up at once, and Linden held her breath; but then she heard his voice echoing back from the other side, 'It's all right. Come on.'

Linden made herself human size again, for courage. Then she steeled herself and plunged into the dark.

She emerged with a stumble into a great oval chamber, airy and brightly lit. Behind her stood an archway identical to the one through which she had just passed – but on this side, the trees and their interwoven branches were carved from white marble. And before her, on twelve tall chairs of the same gleaming, silver-veined stone, sat the Elders of the Children of Rhys.

They were small in stature, like Garan, and like him wore their hair long. But the men were bearded, the women's plaits coiled like crowns about their heads, and the solemn dignity in their faces made Linden feel very foolish and young. Who was she, or Timothy, to come before a great council like this?

'Lord and Lady Elders of the *Plant Rhys Ddwfn*,' said Garan, stepping up beside them. 'I bring before you the faery Linden and the human Timothy.' With a bow he walked off to the left of the chamber and sat down, and only then did Linden realise that the room was full of faeries, hundreds of them, seated in curving tiers that lined the chamber on both sides.

'You have come a great distance to speak with us on behalf of your people, or so you said,' spoke up the first of the Elders, a woman with chestnut skin and a penetrating gaze. 'Tell us, what kind of help do you seek?'

Linden took a deep breath and put her hands behind her back, so that the Elders would not see them tremble. Then she spoke up in her clearest voice:

'We need magic, if you are able to give it. Because my people have lost theirs, and now a powerful Empress wants to conquer us, and unless you help us, we will surely die.'

Linden did a good job of telling their story, Timothy had to admit – but then, she'd had plenty of practice. She told the Children of Rhys all about the Oakenfolk, and how Jasmine had used up all their magic on her mad scheme to 'free' them from humans. Then she went on to relate all that had happened when she and Timothy went to London in search of more faeries, and what they had learned from Veronica and Rob about the Empress. Finally, she explained about the Blackwings coming after them, and how she and Timothy had been forced to flee the Oakenwyld and stake all their hopes on finding the Children of Rhys. But to Timothy's surprise, there was one crucial thing Linden didn't mention: the Stone of Naming, and the bargain she had made with Rob to find it and bring it back.

'This Empress,' said a broad-chested Elder with reddish hair and beard. 'Who is she, and whence has she come? This is the first we have heard of her.'

'I don't know,' Linden told him. 'I just know that she's powerful and cruel, and that all the other faeries are afraid to do anything against her, because she knows their true names. So they have to obey her, whether they want to or not.'

It was then that Timothy realised what Linden was trying to do: she hoped the Elders would see the obvious parallel to their own history, and offer to give her the Stone of Naming without making her ask for it. But though the Elders all looked grave, none took the bait.

'And this Empress refuses to let her subjects associate with humans?' said the dark-haired woman who had addressed them before. 'How does she expect the faeries under her rule to thrive? Where do they obtain their meat and milk and grain, their cloth and pottery, their books and musical instruments? Without human trade we would have none of these things, nor the skills to make use of them, and our realm would be impoverished.'

Silence. Timothy glanced at Linden, but she still looked crestfallen at how the Elders had ignored the obvious opportunity to tell her about the Stone. Well, just because she hadn't succeeded didn't mean he couldn't have a try himself.

'They steal them from us,' he spoke up, and was rewarded with shocked murmurs from every side of the room. 'They pretend to be human, and lure us into trusting them, and then they take our creativity by force. But how are they supposed to know any better? Their Empress is the worst deceiver of all – she tricked all of the faeries into giving her their blood, and then she used that blood to find out their true names.'

The whispers turned into gasps, and many of the faeries sat up in their seats, looking appalled. 'This is evil news indeed,' said a lean blond Elder who bore a strong resemblance to Garan. 'To hear that our fellow faeries have been enslaved against their will cannot help but grieve us all.' He turned his gaze on Linden. 'Yet if this Empress is so powerful and ruthless, what makes you think you can resist her? Her servants are many, and you Oakenfolk are few. It would be ill done if we restored your people's magic only to have the Empress conquer and enslave them, and turn those powers to evil in her service.'

'But the Oakenfolk aren't alone,' Timothy said quickly.

'They have allies – humans like me, and my cousin and his wife. Not to mention a lot of faeries in the Empress's service who would be glad to fight back against her if they could.'

'Yes, and some of those faeries have already helped us,' agreed Linden. 'Even risking their lives to warn us about the Empress's plans, and see us safely on our way. Which is why there's one more thing I have to ask of you.' She clasped her hands imploringly. 'Please – may we borrow the Stone of Naming, so that we can set them free?'

The hall went utterly silent. No one moved or spoke, but Timothy could feel the weight of hundreds – perhaps even thousands – of eyes upon them. The Elders exchanged looks. Finally one of them said, 'You have given us much to consider, and we will do so – but in private. We will return when we have reached a verdict.'

Then they all rose and walked out, and the doors swung shut behind them.

As the murmurs from the audience swelled to a clamour, Garan hurried out onto the floor and drew Linden and Timothy aside. 'You spoke well,' he said. 'My father Gwylan is one of the Elders, and though he questioned you closely, I could see that he sympathised with your cause.' His cheeks were flushed and his eyes bright as he spoke. 'Perhaps it is time for our people, too, to take a stand.'

'What do you mean by that?' demanded a thin-faced faery with a cap of unruly dark hair. He jumped out of his seat and stalked down the steps to join them. 'The Children of Rhys have stood for peace and justice ever since our forefathers first settled these islands. If the other faeries needed guidance they had only to look to us, but they chose to go their own ways instead. If they have fallen under the spell of this Empress, surely they have only themselves to blame.'

'Look to us, Broch?' said Garan incredulously. 'How can they? We leave these islands only to buy our goods and learn whatever crafts may please us, and even then we disguise ourselves and never speak. The humans know us to be generous, but that is all – and what can our fellow faeries learn from the Children of Rhys, when they have not seen or heard from us in centuries?'

'But we cannot leave the *Gwerdonnau Llion*,' protested a girl faery with dusky skin and wiry black hair who looked no older than Linden. 'Not without becoming entangled in the very evils from which Rhys and our forefathers sought to deliver us. Surely you cannot desire that?'

'No, Rhosmari, I do not desire evil,' Garan replied with a hint of impatience. 'But it seems to me that to stand idle while evil is being done is no virtue, either. If it is in our power to help Linden and her people—'

'Of course we will help them,' cut in Broch. 'That much is plain. But what form that help will take is for the Elders to decide.'

'Is it plain, then?' said another male. 'I am not so certain.

230

What do we know of these Oakenfolk? Because one of their number has proven herself honourable, does it follow that all of them are so worthy?'

The discussion became animated as more of the Children of Rhys gathered around, new voices chiming in from every side. But they ignored Linden completely; even Garan was too busy defending himself now to pay any heed to her. All she could do was stand there on the outskirts of the noisy crowd, bewildered and a little hurt.

'Come on,' said Timothy at last, tugging at her arm. 'If they're just going to argue, we might as well go and have something to eat.'

They found a quiet corner on the room's far side, and Timothy handed out the lunches Mrs Jenkins had made for them. A pang went through Linden as she opened her bag and found a jam sandwich, a rosy apple, and a bar of chocolate – tokens of a simple kindness that she now dearly missed. For all their courteous talk, the Children of Rhys had never asked if she and Timothy were hungry, or offered them anything to drink. And for all the sunlit beauty of the white chamber around them, the place was uncomfortable and even a little cold. She thought of the Oak, so humble by contrast, and felt homesick.

She had finished one half of the sandwich and started on the other when the chamber went abruptly quiet, and she looked up to see that all the Children of Rhys – the Elders included – had returned to their seats. Hurriedly she brushed the crumbs from her lap and walked back onto the floor with Timothy.

'We have made our decision,' said Garan's father, and Linden felt a stir of hope. Surely it was a good sign, if the Elders had appointed him to speak? But then she saw how grave he looked, and her confidence faltered as he went on:

'Though it pains us to deny you, we cannot give what you ask. The curse that robbed you and your fellow Oakenfolk of magic has also left you too few in number to resist the Empress, even if your powers were restored. And though you claim to have allies, their loyalty is unproven, and the Stone of Naming is too precious to fall into enemy hands.'

Tears swam into Linden's eyes, and she put her hands over her mouth. She and Timothy had come so far, endured so much...had it truly all been for nothing?

'And yet,' Gwylan continued, 'we are not without pity. It is the will of the Elders that any of your people who choose may come and join us here in the *Gwerdonnau Llion*, where their magic will be restored and they may live out the rest of their lives with us in peace and safety...provided, that is, they pass the test.'

Approving murmurs rose from the audience: nearly all the Children of Rhys seemed to agree that the judgment was fair. But Linden closed her eyes, despairing. What use was an invitation that none of her people could possibly accept? There was no way that a group of small faeries with no magic to protect themselves could undertake such a long journey – and even if by some miracle they did make it this far, how many of them would be deemed worthy to join the Children of Rhys? Much as she disliked Mallow's bossiness and blustering, much as she resented Bluebell trying to set herself up as Queen in Valerian's place, Linden could not bear the thought that any of the Oakenfolk might fail the test, and be left behind.

Timothy's arm came around her shoulders, a wordless gesture of sympathy, and Linden turned to him and buried her face against his chest, a little sob heaving out of her. The chamber grew quiet, the Elders awaiting her reply – but she couldn't bear to look at them, and didn't know what to say.

'So that's what you call pity?' demanded Timothy over the top of her head, and she pulled back, startled, as he continued in the same fierce tone: 'I call it cowardice. Linden's told you what's happening out there – nearly all your fellow faeries are slaves of the Empress, and they're treating my people like cattle. The Oakenfolk are the only ones left who know how to live freely and in peace with humans – and instead of helping them make a difference in the world, you want to make them just as useless and self-righteous as you are?'

'Boy,' began one of the Elders warningly, but Timothy kept talking right over him:

'Why should the Oakenfolk come and live with people who've been so busy congratulating themselves on their own goodness and generosity that they haven't even noticed the rest of the world is suffering? You keep yourselves hidden away on these islands because you're afraid of being corrupted. But what good are your laws if they only help people who are perfect already? What use are your beliefs if they can't stand up to the real world?'

He spoke with passion, grey-green eyes blazing, and Linden gazed up at him in awe. When he had finished the silence in the chamber was electric, and it was several heartbeats before the dark-haired Lady Elder spoke:

'Return to us the magical herbs you carry. You have scorned our sacred traditions and despised our charity, and you are no longer welcome here.'

And with that, she stood up and deliberately turned her back on them. Several other Elders did likewise, and then, after a helpless pause, the rest. Gwylan was last to turn, his face grim and his hands clenched at his sides. Then in a flash of cold light, all twelve of them disappeared.

SIXTEEN

In the dreadful stillness that followed the Elders' verdict, four faeries carrying spears and wearing leather breastplates marched out onto the floor, one from each corner of the chamber. Their faces were hard, their manner imposing despite their small size, and the menace that radiated from them made Linden's mouth go dry with fear.

'So much for your kingdom of justice and peace,' said Timothy bitterly. 'Is that how you keep your people in line here – just throw out anyone who dares to disagree with you?'

'Give us the herbs,' said one of the faery guards, holding out her hand, and with a scowl Timothy swung his rucksack off his shoulder. He opened the side pocket, pulled out the wilted, muddy clump he had taken from St David's churchyard, and flung it at the guards' feet.

Linden looked at Garan, silently begging him to stand up and do something to support them. But he would not meet her gaze, and before she could even speak his name he vanished. Like stars winking out the other Children of Rhys followed his example, and in moments every seat in the chamber was empty.

Her eyes prickled as she stared at the place where Garan had been. His desertion hurt, but it also stunned her to see how easily these faeries could transport themselves from one place to another with a single thought. Surely, if the Children of Rhys had that much power, it would have been no difficulty for them to share some of it with the Oakenfolk. Yet they had not been willing to do even that, except on their own impossible terms...and now her people's last hope of salvation was gone.

'I'm sorry,' she heard Timothy say in a low voice. 'I shouldn't have said anything.'

Linden took his hand and squeezed it. 'Don't apologise,' she said softly. 'You were right.'

'Walk,' said another of the guards, pointing his spear towards the sculpted archway through which they had come. Wiping her eyes on her sleeve, Linden obeyed – and in a few steps she and Timothy emerged once more at the edge of the little wood, with the wildflower-dotted meadow stretching before them. Two of the guards stepped out in front of them, while the other two fell in behind, and in silence they waded through the tangled, hissing grass until they reached the shoreline.

'The boat is there,' the female guard said, pointing imperiously. 'Get into it, and be gone.'

Timothy went first, tossing his rucksack into the bottom of the boat with a thump and climbing in after it. His face was set with anger, but Linden felt only a weary sadness. She was just about to follow when she heard Garan's voice, and turned back to see him standing in the midst of the four guards, gesturing earnestly as he talked with them. They seemed unimpressed, but at last the leader nodded, and he and all but one male guard disappeared.

'I'll just be a moment, Llinos,' said Garan. Then he hurried down the steps to meet Timothy and Linden on the beach.

'I came to plead with you,' he said, clasping Linden's hand between both his own. 'It is not too late for you to accept the Elders' offer. If you return with me now, and tell them you are sorry—'

'I am not sorry,' she said, pulling her hand back and curling it into a fist. 'There is no place here for me or my people, whatever your Elders might say.'

Garan's shoulders slumped. 'Then I can only bid you goodbye.'

'Come with us,' Linden urged, but he shook his head.

'I cannot,' he said. 'For all that I spoke boldly of taking a stand, I am not ready to leave the *Gwerdonnau Llion*, not yet.' He backed away from the boat, one hand lifting in a sad farewell. Then he vanished.

Emotion welled up in Linden, threatening to shatter her composure. Ducking her head so that the watching guard

237

would not see her face, she stepped into the boat and sat down, hands folded in her lap. She had just settled herself when a great wave rushed in, lifting the vessel from the sand and pulling it out to sea.

As they floated towards a set of pillars that looked just like the ones closer to the shore, Timothy rested his chin on his hand, staring into the distance. After a moment he said, 'I didn't take Garan for such a coward.'

'Don't judge him too harshly,' she replied, though it was hard to keep her voice from trembling. 'He did what he could.'

Timothy gave a derisive snort. 'If you say so. It sounded like a lot of useless talk to me.'

Linden forced herself to keep silent until the waves carried them through the portal, and they emerged safely on the other side. Then she broke into a smile, and opened her hand to reveal the parting gift Garan had given her.

'Is that—' started Timothy, bolting upright in his seat, but Linden held a warning finger to her lips. For all they knew, the Children of Rhys might still be listening.

'We'll talk about it later,' she said, trying to sound sad and hopeless – as indeed she had been, until Garan pressed the Stone of Naming into her hand. 'Right now, all I want is to get back to shore.'

The tide was high as they reached the little cove, and their boat pitched and rolled as it rode the breakers in. Linden made herself small and leaped into the air, easily dodging the spray; but Timothy was forced to leap for the cliff-side, and a cold wave drenched his legs at once. Hands numb, feet slipping wetly inside his shoes, he scrabbled for a hold on the rocks and then began edging up the narrow, treacherous path towards the mainland.

'I can't see the Blackwings anywhere,' called Linden from above. After a moment she added hopefully, 'But we were gone for hours. Maybe they've given up?'

'It'd be…nice…to think so,' panted Timothy, all his concentration focused on not slipping. It seemed forever before he reached the top of the cliff, and when he got there he was spent: he collapsed onto the muddy grass and lay there, not even caring whether the Blackwings were coming or not.

'Are you all right?' asked Linden.

Timothy licked the sea salt off his lips and let his head fall back with a gentle thud. 'Yeah,' he croaked. 'Just give me a minute.'

Linden sat down on a rock by his side, the Stone of Naming cupped in her hand. 'I can't believe Garan just gave it to us,' she said softly, turning it over in her fingers. 'He must have known he'd be punished, maybe even exiled, when the other Children of Rhys found out. And yet he wouldn't come with us, either.'

Timothy struggled up onto his elbows and looked out over the edge of the cliff. There was no trace left of the

Green Isles or the boat that had carried them there, just the empty, wind-chopped sea. Even the little cove with the standing stones had vanished, as though it had been nothing more than a dream. 'He's never lived anywhere but those islands,' he said slowly. 'Maybe he just can't bring himself to leave unless he's got no other choice.'

'Maybe,' said Linden, but she sounded doubtful. 'So where do we go now?'

'As far from here as we can, before the Blackwings come back,' said Timothy. He sat up, and the chill wind sliced through his wet jeans like a machete; instantly his teeth began to chatter, and he rubbed his thighs in a desperate effort to warm them. 'I saw...a hostel on the way up from St David's. We could stop there...ask them the quickest way back to London.'

'Yes, but...' Linden's small face wrinkled with concern. 'We don't have enough money to get all the way back home, do we?'

Here we go again, thought Timothy, but without resentment. If he'd succeeded in forcing Linden to pay their way with glamour the last time, they'd never have been allowed to visit the Children of Rhys. 'We could call Paul and Peri. Maybe one of them could drive out...'

Linden shook her head. 'I don't want to do that. They've already risked enough for us. And remember what Rob said, when Paul wanted to come with us before?' She pursed her lips, then said determinedly, 'All right. You get us to the train station. I'll get us home.'

'How are you going to do that?'

Linden put the Stone of Naming in her pocket and stood, flexing her wings. 'I'll make us both invisible.'

How this was any less dishonest than buying a ticket with a glamour Timothy couldn't tell, and he was about to say so when she added, 'And we'll pay for our ride properly later.'

'Right,' said Timothy, oddly relieved that she hadn't abandoned her scruples.

'But we'd better get you some dry clothes first,' said Linden, sounding worried now. 'You really do feel the cold, don't you?'

'Yes, and I hate it,' said Timothy fervently between his teeth.

'Then let's hurry,' said Linden, and with that she flew off. Timothy hobbled behind her, and after stumbling down the footpath for a few minutes he spotted the rooftops of the hostel in the distance.

'You'd better hide in my rucksack again,' he said to Linden. 'Just in case.'

By the time Timothy reached the hostel the last of the afternoon sunshine had disappeared; the sky was the colour of slate, and a thin, drizzling rain had begun to fall. He squelched in through the front door and said to the girl at the desk, 'What's the quickest way to London?'

'Well, there's a train station at Haverfordwest,' replied the attendant. 'But the last bus left St David's at half past five, and there won't be another until tomorrow.'

'How far is it? Could I walk?'

The girl let out a disbelieving laugh. 'Walk? Not likely! It'd take you all night.'

Timothy's shoulders slumped. Now what were they going to do?

'Look,' said the girl kindly. 'Why don't you stay here tonight? We've plenty of space, and it's cheap. You can have a hot shower and a good night's sleep, and take the bus out tomorrow morning.'

'Just a minute,' Timothy told her. He dug a hand into his pocket and counted what was left of the money Owen Jenkins had given them, then hurried outside to speak to Linden. 'Is there a chance we might be safe here for the night?' he said in a low voice as he opened his rucksack. 'Once they lost our trail, the Blackwings might have flown anywhere. Back the way we came, or even back to the Empress, for all we know.'

'I don't see that we have much choice,' said Linden glumly. 'You can't go anywhere like that, in any case.'

Timothy didn't need to ask what she meant. His muscles were trembling with exhaustion and cold, and a little puddle of water had formed around his shoes. He only hoped that he could still find some dry clothes in his rucksack.

'All right,' he said grimly. 'We'll just have to sleep light – and hope for the best.'

*

The room was simply furnished, with walls of grey stone and a bare wooden floor – but it was private, and the bed looked comfortable. As soon as the attendant left, Linden climbed out of the rucksack and jumped onto the mattress, while Timothy grabbed an armful of clothing and vanished in search of the shower.

He was gone a long time. Linden stayed small as she nibbled the last half of her sandwich, so that there would be plenty left for Timothy when he came back. Then she curled up on the pillow, hiding herself with a corner of the blanket while she waited for his return. But she must have been more tired than she realised, because when she opened her eyes again the room was dark, and Timothy was gingerly easing his head onto the pillow in an effort not to wake her.

'It's all right,' she said sleepily, rolling over and curling up against his shoulder. He smelled of soap and sea water, mingled with the earthier scent of his humanity; it was a good smell, oddly comforting. It occurred to her that perhaps one of them ought to stay up and keep watch for the Blackwings, especially now that the iron key was gone and they had no way to shield themselves against another attack. But the pillow felt soft and Timothy was warm and she was so very tired…

Linden dreamed that she was back at the Oak, with all the faeries gathered around her as she cast the spell that would restore their magic. Rob's dark eyes gleamed with admiration as he held up the Stone of Naming and said to her, 'The Empress is defeated. You have saved us all.' Knife, Paul and Timothy watched from the veranda of the House, smiling, and then Valerian came up and embraced her, and said, 'Queen Amaryllis would be so proud of you, Linden. You have truly fulfilled all our hopes.'

It was everything she longed for, and yet it rang false somehow: it was too perfect even for a dream. But she still could not bring herself to wake, even though somewhere at the back of it all lay a feathery blackness, and the sounds of harsh laughter.

Timothy sat in the spotlight, guitar thrumming in his hands as he played before an audience of thousands all clapping and cheering for more. The song was the catchiest tune he'd ever heard, all palm-slapping rhythm and fast-plucked melody, and Miriam stood beside him with a microphone, singing the words in her husky, resonant voice – but her eyes were on him as she sang, and everyone in the audience was watching him too, and he knew that it was *his* concert, *his* song. There was no more uncertainty in him now, no shadow of doubt. He was Timothy Sinclair, world-famous musician, and the knowledge filled him with a fierce and inextinguishable pride.

But when he woke, he found himself a prisoner.

The bed, the hostel, the rocky Welsh hillside – all were

gone. Instead of cosy darkness the room swam with sallow morning light, filtering in through a barred window high above. He was lying on a cement floor without a mattress or even a blanket to cover him, wearing nothing but the T-shirt and boxers he'd gone to bed in. Timothy got up, shivering, and tried to open the door. It was locked.

And yet the room didn't look like a jail cell. There were screw holes in the wall where a blackboard had once hung, and bits of old posters taped to the wall. He felt a muzzy sense of recognition, but it wasn't until he found a blue crayon wedged into the skirting board and a scrap of faded paper reading PPIANS 2:12 that he realised he was trapped in an old Sunday School classroom.

The irony startled a laugh out of him, but he quickly sobered at the thought of what it meant. The Blackwing brothers must have found a way into the hostel during the night – whining pathetically at the door in their dog forms maybe, or just posing as human travellers and waiting for the attendant to invite them in. They'd put a spell on Timothy while he slept, and brought him here to Sanctuary – or at least he assumed it was Sanctuary; how many abandoned churches could the Empress's people own?

Not that it mattered. He had to get out of here, and find Linden. Timothy paced around the room, inspecting every corner for an escape route, or a key, or a weapon. But he found nothing but a few crumbs of plaster, and when he rapped on the wall, no one answered.

He sidled over and crouched in front of the door, shifting uncomfortably as the cement chilled his bare feet, and examined the lock. If only he had something to pick it with—

All at once the door swung inwards, smacking him in the face. He was still clutching his nose and swearing fervently in Luganda when an amused voice said from the doorway, 'Welcome back to Sanctuary, Timothy Sinclair. I trust you slept well? You should feel honoured: I wove that dream for you myself.'

It was Veronica.

The floor of Linden's cage glowed with fiery heat, and when she tried to cling to the bars they burned her fingers. She fluttered helplessly in midair, wing muscles aching with the effort, knowing that she couldn't hover much longer before her strength gave out – and that the moment it did, she would die.

'Tell me, little one,' said the Empress softly. Linden had imagined the Empress would be tall, dark and arrogant-looking like Jasmine, but she could not have been more wrong: this woman was almost childlike, with delicate features and hair the colour of dandelion wine curling about her shoulders. In fact she looked so sweet that it was hard to believe she could be evil – or so Linden had thought, until her torture began. 'Why did you and the human boy go to Wales?'

'We were…trying…to get away…from you!' gasped Linden. Her wings were failing now, and with every breath she sank a little closer to the floor. She could feel the heat beating up at her, searing her skin and crisping the ends of her hair; even the tears that streaked her face were hot.

'You know what will happen if you fall,' the Empress told her. 'This is your last chance to confess before you burn to ashes, and I am forced to interrogate the human in your stead. For I *will* have the truth,' and with a flick of her fingers she set the cage swinging on its chain. Linden shrieked as the hot bars brushed her arm, scorching through the sleeve of her tunic in an instant; panicked, she wove back and forth in midair, trying to avoid another collision.

'We went…to find more faeries!' she cried as the cage spun dizzily around her. 'Ones who would help my people, give us back our magic…but I couldn't.' A sob ripped at her lungs. 'I couldn't!'

The Empress put out a languid hand and stopped the cage; the heat radiating from its metal bars seemed to bother her not at all. 'You see?' she said. 'So much easier. Do you wish me to put out the fire?'

'P-please,' whimpered Linden. The hem of her skirt was smoking, and blisters had broken out on the soles of her feet.

'Then it is done,' said the Empress, and instantly the cage was cool again. Linden collapsed to the floor, faint with relief.

When she had caught her breath, she sat up slowly and

looked at the room around her. It was eerily similar to the Gospel Hall she and Timothy had visited in Aberystwyth: the high, peaked ceiling and narrow windows, the platform over which her cage hung suspended, were the same. Yet this hall was webbed in sinister shadows, with only a few candles to light it, and the only furniture was a single throne in the centre of the platform, facing the empty floor.

The Empress walked to the throne and sat upon it, smoothing her silken skirts. 'No wonder my servants caught you so easily,' she mused. 'For your quest had failed, and in your hearts you had already given up.' She ran one finger across her lips. 'Tell me more about your people. No magic, you say? How did that come about?'

Linden wiped her tear-smudged face on her sleeve – and only then did she realise that there were no scorch marks on the cloth anywhere, just as there were no burns on her skin. The cage had never been hot at all: the whole ordeal had been a glamour, a cunning illusion.

'We were betrayed,' she said shakily. 'By a faery named Jasmine. She stole our magic and used it to change our bodies against our will – all because she wanted to keep us from having anything to do with humans.'

'And rightly so,' said the Empress with approval. 'Or at least the intent was noble, even if the execution was short-sighted. What happened to her then, this Jasmine?'

'She became our Queen, for a while,' said Linden. 'But

then a faery she'd forgotten about came back to the Oak – Amaryllis. She'd been away when Jasmine cast her spell, so she still had all her wits and magic about her, and when she learned what Jasmine had done to the other Oakenfolk, she challenged her to a duel.'

The Empress's eyes widened, like a wondering child's. 'How exciting! Go on.'

'Jasmine lost,' Linden said. 'And Amaryllis wanted to punish her properly for what she'd done. So she took away all her magic, turned her into a human, and banished her from the Oak forever. That's all I know about her.'

The Empress let out a sorrowful breath. 'So cruel a fate, for such a heroine! It is a pity. Had I only known, I would have sought out this Jasmine and taken her into my court. How long ago was this?'

'It's been nearly two hundred years,' Linden told her, adding with a flash of private satisfaction, 'she's long dead by now.'

'And all that time your people have been without magic. Living like prisoners, I am told, inside that Oak of yours; struggling for every mouthful, and hardly daring to step outside lest some predator swoop down upon you. You replace yourselves with eggs when you die, but bear no children; and now fewer than fifty of you are left. Is that not so?'

Linden was taken aback. Where was the Empress getting all this information? Surely the Blackwings hadn't observed all that from one brief flight over the Oakenwyld…but there was only one other possibility, and her mind balked at the thought.

'What a wretched existence,' remarked the Empress, flicking dust off the arm of her carved throne. 'If it were not for your wilful attachment to humans in spite of all Jasmine's attempts to enlighten you, I should feel quite sorry for you all. But as it is…'

'Why?' Linden burst out. 'Why do you hate humans? When you depend on them for so much—'

'I do not hate them,' said the Empress coolly. 'Any more than you hate the sparrows and rabbits you eat for your dinner. But I do not befriend my dinner, either. And it does not please me to see my subjects degrading themselves by keeping company with humans, telling them our secrets, and encouraging them to waste their creativity on their own kind, when those talents would be so much better used by us. And speaking of which…'

She murmured a word Linden could not hear and made a beckoning gesture. Immediately Rob stepped out of the shadows, his guitar slung across his back. He bowed to the Empress, then sat down at her feet and began to play, paying no attention to Linden at all.

'My court musician,' said the Empress fondly, looking down at him. 'And my most loyal subject – are you not, my Robin?'

'Your Imperial Majesty,' said Rob, 'to serve you is my

only pleasure.' There was no trace of irony in his tone, and Linden felt a shiver of unease.

'My Robin is also an accomplished spy,' the Empress continued. 'The night you first came to Sanctuary, he saw you rescue the human boy from Veronica, and set out to discover why you had done it. Imagine his surprise when he learned that you were one of the Forsaken! I could scarcely believe it myself, when he brought his report to me.' She smiled indulgently. 'Of course Veronica was furious with him for stealing her prey, but she soon calmed down when I told her he had acted on my behalf. She appreciates cunning, though she has yet to master it.'

Brought his report to me... Had Rob betrayed them after all? Linden's stomach convulsed, and her hand clenched on the Stone she still carried in her pocket.

'Indeed, if not for dear Robin's vigilance, I might never have guessed that there was treachery breeding among my subjects,' the Empress went on, her fingers twining idly in Rob's hair. 'But he has insinuated himself into their very midst, gained their confidence, so that when the time is ripe I can gather them and destroy them in one blow. And, of course, he has also met with your new Queen and tested her powers, that I might know precisely how many soldiers I will need to send out to add the Oakenwyld to my empire. The answer being, of course, hardly any,' and she let out a merry little laugh.

No, thought Linden numbly. *It can't be. Not after all he's done to help us...*

Then Rob gave the Empress one of his slow smiles, and Linden's last flicker of hope died. Surely no one could look so adoringly at a woman he hated?

'You never know, My Lady,' drawled Rob. 'I may be a rebel myself.'

The Empress smiled back tolerantly, as though this were an old joke. 'He will have his fun,' she said to Linden. 'But what he and I both know is that I own his very soul. Do you know what sets him apart from faeries like Veronica? Poor child, she strives to be like him without knowing his secret: she has enticed one human after another, and yet the talent she steals from them always fades away. But Robin received his gift by tasting the blood of a human musician, murdered for his sake. He took that cup willingly from my hand, knowing full well what was in it; so to deny me, he would have to deny himself.'

Linden's head reeled, and she clutched at the bars of her cage. She had trusted Rob, believed in him – and he had done this? Had he sent them to look for the Stone of Naming on the Empress's behalf, so that she could extinguish all hope of resistance to her power? If so, it was a good thing that Linden had not admitted to finding the Children, let alone getting the Stone from them. As far as the Empress and even Rob knew, their mission had failed...

You mean it hasn't? said a cynical voice in her head that sounded painfully like Timothy, and Linden buried her face in her hands. It was true: all her efforts to save the

Oakenfolk had been futile. Rob had proved a traitor, and Garan a coward. Even the Stone in her pocket was useless, for the secret rebellion against the Empress was no secret at all, and soon it would be stamped out.

Oh, Great Gardener, she wept brokenly. *Help me, please — I'm so afraid, and I don't know what to do.*

But even as she prayed Rob strummed his guitar, while the Empress tapped her fingers and smiled. And in all the whispering echoes of that once-holy place, Linden could hear no answer.

SEVENTEEN

Veronica crouched in front of Timothy, one slim hand bringing up his chin. She inspected his nose where the door had struck it and said, 'How fragile you humans are. Is that blood?'

'Linden,' said Timothy thickly, pulling away. 'Where is she?'

'With the Empress, of course,' Veronica told him. 'And Rob is with them, too – you remember Rob, I am sure?'

He shrugged, not wanting her to guess how much he knew, or cared. But his spirit leaped at the news. The Empress had only to turn her back for an instant, and Linden could slip Rob the Stone...

'It is a shame you didn't let me take your music at the beginning,' Veronica went on, stroking his hair back from his face. 'It would have made everything so much easier.'

Timothy clenched his hands. He could feel the calluses on his fingertips, earned from countless hours of practice; he wanted suddenly, and very badly, to play again.

'I could bring you a guitar,' she murmured, as though she had read his mind. 'Remember the way you played for me, the first night we met?'

He remembered it vividly, for all that he'd spent the last couple of days trying not to. In spite of everything he knew about Veronica, he couldn't forget how it had felt to play with her by his side. Before she'd pushed him, he'd been a pretty good guitarist for his age; but that night he'd been a prodigy, a genius.

'The Empress doesn't want your music,' she went on in the same soft, enticing tone. 'Why should she, with the finest musician in all Faery as her favourite? But I—'

Timothy frowned. 'You mean Rob?'

Veronica's lips pursed irritably. 'Of course I do. Who else? But he can play as well as he likes, whenever he pleases; somehow the Empress gave him that power. Whereas you and I...' Her fingers traced the shape of his ear. 'We need to work together.'

Rob, the Empress's favourite? With a permanent gift of music no other faery possessed? Dread curdled in Timothy's stomach, but Veronica was still speaking:

'What if we were to make a bargain, you and I? You see, I can't take your music just now: it's buried inside you, too deep for me to reach. I need to see the way your fingers move upon the strings, hear you play the melodies that belong to you alone, before I can touch your gift and make it shine. So...'

Her fingers drifted down the bridge of Timothy's bruised nose. 'I will bring you a guitar,' she continued, 'and you will play it for me. It will be a performance such as you dreamed of last night, one that could not be surpassed if you lived a thousand years. And then, when I take your music, you will be grateful.'

'Sounds terrific,' said Timothy sardonically. 'And once you've taken it, how long will it last you? A few days? A week?'

She shrugged, unfazed. 'Better than never being able to play at all.'

'That's a good way to put it,' Timothy told her. 'Because you know what? That's what I think, too. Almost anything would be better than not being able to play. So if that's your idea of a *bargain*—'

'Oh, no.' Her eyes widened in an unconvincing attempt at innocence. 'That was only your part of it. I haven't even told you mine. First, I take your music…'

She stopped and glanced back at the door, her expression furtive. 'And then?' Timothy prompted.

Veronica leaned towards him until her lips almost brushed his ear. She whispered: 'And then I'll let you go.'

'I have been thinking, Linden of the Oak,' said the Empress, rising from her throne and walking back towards the cage. 'Misguided though your attitude to humans may be, you have shown such loyalty towards your fellow faeries as I have seldom seen. You have endured much hardship on your people's account, with little prospect of reward, and I find that admirable. So...I will make you an offer.'

'Offer?' Linden scrubbed at her burning eyes. 'What kind of offer?'

'It is this: if you consent to my terms, I will allow your people to continue living in the Oak as long as it pleases them to do so. I will even send some of my own servants to increase your numbers and make you strong. Your lost magic will be restored, and you will have everything you desire...on three conditions.'

She trailed her fingers around the edge of Linden's cage, spinning it gently as she spoke. 'One: the Oakenfolk will all swear fealty to me by each giving me one drop of her blood. Two: you will no longer associate with humans. You will not linger in their company, nor aid them, nor befriend them; none of you will ever again look upon a human with love, nor take a human child and raise it as your own, but will remain true to your own kind. And three: every faery infant born in the Oak must be brought to me within its first few years of life, that I may assure myself of your children's loyalty just as I am assured of yours.' She stopped the cage and looked at Linden questioningly. 'Is that not generous?'

Linden felt as though her chest was being squeezed between two giant fingers. Her breath came quick and shallow, and a rushing noise filled her ears. Everything the

Oakenfolk needed...she had never dreamed the Empress would make such an offer. Of course the terms were not ideal, but if every other hope was gone... She put her head in her hands, overwhelmed. Could she really afford to say no?

'Perhaps you doubt my goodwill,' the Empress said. 'But consider: have I ever done you any real harm? I commanded the Blackwings to capture you, not to kill you; and even the fire I kindled beneath your cage was only illusion – meant to frighten you into telling me the truth, no more. The human boy I have locked away for safekeeping, but...'

'Timothy!' Linden burst out. 'Please don't hurt him. This was all my doing, he doesn't deserve—'

'Of course not,' said the Empress in a soothing tone. 'I assure you, he is unharmed; no one has so much as spoken a harsh word to him. All I wish is to remove his memories of the past few days, so that he cannot betray the secrets of our people. Then I will set him free...just as soon as you accept my terms.'

Linden let out her breath. That didn't sound too bad. Perhaps Timothy would be happier not remembering Sanctuary, or Veronica, or the dangers and hardships that had followed. And it would be a small price to pay if she could go back to Queen Valerian bringing good news of the Oakenfolk's deliverance. Surely even Knife would understand...

Knife.

The image of her foster mother flashed through Linden's mind, and at once she realised how foolish her temptation to give in to the Empress had been. Knife had dared to love a human, and give up her faery heritage for his sake: her very existence was a denial of the Empress's creed, and all the Oakenfolk knew it. The only way the Empress could respond to such a threat would be to tear Knife and Paul apart, or else kill them both...

Never.

'Great Gardener, give me courage,' she whispered, and then she stood up straight and faced the Empress. 'No,' she said. 'You will not have our blood, or our fealty, or the service of our children, and we will not turn our backs on our human friends. If we die, we die. But we will not surrender the Oak to you without a fight.'

The Empress's face hardened. She smacked the flat of her hand against the cage, sending it swinging high into the air. 'It is a fight you will lose,' she snapped, as Linden clung to the bars in dizzy terror. 'And when you and your human *friend* stand before me for judgment, you will both regret that you did not accept my offer. Robin!'

Rob stopped playing at once, set his guitar aside and looked up at her expectantly.

'Fetch the human boy,' she said. 'Bring him to me.'

'As you will, Your Imperial Majesty.' He rose and bowed, then stepped towards the door.

'Oh, and Robin?'

Rob turned, brows lifted in a wordless question.

'Send word to all the faeries in the city that I wish them to attend me at once – and be sure to include your fellow would-be rebels. Clearly, it has been too long since my people witnessed an execution.'

Linden's heart stuttered. Her eyes flicked towards Rob, silently begging him to do something, say something, to reassure her he was on their side. If he hesitated or looked troubled, even for an instant...

But the only thing that crossed Rob's face was a smile. 'Of course, My Empress,' he said, and went out.

'I don't believe you,' Timothy told Veronica flatly, though his pulse was galloping. 'After the Empress went to all this trouble to capture me, you really think she won't mind if you just let me go?'

'Of course she would *mind*,' Veronica said with a roll of her eyes that made her look almost human. 'If she knew I was doing it. But you are going to escape all by yourself – or so it will appear. Look.' She unzipped the front pocket of her fitted jacket and pulled out a small brown envelope. Opening the flap carefully with her long fingernails, she shook out a loop of leather cord and then used it to draw out the rest of the packet's contents.

It was a cross, formed from two square-edged nails bound together with copper wire. The thong went through a loop at the top of the cross, so it could be worn as a necklace.

It was also, unmistakeably, made of iron.

'Where did you get that?' demanded Timothy. He grabbed at it, but Veronica whisked it out of his reach.

'I found it under one of the beds upstairs, months ago,' she said, dangling it teasingly in front of him. 'One of our human guests must have left it behind, and I thought it might prove useful one day. If you wish, I will give it to you, to use in making your escape – but you must give me your music first. Is it a bargain?'

Timothy sucked in a breath and let it out slowly. His eyes followed the cross as it swung back and forth at the end of the leather cord. It had to be as potent a weapon against magic as the key he'd lost, if not better...and what good would his music do him, if the Empress was going to kill him anyway?

'All right,' he said in a rough voice. 'It's a bargain.'

'No, it is not,' said Rob unexpectedly from the doorway, and the triumph froze on Veronica's face. She whirled, the cross still dangling from her hand.

Timothy saw the opportunity at once, and went for it. He lunged – but Rob shoved him back and grabbed Veronica, hauling her up against the wall. His hands gripped hers and raised them high, swinging the cross close to her cheek.

'Rebelling against the Empress?' he said silkily. 'Conspiring with a human to defy her commands? I wouldn't have expected it of you, Veronica.'

Her lips parted, but she did not speak. Only her eyes

moved, white-ringed with fear, following the shallow arc of the cross as it dangled beside her head.

'On the other hand,' remarked Rob, 'I find the irony amusing. What will you give me *not* to tell the Empress? If you could offer Timothy such an ingenious bargain, I'm sure you must have something even more interesting to propose to me.'

Veronica licked her lips, the first nervous gesture Timothy had ever seen from her. 'I wasn't really going to give it to him,' she said.

'Oh, were you not?' The iron cross inched nearer to her face. 'The truth, Veronica.'

'It is the truth!' Her voice rose to a shriek. 'I only meant to trick him into giving me his music! I serve the Empress! I would never have let him go!'

'I see,' said Rob, plucking the necklace from her grasp. 'Well, then, you will just have to miss the execution,' and with that he tapped her on the forehead, and she collapsed unconscious on the floor.

Timothy stood warily in the centre of the room, watching Rob. 'Execution?' he said.

'I am here to fetch you at the Empress's command,' Rob told him. 'You and Linden are to be put to death. So I suspect you will need this more than I will.' He stepped around Veronica's motionless body, took Timothy firmly by the wrist, and let the cross fall into his hand.

'What?' said Timothy.

'Do not wear it openly,' Rob said, 'but keep it against your skin. It will be of little use as a weapon with so many of my people around you, but it will shield you from the Empress's power until we can find a way to free Linden.'

So Rob was on their side after all. Timothy had begun to doubt it, but the cross in his hand was proof enough. He looked down at himself helplessly for a moment – T-shirt too thin, no pockets in the boxers – then bent and tucked the cross into the side of his sock, folding the thick ankle band down to hide its telltale shape.

'I wish that your quest had succeeded,' said Rob. 'Then I and my allies could fight openly in your defence. Still, we will do what we can.'

Timothy hesitated, then took the plunge. 'We didn't fail,' he said. 'Linden has the Stone of Naming in her pocket.'

Rob caught his breath. 'You found the Children of Rhys?'

'We did, but they wouldn't help us. We were lucky to come away with the Stone.'

'Luck indeed,' murmured Rob appreciatively. 'Well, then, we have only to find a way to get it from her, in full view of the Empress and a hundred or so others. You're the one with the creativity, human – have you a plan?'

The Empress lounged upon her throne, watching her faery subjects with hooded eyes as one by one they stepped up to the platform and kneeled before her. The room was filling rapidly, and in desperation Linden felt around her cage, searching for a catch, a crack, any weakness that might let her escape. But the bars were too narrow for her to squeeze through, too strong for her to bend, and though she had tried to make herself smaller, she could not. She could think of one other possibility, but she was afraid to try it – the cage looked too strong to break easily, and what if she ended up crushed into this tiny space?

'No song for us, little bird?' taunted a voice, and she turned to see Byrne Blackwing grinning at her. Corbin leaned against the wall just behind him, with a half-smile on his lips that chilled her more than his brother's open mockery.

'I may be in a cage,' Linden retorted with all the boldness she could muster, 'but at least I'm not the Empress's slave.'

The amusement went out of Byrne's face, and he started forward. Corbin caught his arm; he snarled and threw his brother off, and Linden shrank back—

But then a door on the other side of the hall crashed open and Rob stalked in, dragging Timothy behind him.

Timothy's wrists were lashed together with rope, and dried blood streaked his face. He was limping a little on his right side, and his head hung down as though he were exhausted. But when he saw Linden's cage he looked up sharply, and his gaze met hers with a fierceness that stopped her breath.

'Stay,' said the Empress as Timothy and Rob reached the foot of the platform. Linden's heart thumped as Rob turned his head towards her, but his gaze only flicked over her indifferently before returning to the Empress.

'Human,' said the Empress to Timothy, 'you are no subject of mine, nor do I wish to claim you. But you have given help to those who would defy me, and for that you must be punished. Kneel.'

'I'd rather stand, thanks,' said Timothy, but Rob grabbed him by the shoulder and forced him onto his knees. With a little surprised-sounding grunt he went down and crouched at the foot of the platform, hunched over his bound hands.

The Empress rose fluidly and addressed the gathered faeries, her voice ringing out across the room: 'You all know the law: it is forbidden for a faery to keep company with humans, or give them aid or comfort. Yet the young rebel you see in this cage before you –' she swung around and pointed at Linden – 'dared to assault Veronica, one of our own people, and deprive her of her rightful human prey. She helped the human boy to escape from Sanctuary, and then she enlisted him to help her seek out other faeries and persuade them also to rise up against me.'

All the faeries' eyes were on Linden now. She searched the crowd of dim faces for signs of sympathy, but though some looked apprehensive and a few even sorrowful, no one moved. The Empress went on:

'I offered her a chance to repent of her crimes, but she spurned it. Such rebellion, such wilful perversity, cannot go unpunished. And the punishment I have chosen, for both this faery and the human she has so foolishly befriended…is death.'

Linden wrapped her arms tightly around her ribs, trying to hold in the fluttering panic. She had heard the Empress speak of execution; she'd had ample time to consider what that meant; and yet hearing the words shocked her all over again. *The punishment…is death.*

'Your Majesty!'

The voice was Timothy's. 'Before you carry out the sentence, I'd like to say a few words.'

The Empress let out a short laugh. 'You, a mere human, address my court? Do you imagine yourself so clever, or so eloquent, that with just one speech you can win my people to your cause?'

'No,' said Timothy, with surprising meekness. 'I mean…just to Linden. I'll talk quietly if you like, so the rest of your subjects don't hear. But if you're going to put us both to death, can't I at least say goodbye to her first?'

'You are in no position to ask for favours, boy,' said the Empress coldly, and began to turn away. But then Rob spoke:

'My Empress, I would ask that you grant his request for my sake, if not his own. I am curious to know what this human thinks is so vital for him to say – and surely you have nothing to fear from words?'

'Fear!' Her tone was acid. 'As if a human could threaten me! Very well, my Robin, for your sake. But –' her hard

266

gaze turned on Timothy – 'be brief, boy, or I will burn out your tongue.'

Timothy bowed his head for a moment. Then he looked up at Linden and said:

'There's a Bible verse that says *"As iron sharpens iron, so one man sharpens another."* I know that's probably not a popular proverb among faeries, but what I mean is, I've learned a lot from our friendship, and I'm grateful for that.'

Despite the dread churning inside her, Linden was touched – but also baffled. Why was Timothy quoting the Bible? Either he'd changed his mind since the last time they talked, or else…

'And there are other verses that make me think of you, too,' Timothy went on more quickly as the Empress began to tap her foot. 'Like, *"How beautiful are the feet of those who bring good news,"* because that's what you were trying to do for your people. And I know you thought you were too young to make any difference, but like Jesus said, *"The least of you shall be the greatest—"*'

His words ended in a choking gasp as Rob grabbed the back of his neck and pushed his head nearly to the floor. 'I beg your pardon, My Empress,' Rob said. 'I had thought he might tell us something useful. Forgive my poor judgment.'

Timothy had been trying to give her a message, Linden realised. But what? Why had he chosen those verses?

*The least of you shall be the greatest…*that meant her, surely: she was the smallest person in this whole room.

Perhaps if she figured out what Timothy meant, she could do something great to save them? But what?

How beautiful are the feet...but there was nothing special about her feet that she could think of. Maybe it was the *good news* part he wanted her to think about? Telling her not to lose hope, because he had a plan to save them? And then there was that first verse he'd quoted, about how *iron sharpens iron*...

Iron! What if he'd found some, to replace the key he'd lost in Wales? But even if he had, why go to the trouble of telling her about it? She was a faery: she couldn't touch iron without losing what little magic she had...

'Enough of this folly,' snapped the Empress. She raised a hand towards Linden's cage, sparks of baleful light flickering around her fingertips. 'As Empress of all Faery, I proclaim Linden of the Oak to be traitor and rebel, outcast and Forsaken, and worthy of no better fate than death. So be—'

Her words ended in a gasp as Timothy leaped up from his crouch, sprang onto the platform, and hurled himself at her. She staggered back into the throne, which toppled over with a crash, sending the two of them tumbling onto the floor. But somehow Timothy had got his wrists free, and while he gripped the Empress's throat with one hand, he reached for his ankle with the other.

Feet! thought Linden, suddenly realising why he'd been limping. But her epiphany came too late. Timothy's fingers had barely brushed the edge of his sock when the Empress brought up her hands and the white lightning of her power ripped through him, tearing him away from her and hurling him into the air. He landed on his back at the very edge of the platform, open-eyed and still.

'No!' Linden screamed. Reckless energy flooded her, sweeping away the last of her caution: she had to get to Timothy, whatever the cost. She clenched her fists and willed herself, with all her might, to grow.

Her head struck the top of the cage in an instant of blinding pain, and then the bars sprang apart and she dropped to the platform, free. She threw herself down beside Timothy.

Thank the Gardener, he was alive. His chest rose and fell, and his eyelids fluttered. Something had protected him from the full impact of the Empress's power. Linden grabbed his right foot, peeled down the sock – and the iron cross fell out into her hand.

It was pure agony. Her heart, her lungs, even her thoughts stopped. Linden crumpled, dropping the pendant onto the stage, as her magic sputtered out and left her helpless.

But she was *still human size*.

'Remove the boy,' the Empress croaked from the back of the platform, rubbing her throat with one hand while she struggled to push herself upright with the other. 'Robin, do you hear me? Take him away!'

Until now Rob had stood motionless, apparently stunned by what Timothy had done; now he shook himself as though waking from a dream, and climbed the stairs to obey. But as he stooped down and his hands closed on Timothy's wrists he whispered to Linden, *'Use it.'*

Use what? The cross? But how could she, when it had crippled her just to touch it the first time, and she was so weak she could barely...

The least of you shall be the greatest.

Was it possible? Could her very weakness, in this moment when the Empress was distracted, become her strength?

Linden's magic was gone; she could no longer change size, or fly, or cast a glamour to protect herself. But the iron cross still lay within her reach. And as Rob dragged Timothy out of the way, Linden seized the leather cord, leaped up, and whipped the cross at the Empress as hard as she could.

The cord snapped. But the cross kept flying, flashing in the candlelight as it spun through the air and struck the Empress's cheek. With a shriek she bent over, hiding her face in her skirts, while a cry went up from the watching crowd.

Rob grabbed his guitar from beside the platform; it blurred in his hand, and became a sword. He leaped in front of the Empress as though to defend her, but it was to Linden that he spoke:

'The Stone! Give it to me!'

There was no way he could know that she had it, unless Timothy had told him. Quickly Linden dug it out of her pocket and held it out to him.

Rob closed his hand around the Stone, and relief washed over his face. 'You were wrong, *My Lady*,' he said with savage triumph as he turned to confront the Empress. 'I can deny you – and I do.'

The Empress raised her head, eyes burning with hate – and Linden gasped.

'Jasmine!' she cried out, scrambling to her feet. 'Rob – she's the faery who stole my people's magic!'

The touch of cold iron had not only robbed the Empress of her ability to cast spells, it had stripped away the powerful glamours she had used to disguise herself. Dark-haired and proud-featured, she was now the image of the portrait Linden had seen in Paul's book. But now the heavy-lidded eyes and sensual mouth were surrounded by deep creases, and the once black hair bore streaks of grey. Signs of age, such as no faery before had ever shown – how many years had she lived as a human before regaining her magical powers?

'Defend the Empress!' rasped a familiar voice from below them, and Corbin Blackwing leaped up onto the stage with sword in hand. Rob sprang to meet him, shouting, 'Rebels! To me!' and the entire room erupted in confusion. Some faeries appeared to be plunging for the exits, others towards the platform, while still more milled about uncertainly.

'The Empress has lost her power!' Linden shouted into the jostling crowd. 'Come here quickly, before it's too late – Rob has the Stone, he can free you!' At first she despaired that anyone could hear her, there was so much shouting and wailing going on; but then she heard a female voice cry out, 'The Stone of Naming!' and another echo, 'The Stone!'

Within seconds the chaos on the floor resolved itself into two sides: the rebels pressing eagerly towards the stage, and the Empress's servants trying to hold them back. Birds wheeled about the ceiling, animals leaped and tussled on the floor; light sizzled and metal rang, and in the half-darkness it was impossible to tell which side was winning.

The Empress clawed at her fallen throne, dragging herself to her feet. She staggered forward and swiped at Linden, who ducked away just in time.

'I should have burned that blighted Oak to the ground,' Jasmine panted. 'And when I regain my powers – I swear to you that I will—'

But at that same moment Rob and Corbin came clashing towards them, all swords and spell-fire. Linden scrambled back, shielding her eyes – and when she looked again, the Empress had flung open the door at the back of the stage and fled, leaving it open behind her.

Linden darted to Timothy where he sat slumped against the wall. She grabbed his shoulders and shouted in his ear,

'Can you move? The Empress – she's getting away!'

He looked at her dazedly, then gave a weak nod. Linden slung her arm around him and helped him struggle to his feet, then yelled, 'This way!' and pointed at the door.

'Just a minute...' Timothy stumbled across the platform and bent to snatch up the iron cross from beside the fallen throne. Corbin's sword whistled towards his head, but Rob blocked the stroke and kicked the Blackwing off the stage. Within seconds an enraged raven came whirring back towards him; Rob dodged the attack just long enough to stoop and clasp hands with someone in the crowd, then shouted back to Timothy and Linden, 'Run! Save yourselves!' and suddenly whisked off into the darkness...

Linden blinked. Had he really changed himself into a *fox*?

'Free!' cried a melodious voice, and Linden looked around to see the faery who had helped them at Euston station holding the Stone of Naming high in the air. Other faeries were fighting their way towards her, plunging through walls of blue fire and dodging fountains of red and green sparks; as the first of them reached the faery she passed him the Stone, and his voice echoed hers in exultation, 'Free!'

With a screech one of the Blackwings dived out of the shadows, straight at Timothy's face. Timothy flung up the iron cross; the raven dropped like an anvil and crashed to the floor as Byrne, unconscious.

'We have to go, Timothy!' Linden called urgently.

Clutching the cross in front of him, Timothy began weaving his way past the other faeries swarming onto the stage – but just as he reached Linden, he stumbled and crashed to his knees.

'Timothy!' cried Linden in alarm, and he gasped back, 'Legs went numb – don't know what's wrong but I can't—'

Linden helped him to his feet again, and together they limped towards the door. They had almost reached it when a slim figure slipped out to block their path, tossing the pale hair from his eyes and greeting them with a familiar mocking smile.

'Martin, get out of my way,' Timothy panted, brandishing the cross, but the male faery only laughed.

'I have no quarrel with you, human boy,' he said. 'Why should I? I have not had such entertainment in many a year.' And to Linden's amazement, he swept them a bow and disappeared again.

A noise like thunder cracked across the room, and all the candles went out. 'Run!' screamed Linden, and she and Timothy plunged through the door. They found themselves at the top of a stairwell, with a second and heavier door before them; Timothy shoved it open, and the two of them tumbled out onto a concrete step, dazzled by the cold blue light of morning.

There was no sign of the Empress, and behind them the battle of Sanctuary still raged. But at least — or so Linden thought, as she clung to Timothy in exhausted relief — at least the two of them were safe.

EIGHTEEN

Timothy sat in the back parlour at Oakhaven, gazing out across the garden. Two days had passed since he and Linden escaped from Sanctuary: they'd huddled in an alleyway for a miserable hour or so until her magic returned, and then she'd turned them both invisible and they'd taken the train home. They'd arrived on Paul and Peri's doorstep filthy, starving, and half-dead with cold – but they were alive.

The only question was, for how long?

Resignedly Timothy opened his Bible to the fifth chapter of Matthew and reached for his notebook. *Blessed are the poor in spirit, for theirs is the kingdom of heaven...*

He had just started scribbling down some thoughts for the essay he owed the Dean when a spasm went through his hand, and his pen tumbled to the floor. He was trying to make his nerveless fingers pick it up again when he heard Paul's voice from behind him:

'You all right, Tim?'

'I'm fine,' Timothy said quickly, sitting up as his cousin rolled into the room. 'Just an aftershock from the Empress's spell.' It had frightened him the first few times, but by now the spasms were weaker and less frequent, and he was pretty sure they'd soon go away. Still, it was a chilling reminder that if he hadn't been touching iron when the Empress blasted him, he'd be dead right now.

'Let's say we just call her Jasmine,' said Paul, wheeling the chair around to face him. 'I don't think she deserves the title, do you? And if Rob can get enough rebels on his side, she won't be holding on to it much longer anyway.'

'That's just the thing,' said Timothy reluctantly. 'I don't know if he can. I don't even know if he and his followers are still alive. For all we know the Emp— I mean, Jasmine, could be coming here with an army to take over the Oak right now, and there's not much any of us can do about it.'

Paul was silent, his fingers steepled against his lips. Then he said, 'True. In which case maybe we should just call your parents and get you on a plane to Uganda before things get any worse.'

'Are you joking?' demanded Timothy. 'I'm not going to run away and just leave you all here!'

'Why not? You've done everything you can to help the Oakenfolk, Tim, and a good deal more than anyone expected of you. Believe me, Peri and I appreciate all you've been through for Linden's sake. But I'm still your guardian, and I'd be a pretty poor one if I let you hang about in the middle of a war zone.'

Timothy dropped his head into his hands, fingers furrowing up his hair. To be forced to confront his parents on such short notice, when he still hadn't decided what to tell them, would be bad enough...but even worse was the thought of being thousands of miles from the Oakenwyld, not knowing if his friends there were dead or alive.

'I want to stay,' he said huskily.

Paul frowned, but then Peri's voice echoed in from the corridor, 'I seem to remember another young man who refused to run away when his life was in danger, too.'

She walked into the room and crouched beside Paul's chair, laying both hands on his arm. 'I know you feel responsible for Timothy, and so do I. But after all that's happened, I think he's got a right to choose where he wants to be.'

'That's easy for you to say,' Paul retorted. 'Unless you're volunteering to call his parents and tell them their only son is dead?'

'No,' replied Peri, 'but you won't have to do it, either. If Jasmine comes to Oakhaven, she's hardly going to stop at just killing Timothy.'

Paul threw up his hands. 'Oh, well, in that case there's nothing to worry about. Good news, Tim! We're all going to die together!'

His tone was sarcastic, but Peri put her arms around his

shoulders and kissed his cheek, and when she let him go his mouth had pulled into a resigned smile. Timothy grinned back, feeling his own tension lift a little.

'I can think of worse ways to go,' he said.

Linden gazed out the slit that was all that remained of her bedroom window – Rob had done that, she remembered, and the thought was laced with regret. He'd risked so much to help them, and she'd never had the chance to say goodbye. Was he even still alive?

The garden below was sombre with rain, the flowerbeds buried in black mulch and the rose hedge a withered skeleton. All seemed quiet, but surely that couldn't last. The Empress had escaped the battle at Sanctuary, and by now she must have recovered her powers, just as Linden had done. And the faeries who'd seen Jasmine's true face, with its telltale lines of age, were just a tiny fraction of the many under her command. How long would it be before she gathered her forces and came back to take her revenge?

Linden leaned heavily against the windowsill. It seemed so wrong that it should end this way. The Oakenfolk still squabbling over who should be their next Queen, most of them still blind to the greater danger; Knife trapped in the Oakenwyld, her fate bound to the faeries' even though she was no longer one of them; and Paul and Timothy, condemned for no greater crime than being human...

Sunk in gloomy reverie, she barely noticed when the

whispering wind changed its tune. A gust swirled through the Oakenwyld, scattering twigs and long-dead leaves across the grass – and when Linden looked out the window again, the Oak was surrounded.

A bone of terror lodged itself in her throat. She jumped off the bed and pelted out of the room, shouting up the Spiral Stair, 'Your Majesty!'

'Queen Valerian's busy,' came Thorn's irritable reply from two landings above. 'What's the matter?'

'They're here,' gasped Linden, and dashed off down the Stair. The window-slits were too narrow for her to climb through, but she might be able to sneak out through the hedge tunnel, fly to the House and warn Knife and Timothy. Yet even as she ran a pounding noise reverberated through the Oak, like a heavy fist demanding entrance, and she realised it was already too late. They'd found the door in spite of all the glamours she'd put around it, and now...

She skidded to a halt in front of another window-slit, squinted out again – and immediately her fears drained away. The faeries outside were far too big to be Oakenfolk, that was true. But they were still *less than half human size*. Linden galloped down the last flight of the Spiral Stair, dashed to the Queen's Gate, and heaved up the bar to let their visitors in.

The first through the door was Garan – but now he stood only a little taller than herself, and when she threw herself into his arms her exuberance nearly knocked him over. 'You came! You came after all!' she cried, and he let out a surprised laugh.

'Get off me, you mad girl,' he said, detaching himself and holding her at arm's length. But his eyes twinkled as he added, 'Mind, had I known to expect such a welcome, I might have come sooner.'

Linden blushed and stepped back as the other Children of Rhys came in. There was the guard Garan had called Llinos, and a few others whose faces she had seen at the great council, including – *Broch*?

'But you – you were against us,' she stammered, looking up into that sharp, sardonic face. 'You said—'

'I know what I said,' Broch cut in impatiently. 'That it was for the Elders to decide how best to help you. But the Council is divided, and there have been nothing but arguments since you and the human boy left. And by the time Garan announced that he had given you the Stone of Naming and that the rest of us were cowards and traitors to our own kind, I'd heard enough shouting to last me the next two centuries. So I came.'

Linden looked at Garan in delight. 'Did you really say that?'

'I am only sorry I could not say it earlier,' replied Garan, sounding a little gruff with embarrassment. 'But I dared not draw attention to myself before I had safely given you the Stone. And I hoped that given time I might be able to persuade more of the *Plant Rhys* to support your cause – a hope which was not wholly vain, as you can see.' He nodded respectfully to his companions. 'We are only thirty-eight men, but we are yours to command.'

'What,' said Thorn's flat voice from the Stair above, 'in the name of all that's green and growing—'

Linden whirled towards her, dancing with excitement. 'The Children of Rhys, Thorn! They've come to help us!'

Thorn stalked around the last bend of the Stair and stopped, surveying Garan and his companions. Her gaze darted from one male faery to another, taking in their strong features and close-trimmed beards, the swords at their belts and the bows slung across their shoulders. Then she sat down slowly, her eyes glassy with disbelief, and for once she didn't say anything at all.

'If we restore the magic Jasmine took from you,' said Garan, as he and his followers stood before the Oakenfolk gathered in the Great Hall, 'the task will cost us dearly of our own magical strength, and we will need several days to recover. We will never be as powerful as we once were, nor will your own magic be as great as that of the Empress and her followers – but yes, it can be done.'

Linden threw her arms around Wink and hugged her, and Thorn actually whooped before turning it into a cough.

'We would be glad,' Valerian began – but Bluebell's voice cut in:

'You forget yourself, Healer! We are not humans, to take

from each other without giving in return: we are faeries, to whom a bargain is sacred. How dare we accept help from these strangers, when we have no means to repay them?'

The pleasure faded from Valerian's face, and her grey eyes became downcast. 'Bluebell is right,' she said. 'Forgive me, I beg of you – I spoke too soon.'

'There is nothing to forgive,' said Garan, with a swift glance at Bluebell. 'We did not come to you seeking wealth or goods that we could take back to our own land; rather, it is our hope that you will accept us as your subjects, and allow us to dwell among you. For by leaving the *Gwerdonnau Llion* we have made ourselves exiles, and if you do not give us a home, then I cannot think where my men and I will go.'

Valerian's smile returned, wavering with emotion. She stepped forward and held out her hand to Garan.

'There is ample room for you all here,' she said. 'And as Queen of the Oakenfolk I welcome you, with all my heart.'

Garan took Valerian's hand and kissed it, then bent on one knee before her with head bowed and both arms spread wide. Immediately all the other men in his company did likewise, although Broch's mouth gave a self-mocking twist as he went down.

Valerian looked back at the crowd of Oakenfolk behind her. No one moved, until Wink hurried forward and kneeled as the Children of Rhys had done. Thorn joined her, and Campion quickly followed. One by one, and then in pairs and clusters, all the Oakenfolk kneeled until only Bluebell and Mallow were left standing. And when after an uncomfortable pause the Chief Cook shrugged and bent her knee as well, Bluebell let out a little sob and collapsed to the floor beside her, defeated.

The Oakenfolk had acknowledged their rightful Queen at last.

The moon hung high over the Oakenwyld, bathing the garden in silvery light. Timothy stood on the veranda with Peri and Paul, watching as a line of tiny, winged figures emerged from the roots of the Oak and joined the waiting Children of Rhys on the lawn. Even from this distance it was easy to recognise Linden by her brown curls and the eager spring in her step; he waved to her, and she waved back.

He turned to Peri, wanting to ask her if they couldn't go a little closer – but then he saw the wistful look on her face and swallowed the question. Paul must have noticed his wife's expression as well, because a moment later he said quietly, 'You could ask them, you know.'

Peri did not move her gaze from the Oakenfolk. 'Ask what?'

'To make you a faery again.'

That got her attention; she swung around to look at him, frowning. 'What makes you think—'

'I don't think,' said Paul. 'I know. Of course you miss it sometimes; why wouldn't you? I'm just saying that if the

Children of Rhys have enough power to undo Jasmine's spell on the Oakenfolk, maybe they have some to spare for you, too.' Then, as Peri looked troubled, he added gently, 'It's not as though I'm asking you to leave me. You're still my wife, whether you can change size and do magic or not. But they're your people.'

For a moment Peri did not reply; then her lips firmed, and she shook her head. 'No,' she said. 'If the Oakenfolk are going to survive, they'll need every bit of power that Garan and his people can give them. Besides –' she took a deep breath – 'I made my choice to become human fourteen years ago. I won't go back on it now, even if I could.'

'Not even if it meant you could fly again?' Paul asked.

Timothy held his breath, but to his surprise, Peri smiled. 'Who says I can't fly? The moment this business with the Empress is over, I'm buying a plane ticket.' Then her face grew serious again and she said, 'But truly, I wasn't feeling sorry for myself. I was feeling sorry for them. Look at their faces.'

Timothy studied each of the faeries in turn, and he could see what Peri meant. Linden and Wink were both glowing with excitement, and even Thorn looked grudgingly pleased; but many of the other Oakenfolk seemed nervous, and a few – like Bluebell, and the hard-faced faery next to her who had to be Mallow – appeared wary and even resentful about what was taking place.

'I'm afraid Valerian's going to have her work cut out for

her,' Peri said. 'A lot of the Oakenfolk don't like change...and now, everything about their lives is changing at once.'

'But having the Children of Rhys join them, and getting their magic back again – it's so obviously for the better,' said Timothy. 'How can they object to that?'

'Because it's new,' said Peri. 'It's different. It's frightening. And no matter what happens now, there's no way any of them can go back to the way things used to be.'

Timothy was silent, digesting her words. Then Paul said, 'It looks like they're about to start. Come on, let's move a bit closer.'

By now Garan had shepherded all the faeries into a rough circle, arranging it so that all the Oakenfolk had at least one of the Children of Rhys beside them. As the last thin veil of cloud slid from the moon's luminous face, he turned and addressed them.

'The time has come.' He stepped back beside Linden, holding out his hand to her; she took it, and stretched out her own hand to Wink on the other side. The other faeries hesitantly did likewise, and in a moment the whole circle was joined.

Linden's heart pounded, and her breath came shallowly between her parted lips. She'd received magic from another faery before, but Amaryllis had been just one dying woman, and the Children of Rhys were strong and many. Would it hurt? What if one of the Oakenfolk panicked or changed her mind at the last moment, and broke the circle?

'Linden,' murmured Wink in a pained tone, 'you're squeezing my fingers.'

'Sorry,' Linden whispered, and forced herself to relax.

Beside her Garan stood with eyes closed, his brow furrowed in concentration. For a long moment no one moved, and the Oakenwyld was eerily silent. Then Linden saw it: a glimmer of light on the far side of the circle, a slowly expanding radiance that spread from Broch to Thorn and Campion, from Llinos to Mallow and Bluebell…and now the magic was glowing around her too, tingling hot and cold as it swept over her skin and swirled into her muscles and bones. Amaryllis's dying gift of glamour had thrilled her, but that had been a scant half-share of a magic already weak with use and age. To compare it to the power flowing through her now…it was like comparing water to wine.

Still the energy built until every pore in her body sang with it, and the circle of faeries blazed so bright she had to shut her eyes. The magic was too strong now, too much, any more and she would faint, or explode—

Garan's hand slackened in hers, and the light died abruptly as the circle wavered and broke. One after another, the Children of Rhys sagged to their knees and toppled onto the grass, unconscious.

The Oakenfolk all looked at one another, and Linden

saw an apprehension on Valerian's face that mirrored her own. Had the magic transfer worked, or not?

'Look!' came a hysterical-sounding voice from beside her, and she turned to see Wink spreading a length of shimmering, gold-toned silk between her outstretched hands – cloth that seemed to have spun itself out of nowhere. On the other side of the circle Campion had grown to human size and was regarding her far-off toes in amazement, while Thorn rubbed her hands at a bonfire she had kindled on the grass. Faery lights danced through the air; a cluster of violets pushed their way out of the cold ground and stood nodding in the midnight breeze; a roast fit for the Midwinter Feast floated by, so real-looking that Linden could almost smell it.

Jasmine's curse was undone, and the Oakenfolk had their magic again.

EPILOGUE

'Here,' said Timothy, slinging the strap of his guitar around Linden's shoulders. They'd just finished having tea with Paul and Peri and were sitting on the veranda, savouring the first warm day of spring. 'You've been listening to me play long enough – now you have a go.'

Linden hesitated, hands hovering above the strings. Then she shook her head and handed it back. 'It's all right,' she said. 'I don't think it's for me, somehow.' Much as she enjoyed hearing Timothy play, she felt no compulsion to do likewise; unlike the powerful bond that had drawn Paul and Peri together and sparked them both to artistic brilliance, the best her faery powers could do was make Timothy's natural talent for music a bit stronger. But that was quite normal, or so Queen Valerian had assured her; and seeing that Timothy would be leaving Oakhaven in another few days, it was probably for the best.

'If you say so,' said Timothy as he took the guitar back,

but he looked a little disappointed. 'Anyway, how are Garan and the others?'

'Doing better, but they're still tired most of the time. The Queen says it'll be a few more days at least until they all recover.'

'Good thing there's still no sign of the Empress, then.' Timothy ran his thumb over the strings, winced and adjusted one of the tuning pegs.

'I just wish,' said Linden as she watched a robin flutter down to land on top of the box hedge, 'that we knew what had happened to Rob.'

Timothy gave a little laugh. 'Me too. Especially since I'm going to have to go back through London next week, and if I'm going to be attacked it would be nice to know about it. I think I'll stuff a few bits of iron into my pockets, just in case.' He slipped the guitar strap over his head and began to play again, softly.

'Did you ever talk to your parents?' asked Linden. 'About...you know.'

'I sent them an email this morning,' Timothy said. 'I told them I'd been suspended for a couple of weeks, but not to worry, I'd be fine.'

Linden looked at him curiously. 'And are you?'

Timothy was silent a moment, his hands flat on the guitar. 'I don't know,' he said at last. 'I still miss Uganda. I still don't fit in with the other boys at school, and I'm not sure I want to. I still wonder whether everything I grew up believing is really the truth, and I know it's going to take me a lot of searching and thinking to decide. But...' He took a deep breath. 'I'm here now, and I'm going to stick it out. At Greenhill, I mean, unless they decide to expel me. I've had enough of running away.'

Linden tucked her arm into his and leaned her head on his shoulder. 'I'm glad,' she said.

Timothy looked down at her. Then he took off the guitar and carefully put it aside. 'Look,' he said. 'I don't want to...what I mean is...I like you, but there's this girl back home, and...'

'Miriam,' said Linden. 'I know. I saw the way you looked at her picture.' She let go of him and sat up. 'I'm sorry, I didn't mean to make you uncomfortable. I suppose I still have a lot to learn about how to behave around males.' She thought of the way she'd flung herself at Garan when he'd first arrived, and her cheeks grew hot. Did he think that she had *those* kinds of feelings for him, too?

'Well, with thirty-eight of them in the Oak now I'm sure you'll figure it out eventually,' said Timothy. 'And believe me, if I ever get girls figured out, I'll let you know.'

Linden laughed – but the sound died on her lips as the robin in the hedge flapped down onto the veranda, shimmered, and became a lanky young man with fox-coloured hair. His eyes were shadowed with weariness and he bore a thin white scar across one cheek, but when he spoke he sounded as wryly self-possessed as ever:

'If you do that, human boy, you will have achieved a victory indeed.' And with that he pulled a wallet out of his pocket, and tossed it to Timothy.

'Rob!' Linden leaped up to greet him – but then she faltered and hung back, suddenly shy. 'I'm glad,' she stammered. 'To see you, I mean.'

He held her gaze steadily, brows lifting in speculation; then he took her hand, and brushed it with his lips. 'And I to see you,' he said, his smile deepening as he watched her blush. 'I would have come sooner, but my allies and I needed time to regroup and discuss our plans – and I also wanted to be certain that my feet would be sufficiently beautiful when I came.'

'Your feet…?' asked Linden dazedly, but then Timothy snorted and she realised Rob was quoting one of the Bible verses Timothy had used before the Empress. *How beautiful are the feet of those who bring…* 'Oh! You mean – you have good news?'

'For now,' Rob said. 'The Empress and her followers have been forced to abandon Sanctuary, and seek a new stronghold elsewhere. We rebels are still few in number compared to her forces, but our strength is growing by the day – especially now that word of the Stone of Naming is beginning to spread.'

'So the Empress is in retreat,' said Timothy, looking up from his inspection of his wallet. 'Which means we're safe for now.'

Rob nodded. 'But that peace cannot last long, especially when the Oakenfolk have no magic to defend themselves. Which is why I thought—' He stopped short, staring, as Linden picked up a dry twig from the ground and touched it into bloom.

'I think you'll find,' she said, 'that problem has already been taken care of.'

'What?' demanded Rob. He snatched the twig from her fingers and examined it incredulously. 'This is no mere glamour. How did you get this power?'

'The Children of Rhys,' replied Linden proudly. 'Or at least, a few of them. They've decided to join us and help us defend the Oak.'

Rob let the twig drop, and now he looked bitter. 'Then I have come too late.'

'Too late?' Linden was puzzled, and then she suddenly understood. 'Rob! You mean that you and the rebels – you'd decided to help us by giving us some of your magic, too? But I thought—'

I thought you still considered us the Forsaken. I thought you didn't want anything to do with humans, or faeries who would befriend them – and that you'd only helped us so that you could get the Stone. Not to mention what the Empress had said about where Rob had got his musical abilities...

'For years I have tried to convince myself that humans are inferior,' said Rob, 'and that faeries do no wrong to use them. I had my own reasons for wanting this to be true, but

I prefer not to speak of that.' A muscle jumped in his cheek. 'Suffice it to say that on the night you and I first met, even as I parroted the Empress's doctrines to you, my heart knew them to be false.'

Linden felt a rush of amazed relief. To think that Rob had seemed so certain of his beliefs about humans, even treating her condescendingly for thinking otherwise – she would never have guessed he was hiding such deep-seated doubts.

'I will not pretend to believe as you do,' Rob went on, his eyes still holding hers, 'that the Great Gardener created us to help humans. But I do agree that neither of our peoples can prosper unless we work together.' He drew himself up straighter. 'So I came to offer the Oakenfolk whatever magic or other help you might require – but I also hoped that by doing so, I might earn the right to bargain.'

'Bargain?' asked Linden. 'For what?'

'Sanctuary is no longer ours,' said Rob, 'any more than it belongs to the Empress. We need a new place to live and make our stronghold, and I had hoped the Oak—'

Linden could contain herself no longer. She darted forward and threw her arms around Rob, hugging him exuberantly. At first he stiffened in surprise, but then he relaxed and returned her embrace, dropping his face against her hair.

'I take it,' he murmured, 'this means we are still open to negotiation?'

Timothy watched, half smiling, as Linden took Rob by

the hand and led him across the lawn towards the Oak, enthusing about magic and battle strategy all the while. Then he picked up his guitar and went back into the house.

'Is that what I think it was?' said Peri, emerging from the corridor. Her pale hair was dishevelled and she looked flushed, as though she had been working.

'Not sure,' said Timothy as he headed for the kitchen. 'What were you thinking?'

'I'm thinking that Linden is fifteen,' said Peri darkly, 'and that Rob had better watch his step. But aside from that – what are you doing?'

Timothy dropped his wallet on the counter; then he picked up the telephone receiver and started pressing buttons.

'I'm calling home,' he said.

ACKNOWLEDGEMENTS

My heartfelt thanks to my agents, Josh and Tracey Adams, and to my editors Catherine Onder at HarperCollins US and Sarah Lilly at Orchard Books UK for their support and guidance. I am also indebted to my Canadian publicist Melissa Zilberberg for all her hard work on my behalf.

I am grateful to Claudia Gray, who helped me brainstorm and refine the plot in its earliest stages; to my crack beta-reading team of Liz Barr, Brittany Harrison, Meg Burden, Saundra Mitchell, Kerrie Mills, Erin Fitzgerald, Teri (Krenek) Guill, Emily Bytheway, and Sylvia Thomas for providing encouragement and insightful criticism along the way; and also to the 2009 Debs a.k.a. the Feast of Awesome, for helping me sail the choppy seas of publication.

This book demanded a considerable amount of research, and I would have been lost without the help of the kind folks on District Dave's London Underground Forum (subwayrail, stuartpalmer, Colin, undergroundgal, solidbond, Dmitri and Sean B.), who advised me on mechanical and security issues related to the Tube; as well as Jovia Crooks, Carlo Kutesa and Tumwijuke Mutambuka, who graciously answered my questions about life in Kampala and corrected some of my more egregious misapprehensions. Any errors which remain are my fault, not theirs.

And finally, to my dear friend Judy who helps keep me healthy and sane; my wonderful husband and boys who put up with my crazed scribbling at all hours of the day and night; and my wise, godly, and supportive parents who have always made me proud to have been, however briefly, a 'missionary kid' – I love you all.

R.J. Anderson, 2010

ABOUT THE AUTHOR

R. J. Anderson (known to her friends as Rebecca) was born in Uganda, raised in Ontario, went to school in New Jersey, and has spent much of her life dreaming of other worlds entirely.

As a child she immersed herself in fairy tales, mythology, and the works of C.S. Lewis, J.R.R. Tolkien and E. Nesbit; later she discovered more contemporary authors like Ursula LeGuin, Patricia A. McKillip and Robin McKinley, and learned to take as much pleasure from their language as the stories they told.

Now married and the mother of three young sons, Rebecca reads to her children the classic works of fantasy and science fiction that enlivened her own childhood, and tries to bring a similar sense of humour, adventure, and timeless wonder to the novels she writes for children and young adults.

Rebecca currently lives in the beautiful theatre town of Stratford, Ontario.

Visit www.rj-anderson.com to find out more!

DON'T MISS
THE BRILLIANT

Read on for an exciting extract...

Knife woke in a cold sweat, the torn edge of her wing sizzling with pain. Hunger gnawed at her stomach, and her throat burned with thirst. But the moment she tried to sit up her head spun like a weaver's bobbin, and it was all she could do not to be sick.

How long had she lain unconscious? In the darkness it was impossible to guess. The last thing she remembered was Old Wormwood's talons ripping through her wing, and the ground rushing up to meet her as she fell...

I will never fly again. The realisation came to her with cruel clarity, and for a moment she wanted to curl into a ball and weep. To live without the thrill of the hunt, or the joy of soaring through the air...short of death itself, Knife could imagine nothing worse.

Yet there was nothing she could do about it. No poultice could heal a torn wing; a hundred stitches would never close the wound. She had been the youngest and the best Hunter ever to serve the Queen – but without the ability to fly, she would be useless. Thorn would take over her duties, and she would go back to being Bryony, a nobody. She would spend the rest of her life trapped in the Oak—

No. She would not, *could* not. If Queen Amaryllis refused to let her go outside, then she would simply run away, and live as best as she could, as long as she could, alone.

Breathing deep to quell her nausea, Knife tried to swing her legs over the edge of the bed. The room was so dark, her wits so blurred with pain, that it took her several attempts to realise that there was no edge – that the soft thing on which she lay was in fact the floor.

Knife's stomach tightened. No wonder it was dark; no wonder the room smelled strange. Instead of lying on her own bed in the Oak, waiting for Valerian to come and tend her, she was in some unfamiliar place, all alone.

But where?

Cautiously, trying not to jar her injured wing, Knife crawled forward into the blackness. She had shuffled only a few beetle-lengths when her hand struck something cold. She felt her way up its smooth surface to find a huge glass bowl, filled with—

Water. Oh, Great Gardener. Clambering to her feet, Knife leaned over the bowl and drank thirstily, then plunged her hands into it and splashed her face and neck. By the time she had finished washing, she felt almost alive again.

Beside the bowl sat a plate heaped with chunks of some

spongy, cakelike substance. It smelled peculiar, but it seemed to be food. Tentatively, Knife took a bite and began to chew.

After a few more mouthfuls she no longer felt light-headed, and her queasiness began to subside. Her wing still hurt, but she could bear it. Feet braced wide for balance on the too-soft carpet, Knife set off into the darkness again.

Three or four steps in any direction brought her up against the wall: not wood, not stone, but a tough papery substance. It gave a little when she pushed against it, but as soon as she let go it sprang back. There had to be an exit somewhere...

Pick up a copy of

Knife

to read on!

LOOK out for the amazing
sequel to **K**nife and **R**ebel

no ordinary fairytale...

OUT NOW!

ORCHARD BOOKS